SNOWFLAKE, AZ

For information about permission to reproduce selections from this book, write to
Permissions, W. W. Norton & Company, Inc., 500 Fifth Avenue, New York, NY 10110

For information about special discounts for bulk purchases, please contact
W. W. Norton Special Sales at specialsales@wwnorton.com or 800-233-4830

Manufacturing by Sheridan
Book design by Chris Welch
Production manager: Anna Oler

ISBN 978-1-324-00441-7

W. W. Norton & Company, Inc., 500 Fifth Avenue, New York, N.Y. 10110
www.wwnorton.com

W. W. Norton & Company Ltd., 15 Carlisle Street, London W1D 3BS

1 2 3 4 5 6 7 8 9 0

SNOWFLAKE, AZ

Marcus Sedgwick

Norton Young Readers

An Imprint of W. W. Norton & Company
Independent Publishers Since 1923

For the Sensitives

AUTHOR'S NOTE

Inspired in part by my own experience of a disputed illness, and named for a real community afflicted by multiple chemical sensitivities, *Snowflake, AZ* is nonetheless a work of fiction. All of the people and animals appearing in these pages, and all of the incidents, events, scenes, and dialogues concerning them, are products of my own imagination and not to be construed as real. What *is* real is the suffering caused by environmental illness, and the ingenuity required of those who live with it. May this story do them justice.

SNOWFLAKe, AZ

As I sat on line for the water pump the other day, perched on my plastic barrel, the man behind looked me up and down and said, "So what's your story?"

I shrugged and told him it was probably the same as anyone else's, more or less, just perhaps with more gas masks and a goat. We all know what happened to the world, and that's a story that won't be forgotten. But not every story happens to everybody in the same way, and that set me thinking that maybe I should write my story down, so there's a record of what happened to one person.

All histories take place in the past, and this one is more past than some; it took place in the old days, before what happened. It's longer than some, too, but it's gonna take me just as long as it needs to get told. Maybe more than seven days, maybe even seven months. Heaven help me if it takes seven years.

CHAPTER 1

AWAY

The goat ate my sneakers. As I recall, that was the first thing. And I can't promise you for sure, since it's all so darned long ago now, but I always figured that set down the next seven years of my life. More or less. You can't be too certain of things like that. But I do know this. I'd been in Snowflake less than ten minutes and already I was wrapped in nothing but a towel on a storm-wet porch, and when I looked around, Socrates had gone and ate up one of my sneakers and was halfway through the second for dessert. Socrates was the goat. By the way.

There was me. Just off the overnight Greyhound. Halfway around the great nation, till I got to the bus depot in the little town with the funny name, and I thought to myself, well ain't it supposed to be hot and sunny in Arizona, for it was not. It was hot and wet, and the rain did not want to stop, I could see that without asking. Then I walked near enough eight miles out of town, till I reckoned I was lost, so I started trying to hitch a ride and you don't get no prizes for thinking that no one stopped, but as it turned out, in the end someone did. Strangest-looking car I'd ever seen. Like an SUV that had gotten shrunk by the rain. Tiny rusty yellow thing. Kinda funny. Mona told me later it was Japanese and that once upon a time hers had been on a Soviet Antarctic expedition, but she might have been funning me. It was always hard to tell with Mona. Anyway, she said it was as good in the desert as it had been for the Ruskies in the snow, and it was even good in monsoon season, Arizona-style, that is.

So the car stopped and Mona peered out at me through the wound-down window and asked me where I was headed, and when I showed her the postcard with the address on it she said, "Bly's your brother, am I right?" Then she burst out laughing like she was a Pez dispenser. I didn't see what was so funny. I was just wondering how she knew who I was.

So I nodded and said, "I'm Ash."

Then she said, "You sick?" just like that and outta nothing. And I didn't understand but maybe I looked all washed up. So anyway, I shook my head and said, "No, ma'am, I am not," because I figured she was wondering about giving me a ride. And still she kept staring at me, and I felt I had to say something else, so I said, "Nothing wrong with me, ma'am. I am perfectly healthy." Which I know sounds dumb but I was real desperate for that ride and that's what I said.

Then she fixed me and said, "Never met no one perfectly healthy," and she took one more long look at me and finally she said, "Well, I suppose it's raining" and shoved the door open.

"You better come along with me," she said, and that I did.

As it fell out, I wasn't lost at all. I'd come straight to the place. We were in her car for less than ten minutes all told, off the highway and down a dirt road across the bumpy old desert which was going underwater in parts, and it just about gave Mona time to say "So I'm Mona" and not much else. But

I could see I was bothering her. Me being there, I mean. She kept glancing sidelong at me. Frowning and such. Plus I had the feeling she was trying not to breathe too much. I found out later what she meant by "I suppose it's raining." It didn't mean she picked me up because I was getting wet. It meant she figured that because I was wet like a fish I might be a tad safer.

The second we pulled up in front of her house she said, "Right, kid, out you get," which I did and then she said, "Wait here, huh?" and pointed at the porch where I stood with my bag. Inside the house I heard voices, Mona's and someone else, but both so low I couldn't make it out. I dawdled on the porch, wet and wondering what they were saying, because I knew that they were talking about me. That didn't need no explanation. I snuck a peek through the screen door, and there was Mona and a younger lady, and they were putting their heads together and figuring out something complicated, as much as I could tell. Hands were getting waved around. Then Mona turned and out she came to the porch and said, "To the showers!" and pointed in the air dramatically and giggled all at once.

I guess I didn't move then because I was confused. Because I was already wetter than the ocean.

Then Mona said to me, real slow, "You have to get clean."

Real, real slow. Like I was stupid. Which I guess I was, back then. I started to head inside through the screen door and she took a coupla quick steps back and held out her hand like a traffic cop, and then she said, "You have to take your clothes off *here*." Again, *real* slow.

There was a bit of business then while she explained about off-gassing and venting and the dangers thereof, and about Mary (who was the other lady) being in the house and being super-sensitive and all. Then she explained how they'd be out back looking at Mary's papers and how the bathroom was just through on the right and how I'd find a towel waiting for me when I got back to the porch. And when I asked why maybe I couldn't take the towel with me in the first place, Mona explained that I was an "unknown quantity" and they didn't know if I could follow instructions and right now the instructions were not to touch the towel until I had gotten myself all washed up.

Then she left and I stood looking out at the bumpy old desert, which was still being pounded by the rain, and it all looked pretty darn empty. I could see some other houses, low single-story ones like Mona's with metal sidings and dirty red or pale green tin roofs. But they were a good ways off, and I figured that unless they had a telescope trained on this particular porch I was safe enough, so I started pulling my pants down and then Mona stuck her head around the corner of the porch and said, "Don't forget your hair!" and then went off giggling before I had a chance to pull 'em back up again.

I put my clothes on a set of metal shelves there on the porch and went inside, hoping to find the bathroom straight off. But I didn't. First I tried a door on the right and that was the room with the laundry in it, and then straight ahead was the main room, with a kind of a kitchen at one end, and a desk and a bed at the other. Through a door to the back I could see Mona and the other woman, so that was Mary, and they were only just outside on the back porch but they were poring over a bunch of paperwork or something, so even though I was as naked as when I landed on the planet, I stood and wondered where the hell I was.

What I mean is, the walls were papered with tinfoil. All of 'em. Right around the big room, and the ceiling, and when I finally found the bathroom, it was the same. Tinfoil wallpaper. The whole house. Huh.

You know, I washed pretty darn good. That thing Mona had said about following instructions, well, I sure was gonna prove I could follow instructions, that I could do what I was bid, so I washed up good. Though not with any kind of shampoo I'd ever seen before. I stood in the bathtub with the shower running, reading the bottle of shampoo and wondering what it all meant about paraben-free and sulfate-free and everything-free and then I was thinking about the tinfoil and then what Mona had said about the possibility that I might go and *vent* all over 'em. Whatever that was.

So by the time I got back outside, I was confused all to bits and I was just noticing that my clothes had disappeared and reaching for the towel Mona had left for me when a truck pulled up and out stepped a guy in a faded red T-shirt and wearing a mask, like the kind you wear when you do home improvements or something. And for a split second I wondered if he was here to rob the place but then he pulled the mask off and it was Bly.

And I don't know what he thought but I know I was embarrassed enough for both of us, because sure, we used to take baths together, but that was when he was six and I was four, and when he's twenty and you're eighteen, it ain't the same. It surely ain't. But Bly was always a good kid to me, kinda like a brother. Which is me making a joke, because that's what he was. My stepbrother, but like we always used to say, what's the step got to do with it? Yeah, I know I ain't funny.

Bly looked away until I was wrapped up and then he ran from the rain and the dog who'd been in the truck with him came too, and they both bounded onto the porch and Bly gave me a quick hug and said "hey" like I'd only seen him yesterday and the dog started licking my toes. Must've been the no-nothing shampoo.

I laughed at the dog and looked at Bly and then I said, "So, how are you?" and he shook his head and looked away and I felt bad for asking but, hell, that was why I'd come all this darned distance.

Then we stood looking at each other and grinning because it was great to see him and I guess it had been more than a while and then his face suddenly went all funny looking and he shouted, "Socrates!" That was when I turned and just around the corner of the house saw a goat finishing off my sneakers.

Mona told me later why he was called Socrates. It was on account of the Greek philosopher (approx. 470 BC to 399 BC, she told me, which was a kinda weird thing to say. She even said "approx"). Seems the old Socrates had this trick, they call it Socratic irony, which was where he pretended to be dumb while he debated with someone, but really he was much smarter than them, and by letting them run on and on and then by him saying one or two apparently dumb (but in point of fact smart) things, he'd make *them* look stupid. Mona said it was the same with the goat. And he sure was smarter than he looked, because he'd taken my sneakers off of the shelf where I'd left them and gone out of sight around the side of the house to get to work on 'em without interruption.

And it was still raining. But Mona said it was all right and I could go inside now, so I did, in my towel, and Bly disappeared straightways off and went to get a shower because he said he'd been with the normies.

I said "er, hello" to Mary, and Mary said hello back. She had a roll of papers in her hand that she waved at Bly as he went, and she said "morons!" and Bly said, "Ain't that the truth" and I thought "what?" because I couldn't tell if she was joking or not.

Mary was skinny, like Mona, but she had wavy brown hair while Mona's was goose-gray, and longer. Mona was tiny, at least I thought so for an age, until I realized she often just *acted* tiny. If that sounds stupid, I can't explain it no better. Like, if she stood up and slowed down, she wasn't so tiny after all. And when she slowed down I could see she'd once been real pretty, still was, I guess, but you never got to see that because she was always rushing around in a blur. Almost always. She was maybe fifty-something, which I figured was old, but Mary was only old to me because I was a kid then. I don't know for sure, maybe she was early thirties. Ancient. Now I know better what ancient feels like; I guess most of us do.

Mona couldn't seem to make one whole sentence without laughing at the end of it, or maybe halfway through, but Mary didn't barely smile, just a tiny bit when she said hello, like she was scared. Which it turned out she was, of me, because after about ten minutes she looked at Mona and Mona looked at her and nodded and then they told me I was still giving something off that was upsetting Mary, but Mary said, "It's okay, I have stuff to do, and anyway, thanks for the tea and all."

She picked up the stack of papers and I only found out later what that was all about, namely she was having trouble with her health insurance company. Anyway, after she went that left me looking at the floor, mostly, and Mona looking at me, smiling. Then the smile went a little and she said, "Hey, did Bly tell you your mother was here?" and I said "nope" and she said, "He didn't tell you yet?" and I shook my head and was thinking what-the-heck-my-mom-was-here but out loud I said, "Oh. Uh, when was that?"

Mona said, "Recently," and when I asked how long that was, she thought and said, "About six months."

Then Bly came out of the shower, and he'd changed his clothes, so I asked Mona if I could have my clothes back and she said, "Sure," but she didn't get up to get them or anything and so then I asked "when?" and she said "soon." Then I asked how long soon was and she thought about it and said, "About six months." Then she thought some more and added, "I guess. It sort of depends." And then she laughed.

Then Bly looked at me and tried to explain how my clothes would need to be off-gassed for a few months, which meant getting all the chemicals out of them and getting 'em safe to wear again. When I asked what that meant, he said they'd leave them in a tub of water in the yard, and after that they'd dry them out in the sun, and then they'd be okay.

I looked at him and said "for six months" and he just shrugged.

So then I was ready to ask a question, which was "where the hell am I?" (only I didn't say hell) and Mona chuckled at my bad language and said, "You're here!" and when I asked where "here" was, she said, "Away. Here is Away." I guess I looked confused again because she explained, "That's what they told us. All of us, sooner or later."

"Who?" I asked.

"The people. Normies. Any people. Sooner or later, they'd say, 'If you don't like the darned world so much, why don't you go away?' So we did. We went here. Away."

She giggled and said, "Let's have that tea," and Bly went off and came back after five minutes with some clothes to wear which were his and weren't so bad, just a little big for me, but the only shoes they could find was a pair of work boots that were approximately sixteen sizes too big, and when I put them on Mona said if only they could paint my nose red I could join the circus, so I decided I wasn't going to be leaving any day soon until I had some proper-sized shoes back.

Then Mona said, "I wonder what will happen next." And laughed.

CHAPTER 2

BUT YOU DON'T LOOK ILL

Mona said it a lot.

"I wonder what will happen next."

If she didn't say it half a dozen times a day, she said it ten.

At first I couldn't tell whether she was fooling around or being serious, but as time went by, I sorta started to learn that it was both at once. That was Mona. Fooling around and dead serious, both at the same time. All the time.

Like I told you before, she was a skinny creature. Mona Mochsky. Long gray hair. I figured out later from something she said that she was around fifty-one, but you sure wouldn't've known that. No. And she might've been thin but she was tough. And taller than it appeared at first, but you didn't see that because most of the time, she was more like seven, like a little kid, messing around, joking. She even moved like little kids do. You know, the way adults move one way, and little kids, they move different? Like they never set still, even when they're setting, they wiggle a leg or two, or rub their hands on the back of their head or something. Mona was like that. And then once in a while she'd stop, like when she was dead beat, and then you'd see a real elegant lady, and these tired blue-gray eyes. Next to Bly, I guess that made her look even tinier too. Because he had grown since I last saw him, he had grown. Not just up, but out. And I tried to figure when exactly it was I'd last seen him and it was more than one year and less than two.

"Hey look," said Mona, "the rain's easin."

So we took our tea out onto the back porch and sat in red plastic chairs looking out at the desert. The desert was red too. There were scruffy little plants on the ground, here and there, and one scrawny tree every three million miles. The dog came out to say hi, and his name was Cooper. Mona rubbed him on the head and said, "Cooper, this is Ash." Then she looked at me and whispered, "He's kind of a mongrel" as if I'd asked what sorta dog he was, though I hadn't. Then she said, "But ain't we all?" and Bly smiled, and I thought, yeah, well I guess you got that right.

It was better outside. That is to say it was overly warm in the house, even with the windows and doors all open, and even with the rainfall it was still too warm, but Mona said it would pass and I asked when and she said "soon." Which I started to learn meant something different up here, and when I say "up here," well, that was the next thing I learned.

"We're over five thousand feet," Mona told me. "Well, heck, almost six. That's pretty up." And chuckled, of course. "Up, up, and away."

"Might take you a while to get used to it," said Bly. "You'll be tired."

Mona nodded. "You might get a nosebleed or two."

"Ma'am, I don't think there'll be time for getting used to it," I said. "I just came to find my brother and see what . . ."

But I didn't know how to finish that sentence I'd started, because I could already see Bly looking uncomfortable. I figured there'd be time later for finding out what was happening. With Bly, I mean.

Mona said, "How long you staying, Ash?" and I had no answer. Not really. "I just came to find Bly," I said. And I was thinking I guess I might stay a night or two, but anyways I ain't going nowhere without ditching the circus shoes.

I looked at Bly.

"Well?" I said. "What happened?"

But he shook his head again, just like the first time.

Then no one said nothing, during which time Socrates wandered by, and I wondered if they never tied him up and why he didn't just escape. I mean, there was this bit of fence around the back of the house, the inside of which Mona called the yard, though what was inside of the fence didn't look to be no different from what was outside of it. But it had two gates and they left the gates open all the time, so there was nothing to stop Socrates just rolling off into the world. Going to Vegas or something. But then I looked out at the desert and I thought, huh, where the hell is there to escape to? Nowheres. Not really. And anyhow, I couldn't picture Socrates at Vegas. I could already see he was way too classy for that. So maybe Mona was right, maybe he was smarter'n he looked.

Mona said, "That sure was a coincidence, me picking you up on the road there!" and I thought not really, since about three people live out here. But I nodded, and anyway, she was right about coincidences. Because it wasn't the first, and Bly must've been thinking the same thing because he turned to Mona and said, "You know what they used to call Ash at school?"

So then her eyes widened up at what was coming and then when Bly told her she burst out giggling like her neck was faulty. She said "no" in that way that people do when they mean "what? really?" and then she said, "What? really? They called you Snowflake?"

I turned red, which meant yes. I hated that. Was I not sorry to leave my education behind.

"Why'd they call you that?"

Good question, I thought.

"I guess you'd have to ask them."

Mona nodded.

"Idiots, huh?" Mona said and I nodded.

"I guess Ash just didn't fit in there," Bly said and looked at me. "Did you?"

"You two were at school together?" Mona asked.

Bly just shrugged, so I said "some" and that set Mona pondering, I could tell.

I guess I lived in eight states by the age of nine, not one of 'em fancy. Mostly on the road, mostly on to the next place, until for a while we settled: me and Mom and Bly and his dad. Then my mom announced that she was leaving Bly's dad and that she'd send for me, but she didn't. So yeah Bly and me went to the same school for a while, and that was the last time I saw my stepbrother, right before he went off to be a police cadet, which is what he'd wanted to do since before I could remember. And now he was here, in the middle of the desert instead, and I was expecting some kind of answer about that.

I tried a third time.

"Well?" I said.

By now you'll see that Bly had gotten to have this new habit for shrugs, because that's what I received by reply, and pretty much all I had learned was that Bly was not keen on explaining why he was not in San Francisco being a police cadet.

So I changed tack.

"Uh, Bly, Mona says Mom was here."

"Uh-huh," he said, "she was just passing through . . . with the love of her life."

Then there was a pause and then we both burst out laughing at the same time.

Mona stared at us, so I explained to her all the stuff how my dad had been the love of Mom's life, even though they'd only known each other for a week before he hit the road. And after that how *Bly's* dad had been the love of her life. And then how she'd found a whole bunch of guys, each and every one of 'em the love of her life, till the next came along.

"So I guess she found another one, huh?" I asked and Bly nodded.

"Trucker down from Nashua."

"Nashua?"

"Nashua, New Hampshire."

"Nashua?"

"Nashua."

I guess Socrates might've had something real smart to say about that, because he just sat on the edge of the porch looking dumber than ever, chewing. The last of my shoe, I figured.

And I was about to open my mouth again when Bly beat me to it and said, "Nashua" in a dumb voice and we both lost it again for a time.

"How'd she know you was here?" I asked when I stopped snickering, and Bly shrugged and said, "I guess Dad told her," which told me that I had been the last goddamn one to find out what had happened to Bly.

So I got a mite angry then, and I said, "Bly. I don't get it. You were gonna be a police officer."

You are a ways ahead of me if you know what answer that got me. But after he'd done shrugging, it started to come out. Couple years before, there was Mom and me and Bly, living with Jack, his dad. And I will say this, Jack was a good father, even if we shared not one drop of blood. When Mom set off down the road again, Jack kept Bly and me with him. Signed papers and everything to make me his own. Legal. You know many people who'd do that? I surely don't. My mother didn't object. You know many people who'd do that either? Maybe you do.

But this couple years ago, Bly had gone off to become what he had always wanted to be, while I turned myself in for one last year at school. And then as soon as I could, I stopped going to school and got myself the job in the shoe store. And Jack was fine with that and I lived with him until I found the postcard and then it all came out. Or some of it, anyhow.

I waited a bit longer and saved some money and got me a great pair of shortly-to-be-eaten sneakers on staff discount and then when I knew I couldn't wait no more I quit my job and got on a Greyhound bus to the last place I was expecting Bly to be. That being Snowflake, Arizona.

So Bly shrugged, and when he'd quit with that, he said, "I got sick, Ash."

"Sick? You okay?"

And yeah, he shrugged, so Mona took over and said, "Everyone's sick, Ash. That's what we're doing here. Who else would want to live in the god-danged desert? We're all sick."

I looked at Bly.

"But you don't look ill," I said. "You look great." And come to that, I didn't think Mona looked too shabby either. Not for fifty-something.

"You can tell someone has cancer just by looking?" Mona asked.

"You have cancer?" I said to Bly, scared to heck.

"No," he said. "No, Mona's just making a point. Like before someone knows they have cancer, they might look normal. But really they're sicker than hell."

"Oh," I said. "Yeah. Of course not. So? What's wrong?"

Mona laughed and said, "What ain't?" and Bly smiled but I didn't see why he was smiling.

"Hey, Snowflake," he said, "remember how we used to run away from home?"

I ignored the "Snowflake" part and said, "Yeah." Then, "No, wait. That was just me. I know I did, but—"

"Yeah, I did it too. We did it together a couple times."

"You guys ran away from home?" said Mona. "How old were you?"

"Like, six and eight, or something," Bly says. "And we were serious about it too. Sometimes we'd get all the way to the end of the block, and then we'd sit there."

He started laughing and I started up too.

"So why'd you run off like that?"

Bly lifted his shoulders in that thing we call a shrug.

"I dunno. I guess it was near the end of them being together. My dad and Ash's mom. Jamie. I guess they argued and we didn't like it."

"So what happened?"

"So in the end Mom would come down and haul us back."

"Was she mad?" asked Mona. "She must've been mad. Or worried. Mad or worried. Or both. I guess both."

And yup, Bly and I thought about that because it was not something we had thought about before, and then I said, "No, I guess not. She used to laugh at us."

Mona opened her mouth and then shut it again, and Socrates kept whatever he was thinking to himself. And I wanted to ask what was wrong with everyone up here, but I didn't know how. Because it's hard to ask about illness, because perhaps people are dying, or perhaps they're sad about it, but I wanted to know what was wrong with Bly, so I said, "Is that lady Mary sick?"

Mona nodded.

"Sooo-per sensitive. Anything gets to her. Everything. See, she could smell that perfume on you."

So I was about to say do I look like someone who wears perfume? But that would've come out rude. Instead I said, "But ma'am, I don't wear perfume. Generally."

Mona shrugged and said, "Wouldn't have to be you. Like maybe you hung out with someone who wore a lot. Truth to say, I can feel it a little bit, that's why I thought we'd be better set out here on the porch, with you downwind an' all and anyway, it might just have been someone you worked with, or whatever."

All through this I was thinking, well, this is a load of hokey, and then when she said that part about working with someone I remembered Sue, the boss at the shoe store, who was kinda sad and I think that was why she wore a ton of perfume, and I mean *a ton*, and we all used to gag behind her back when she passed by. It was real bad, that perfume of Sue's, it made your nose itch for an hour or more, even after you left work, and it was not even something decent, it was like old roses or whatever, but it was about a week since I'd quit the store and headed to Arizona so this all had to be hokum, right? And yes, I was just thinking that to myself when Mona said, "Like flowers, right? Yup, flowers. Roses."

So then I shut the hush up.

We set in silence, and I was thinking about what they'd said. About how sometimes people don't look sick, even when they are. And if I had known then what we all know now, I might've worked out that sometimes the whole world don't look sick neither, even when it is.

But I didn't. Not then. I guess almost no one did. Those days were still ahead of us.

CHAPTER 3

CANARIES

The rain. There was that. The rain was not to be thought irrelevant. It had started on up again. It came from the sky like ten thousand bullets fired from a thousand guns and I had had enough of getting wet for one lifetime. And then there was the fact that I was wearing circus shoes. Plus the fact that I was dog-tired. Anyway, why do they say that? Do dogs get more tired'n other folk? Cooper seemed okay to me. . . . But most of all, there was Bly and how good it was to see him. I'd come all this way to find him, and here was the thing: I hadn't got no plan for after that. Somehow that was as far as I had been thinking. Find Bly. And now I had, I had no good-God idea what to do next. So add all these things together and what you got is that I stayed put.

I guess I coulda turned right around and got on the Greyhound and gone back to Jack. Now, Jack had gone and met someone, finally met someone after Jamie, and I couldn't fault him. He'd given years to me and I wasn't even his kid. But when Suzanne, his new lady, came along I knew he wanted to make a new start. He never said nothing. Not one thing. But I knew he needed his new start and that seemed fair because don't we all? Sometimes. So I'd come all this way for something too, and now I had it, I had no more plans. And yeah, I coulda gone back and Jack woulda had me. But I didn't. Not for the longest time.

"You can stay here, Ash," said Mona, as we sat in the red plastic chairs. "Wouldn't be the first. Right, Bly?"

Bly nodded.

He said, "Mona is everybody's first home out here," and explained how he'd been here till he got his own place, and I was thinking what, can't I stay with you, but I didn't wanna seem rude to Mona.

Instead I asked where his place was and he said, "Over that way" and nodded to somewhere I couldn't see out beyond a coupla sheds on Mona's land. And I still didn't know how Bly got sick, no more'n I knew what was wrong with him.

"So you can stay here," said Mona and I panicked a mite and said to Bly, "You don't got enough space for me?" and Bly laughed. So I took that as a no.

"Okay, well," I said, "thanks then, Mona. But just a night," and Mona giggled and Cooper looked at her and she looked back at Cooper and said, "Come for a day, stay for a lifetime," like it was the funniest thing anyone ever said.

She sat up straight and said, "I have a great idea! Bly, why don't you take Snowflake on the rounds with you?" and Bly nodded and said, "Sure, come on Snowflake," and I started wondering why everyone thought it was funny to start calling me that when I'd left school because of it. Well, not exactly because of it, but it showed why I had to leave. I guess.

Bly was up and around the side of the house and I saw Socrates there and asked Bly where we were going and he saw Socrates too and said, "Maybe you wanna put your bag right up high on that top shelf," so I did, because I did not want to come back to find the last few things I owned in the world end up inside of a goat.

Then Bly got this funny kinda look in his eye. He made a big deal of checking for Mona first, even though she was still out back somewhere.

"Look," he said, "next time he gets at something he oughtn't . . ." and then he ran straight at Socrates, who was struggling on chewing one of my laces and the goat did a darn-crazy thing; it fell over and rolled onto its back with its legs straight up in the air and lay there stiff as a table that had died, and I yelled, "Bly, what'd you do? You killed him, Bly, you—oh—" because Socrates was already getting up again. Just like that. Bly was grinning from one ear to the other and then he saw my face and said, "It's okay, it's okay, it's just that Mona don't like me doing it."

"Doing what?" I said. "What the hell just happened?"

Bly pointed at the goat.

"That there's a Tennessee fainting goat."

"What?" I said, and then Bly explained how it was a Tennessee fainting goat, just like he said, so I said, "And what the heck is that?" and Bly pointed at Socrates and said, "That is." And I could see we were getting nowhere. Then Mona came around the side of the house and said, "Ain't you two left yet? You ain't funning my goat, are you?" and she looked kind of mad but I had no idea if she really was or not.

"No, ma'am," said Bly, "I was explaining to Snowflake about

how Socrates doesn't like getting scared. What's it called now? I always forget that word."

"Myotonic. Socrates is a myotonic goat and Bly, you oughta know better than to mock the afflicted."

"Who's mocking?" said Bly, who, to be fair, was only grinning. Then Mona said, "Git!" so we got.

In Bly's truck he explained how Socrates was a kind of rare breed and for some reason, but no one knew why, when they got scared their legs would lock up tight and for a few seconds they'd lie there, feet sticking up to heaven like they'd chewed their last article of clothing. And then, bam! they'd pop right back into life again, and he explained that Mona didn't like anyone playing that game with Socrates.

"I guess it's kinda mean on him," I said, and Bly nodded but said the real reason Mona didn't like it was that she was embarrassed to have bought a defective goat, for one thing, and for a second thing, she was embarrassed twice over because she thought she was buying a nanny goat and would be able to have milk from it, and then, when the man brought it, it was a billy goat and good for nothing except maybe as a garbage disposal unit with a white beard and attitude.

We were riding down the dirt tracks now and Bly waved his hand at the wet desert.

"These are the Forties. Forty acres each. That's what Mona's got. Forty acres of sand and nothing. And Mary too. But first we got rounds to do down in the Twenties."

"So what are we doing?" I said, and instead Bly explained how Mona gave him somewhere to live when he arrived. Then he explained how Mona had let him go on living on her property and even paid him to run errands for the people who were too sick to go to Snowflake and get their own groceries, or whatever. And that's what we were doing now, taking groceries to a bunch of the sickest folks.

"I been into Snowflake this morning. Got stuff for four of the guys. Hey, I might've been the one to pick you up, instead of Mona. That would've been an even bigger coincidence, right?" and I thought "not really" but I never liked to disagree with Bly, not ever.

Instead I said, "Why the heck is it called Snowflake?" and he said, "That is a weird story, kind of another coincidence. It was named after these two gentlemen, Mr. Snow and Mr. Flake. This is eighteen-something I'm talking about. Mr. Snow and Mr. Flake. What are the chances? And anyway, they were the founders of the town, so they got to choose and they decided to call it Snowflake."

"They coulda called it Flakesnow."

"Yeah they coulda, but I guess that would've been dumb."

"Just saying."

"So'm I."

"Funny kinda name, though, right?"

"That's nothing. There's a town down the road called Show Low. Named after two men playing poker. Gambling for the land, and they couldn't get a winner, so finally one of them says,

'Lowest card wins?' and then this other guy drew the deuce of clubs. Show Low."

Well, there was nothing to say about that, so I shut up and looked at the desert for a few minutes more until I couldn't look at it no longer and I said, "Bly, what's wrong with you?" but he said, "Here we are! The Sick Birds!" because we were pulling into a yard between two little houses, metal sidings and roofs like Mona's but even smaller.

Bly leaned over to me.

"Mona calls 'em the Sick Birds but we don't say that to their face. It's just on account of their name's Byrd, is all. They're sisters."

"I can see that," I said, because through the wet windshield I could see the two women, one on each porch, keeping outta the rain, and they might have been identical. Bly said they weren't, they just looked almost like it. Then he said, "Help me with their stuff?" so I did.

We got two boxes out of the back seat of the truck, one for each of them, and Bly whispered, "That's Sally and the other one's Dolly. You take Dolly's and I'll do Sally," and we went over and Bly called out, "That there's Snowflake," nodding at me as he went into Sally's house and I was trying to avoid falling over in my clown shoes and I wanted to say, "No, I'm Ash," but by then Dolly was saying hello and asking if Bly was my brother and I said yes but was wondering how she knew about me and then Dolly said, "Mona just called to say you were coming," so that explained that.

I kinda tried not to stare at Dolly, but it was hard. She was real pale. Pale, like she was covered in flour. And she looked kinda dry, which added to the flour thing. She had real dark rings under her eyes too. But that wasn't the worst of it. The worst of it was that she seemed confused, like when you just wake up and you don't know where or what the hell you are? Dolly seemed like that, confused, over nothing, so when I said, "Where'll I put your box?" she said "box?" and looked like I'd asked her the hardest question in the world.

"Pleased to meet you," I guess I said then, and I repeated, "Where'll I put your box?" and Dolly showed me through into the kitchen that was just a corner of the main room, like at Mona's. And like Mona's this place was covered in Reynolds Wrap too, floor to ceiling. Apart from that, well, it looked more or less normal, and newer than Mona's.

Dolly looked at me, still with that look on her face. Confused. Then she said, "You sick too?" and I shook my head and assured her that I was not sick. Maybe tired from the bus.

Then I saw something to make me wonder. As I was leaving, I saw a table in the center of the room, a large round table, and the whole darned top of it was covered in bottles, those little white plastic bottles, like medicine comes along in, and I guess there were two hundred bottles set right there. A sea of plastic bottles. An ocean. Now you might be thinking "so what?" but I think back and I can recall that there was something not right about it. I stared at the table and felt guilty like I was looking at her unmade bed because there's also something not right about seeing an unmade bed, the bed of someone you don't know. I believe.

And I think Dolly caught me looking so I looked away and said, "Where's that Bly got to?" and headed out. We got back in the truck and Bly said, "Well, what did you make of them canaries?" and I said, "Because they're called Byrd?" and Bly shook his head.

"No, that's more coincidence, I guess. They're called Byrd. But we're all canaries."

To which I said nothing but must've looked kinda dumb because Bly started the engine of the truck and said, "We're all canaries, Ash. Everyone here."

We rolled out into the desert again, and he started to talk. "You know," he said, "in the olden days, when there was a coal mine, there was no way of knowing if there was poisonous gas down there, gas that would kill the miners, because you couldn't smell it. So what they did was, they'd get a canary in a cage and lower it down the mine shaft, and if it came up singing, then they knew it was safe, but if it came up dead, then they knew there was gas down there. See?"

And still I did not see, not at all. Not then.

DEAD ELF

Sure, I can tell you now how stupid I was back then. And I guess I wasn't stupid, just ignorant, which ain't the same thing, they say, and for once they're right. I had done with school but I hadn't begun to learn nothing, not yet. That time was coming. And what a fine and eager kid I was, I was then. From here, believe me when I say, I can still see all the way back to my brightness and feel it like yesterday, my chomping child, o eager little scout of the world's adventures! And, yes, I'll guess there was already a little tiredness in my bones, but I was ready to learn something, and Snowflake was the place I learned it.

Then Bly said to me, "We're gonna go see the dead elf," but I wasn't listening. I guess I was still thinking about what he asked me before, about the sisters, and I said, "I guess Dolly seems kinda sick" and I thought about the table full of bottles and I said, "She has all those pills. She needs all those pills?" and Bly shrugged and said, "If she wants to get well" and I said, "But that's crazy. No one needs all those pills," and Bly didn't reply.

Then I caught up and said, "Did you just say dead elf?"

Bly looked at me and said, "You feeling all right?" and I reckoned I was just dog-tired. That's why they call them Greyhound buses, I guess. You don't get much sleep. Maybe none.

"We're going out to see Dead Elf," Bly said. "He's this German dude. He built his own house, way out. To be sure it's safe. Actually he's called Detlef, but I call him Dead Elf sometimes, because that's what Mona calls him sometimes."

"He built his house?" I said, as we bumped down the road, but when I say "road," you don't go thinking it's the interstate or something. It was a dirt track, like all the rest I'd seen, and it was bumpy as hell and filling up with water in places, and it went on for miles.

"Who, Detlef?"

"Detlef, right. He's sick too?"

"Uh-huh, yes he is."

"Then how'd he build his house?"

Bly looked at me for a time, across from the wheel, then back straight ahead.

"There are all different types of canary, Snowflake."

"Will you quit calling me that?" I said and Bly said, "Maybe."

Then he said, "Thing is, Detlef was real, real sick. I mean one of the worst Mona's ever seen, she said, when he got here. He lived with her a coupla years and got himself cleaned up, and then he built his place. He was real careful about how he did it. And he's way off grid here, so that helps with everything. So, if he stays out here, and doesn't go to flatland, then he's pretty well. But if he goes back and hangs around with normies, he gets sick again pretty quick."

"Flatland?" I said then and Bly said that flatland was where the normies lived, which is to say, normal people, people who weren't canaries, and flatland was anywhere that wasn't out in that patch of desert outside Snowflake at five thousand feet, well heck, nearly six.

"Oh," I said. "Is that like you?"

Bly nodded.

"And Mona. And some of the others. If we stay here and keep ourselves clean, things ain't too bad. I mean, I still have bad days. Like if I spend too long in flatland, I'll pay for it later. But I'm careful as I can be." And he pointed at the mask I'd seen him wearing before, which had been setting on the dash the whole time. Then he went on and said, "And Detlef is more or less the best of us if he stays out here, but last week he had to go to New Mexico. And he's been laid up ever since he got back. Which is why you and I are bringing him his groceries."

I guess you can tell I wasn't really buying any of it. This canary stuff. But I also knew Bly and I knew he wouldn't make something up like being ill. He wouldn't fake it. But maybe some of the other folks were. So what I thought was, well, let's just see where this is all heading.

So I said, "But why go to New Mexico, if it's gonna make you sick?" and Bly said "funeral." I looked at him real close, and I could not figure out what the look on his face meant. But something told me to shut up.

After two or three miles of bumping we pulled off the dirt turnpike. Now I knew for sure we were in the middle of nowhere, because not only was there the damn desert, but you couldn't see one other house, not one, whereas at Mona's you could see two from the front porch and one from the back, way off in the distance.

I looked around as I got out of the truck. The rain had left us for a time, and over on the horizon in the haze were some low mountains, which I guess is where the six thousand feet came into it. But as far as you could see, in any direction, there was no sign of human life, nor barely anything else neither.

"Why'd anyone want to live out here?" Bly said, looking at me. "That's what you're thinking, right?" And I nodded, because yes, that was exactly what I was thinking. Bly said, "This is nothing. This is the center of the freaking world compared to some folks. There's the first guy who came here. Mona was one of the first, but this very first guy, he used to live in the Forties, but now he lives way out in the deep."

And Bly nodded towards the mountains. The deep.

"Twenty miles that way." He paused.

"Twenty miles, huh?" I said. It was the first time I'd heard of this first guy, but I wasn't really paying attention. And when I speak about him again . . . well, by then things had gotten real weird. Before I could say anything else, Bly fixed me real serious and said, "No one wants to be sick, Snowflake. No one. Don't let anyone ever tell you different. Grab the box."

I had no time to wonder what Bly meant because I was peering at the back seat again and there was one box that had "Dead Elf" with a smiley face after it written on the flap and it was full of candy bars and hot dogs and boxes of Twinkies and bags of chips and tins of beer, so I said, "We having a party?" and Bly said, "Nah, that's just what he eats."

Then we met Dead Elf.

He came out on his porch and held up his hand when he saw Bly coming. He was a big blond guy, skinny, but way over six foot, and he had one of those open kinda faces that make you relax straightaway. He stuck his hand out for a hello and I was scared he was gonna break my fingers because his hands were like shovels or something, but I guess he was one of what folks people call a gentle giant.

"You out of bed today?" asked Bly, and Detlef said, "Getting there" and then "You must be Snowflake," so I knew Mona had rung ahead again.

"My name's not—" I was saying, but Bly and Detlef were yakking away about this and that and a lot of nothing. Bly said to me, "You wanna see his place? It's cool, he built it himself."

"You're German?" I asked Detlef and he said that, yes, he was but he'd been living in the States for about thirty years and maybe I could still hear his accent, which I could, a little. It was more in the way his sentences trotted along than in any one word.

I told him how there was supposed to be some German blood in my family, a ways back.

"On my father's side," I added, looking at Bly, and he was probably wondering how the hell I knew that when my mother had only known my father for a week and he was also probably wondering when I had learned to make dumb conversation like that. But Detlef was friendly, like the fact that my mother spent seven days with a guy whose third cousin might've once seen Munich made us old family friends. And he showed us around the house.

He pointed at the walls.

"Pretty cool, huh?" he said, and I couldn't see nothing but a wall and then he explained that like Mona's they were covered in Reynolds Wrap but he'd figured out how to paint it with white clay watered down, which covered it up and looked just like normal white plaster. And still I had no idea why you'd paper your house with tinfoil.

Then he showed us his phone. See, he said he got buzzy even if he used a landline telephone. Buzzy. He said lots of canaries did. So he'd invented a way around it. He had a wooden telephone, like the part you hold in your hand, and he'd carved that himself. It had holes where the earpiece and the mouthpiece would be, and from these holes there was two tubes that ran off and was connected to the actual telephone handset. So you could use that and keep the real one away from your head.

"Wanna call someone? It works!" he said, like I had doubted it for one second. "I made them for a bunch of folks now."

He showed us around the shed out in the yard, and inside was everything electrical, kept away from the house so all the "bad stuff" was far enough away not to give him any trouble. And when I started thinking but he still has an oven and a kettle and what all in the house so there must be electricity there, he saw me thinking that, because he explained that unlike most other houses, he'd built a special converter that turned AC into DC and his house was run on DC which was just fine, because it was only AC that gave him trouble.

Well, that seemed neat, and Detlef sure was a smart guy, because he'd done it himself. He said he'd been an engineer in flatland, so he knew how to do this stuff. He'd fixed up his car too, by which I mean he'd stripped out all the electrics he could and left it as basic as could be, and that way the electromagnetic radiation and so forth was way down as low as it could be.

We stood looking at his car, the three of us, hands on hips, like we was connoisseurs of motor vehicles, which was hilarious because I knew precisely nothing about cars. Still don't. Anyways, we were looking at this big old dirty heap of a thing, and though you might think the rain had cleaned it up it looked like the rain put as much dust on the car as it took off of it. Monsoon season, Arizona.

"You're gonna see a few of these around here," said Detlef. "1984 Mercedes. The color was called 'Icon Gold.' These cars, they last forever. But the real thing is that they were the last car to be made simple enough. You can strip out almost all the electrics, make 'em clean. They still run good."

Then he said, like he was only just figuring it out, "Bly's your brother?" and I said yes and he said how it was real nice to meet me. Then he said, "You'll be staying a while?" and I said no, and then he looked confused and said, "But you're sick too?" and I said no, I wasn't. And I was thinking why does everyone keep asking me that?

"Not sick?" said Detlef.

"I'm fine," I said. "I mean, I'm tired," and I explained how I'd come in on the overnight Greyhound and that you don't get no sleep on a Greyhound and then I said my joke about how that's why they call them Greyhounds because they leave you sick as a dog. And then I figured no one was laughing and I said, "I mean, tired as a dog. Dog-tired," and then it was even less funny.

I really did feel tired by then and Bly said we'd better go home and by that he meant back to Mona's.

So we bumped our way back down the dirt interstate and I was looking out at the desert and the shrubs and the occasional house in the distance and the rain had still left but it was hot and sticky and I felt my head swimming round like I was underwater, and I remember thinking one thing to myself, which was along the lines of "what the heck is going on?" and then I blacked out.

CHAPTER 4

ENVIRONMENTAL ILLNESS

So. As I was saying, I passed out on the way home from Detlef. But I wasn't out for long. Leastways, I woke up and figured out I was on the porch at Mona's. They had me set in one of the red plastic chairs, with my feet on another. That sounds like we was two different things, my feet and me, but that's okay, because that's more or less how I felt. They'd propped me up so my head was against the wall and put a blanket across me, and I opened my eyes and said, "Huh, it's raining then," and there was Mona and Bly looking down at me with their hands on their hips like I was a 1984 Mercedes that some German guy gutted.

I wasn't awake for long either. I just had time to hear someone say, "I wonder what will happen next" and then I went off to sleep. Guess I was dog-tired, and maybe there's something to that, because of the two of 'em, it was Cooper that spent most of his day lying around with his tongue hanging out and Socrates who was always busy nosing around for the next item of clothing to consume.

I slept long, making up for all the time I wasn't asleep on that Greyhound, driving through the night and thinking that if no one was gonna tell me where Bly was at, I sure had the right to go and find him.

Now my long sleep, it was one of those sleeps, you know 'em, where you can be half-woke, kinda, and during that half-woke-up time I recalled something from Dolly's house. You'll know that too, how you can sometimes see something or notice something, but at the time you notice it you don't have time to notice you noticed it? And it's only later that you get around to noticing what you noticed. Yeah, that's how it is. And I recalled seeing a calendar, the kind with one month on show at a time and a big picture of something on the top half. Like a mountain. Or a horse. Or a goat, that kinda thing. So this calendar, it was hanging on Dolly's tinfoil wall, opposite a window with no curtains or blinds or anything looking out across the whole damn desert. And in my mind, I saw that there was not one thing writ upon that calendar. Not one. And this is the point, as I lay there, half-dreaming and half-thinking, the point is I wondered if there was anything writ on any of the other months either.

When I woke up for real it was still raining and I felt cold, never mind the blanket. It was still daytime, but the sky was dark. There was no one around. The house was dark too, and I wondered where everyone was at. Mona, Cooper, Bly. Even Socrates seemed to be taking time off hunting for people's footwear.

I wondered what the hour of the day it was and that's funny because why did it matter? I wasn't going nowhere, not that day, I knew that. Why did we always need to know the damn time?

What were we so fussed over? We were none of us going far, even then. And I guess we know better now. But I went to find my bag, around at the front, getting splashed some by the rain hitting the ground just off the porch.

I found my bag and found my phone and it was still alive and it said it was around five. I put my hand to my face and felt my nose, which felt kinda funny, and I found there was blood all crusted up around my nose and my lip and I'd had a nosebleed of some kind. I snuck back into the house, just like the first time, and even though there was no one there, I snuck in quiet and careful like I had when I was naked. I went into the tinfoil bathroom and washed up my face in the basin and there was my towel from before so I took it and dried myself up, but careful, in case the bleed came back, which I didn't want it to, this not being my house.

I came out and stood and took a proper look at Mona's place. It was dark, like I said, so I stood for a time and waited to see if I could see a little more. It was a funny kinda home. There really was just the kitchen at one end of the main room, with the sink and the refrigerator. Heck, you know what a kitchen looks like, right? Though I will say there was no kind of cooker, not a proper one, just an electric ring for one pan, setting on the worktop. Then there was the rest of the main room, with stuff all around. The desk, which had a phone on it, buried under piles of paper. There was Mona's bed but I didn't look at that, even though it was made. And there really was nowhere else to sit, but all around the walls were bookcases and I saw more books than I had ever seen in my life put together. It was like she had her own library, Mona I mean. I stared at the books, standing there in the darkness, and the books setting there on the shelves and the rain hammering down on that tin roof like the mighty world was ending and I wondered what was in them. For I had never been a book lover. No, I did not open a book very often, not once since I left school, that's certain. Truth to tell I was a mite scared of a book. But there was no one around, and it was dark, so I started to feel brave and I wondered who could have so much to say that you needed a few hundred pieces of paper to say it and not just a couple. Or even one. Or even the back of a postcard, which is how parts of my so-called family seemed to like to communicate.

So I snuck to the bookcase and I was trying to read the titles, and I read a few and I could see that most of 'em, the ones I could see, were books about being sick or about how to get better from being sick. But I couldn't really see so I pulled my phone out of my pocket and lit up the screen for a flashlight and was just reading one thing that said *Multiple Chemical Sensitivity: A Sufferer's Memoir* and then I jumped a mile. Because out of nowhere Mona said, "It's going to be better if you don't use that thing around here," and I knew she meant my phone. There she was setting in the dark in a corner I hadn't seen, half hid behind a bookcase and curled up tiny in a chair with a book on her lap reading though how she could read in that light I have no idea, I surely don't.

"What?" I guess I said, and she explained that the phone was bad for her, my cell phone, and had I heard that in Italy, some judge just awarded four million somethings to a guy who said using his cell for work all day had given him a brain tumor, and the judge agreed, yes, yes it had. So that was the first time anywhere in the world where someone with the law on their side had said that cell phones were bad for you, and Mona finished up by saying she figured it wouldn't be the last one neither. And I said, "Uh, no, I didn't hear that," and then I thought for about two seconds and I said, "I'll turn it right off." Which I did.

There was this real long pause and I felt uneasy but Mona was, well, Mona was something else, you know. She knew right away what was up and she said to me, "Snowflake," but she said it gentle and like she liked me, "are you okay, kid? I guess all of this is kinda strange, huh?" and I said, yes, yes it was and would she please tell me what was going on and why were everybody's walls covered in Reynolds Wrap and why did Dolly have two hundred bottles of tablets and why was electricity bad for you and what the hell was wrong with Bly, because I did not want anything bad to be happening to him, not my big stepbrother.

So Mona says, "Here, sit down. You had a day, huh? Out here in the desert with us canaries. But don't worry about nothing. The altitude takes some getting used to, and the air ain't right, not with all this rain. Though I am pleased to say you've missed the worst of it. It's been a bad one this year. The monsoon." She looked out the window and said, "This is just the pointy tail end of it."

I sat down on the chair at her desk and stared at the papers there and while I did that, she told me all about it.

She told me how they had environmental illness. And how that can mean different things.

"Some of us," she said, "we got multiple chemical sensitivity, and we get affected by chemicals. Things like fragrance and perfume, things like what they put in soap powders, things like pesticides and herbicides, things like pollution, gas fumes, glue, you name it. Now, normies, they can cope with this stuff, but we can't. And it ain't the same stuff for everyone. For someone it's this, but for someone else it's that. See? It's like being allergic. Some people are allergic to peanut butter, right? And others ain't, they're allergic to cats. See?"

I was thinking "sorta," but Mona was going right along, and next she told me about the electromagnetic hypersensitivity syndrome.

"I ain't too bad with that, but cell phones make my head start buzzing in a few minutes. Detlef, he's gotta be *real* careful. So some of us here got MCS and some got EHS and the lucky ones got both," and then she started giggling right there. "Real lucky," she said, and then she went on. "And then there's people who got all of that, and maybe something else, like undiagnosed Lyme, or Bartonella, or mold issues, or what-have-ya."

And she went on and she went on and she told me that the walls were covered in tinfoil to keep all the chemicals inside them just that: *inside* and away out of the air. She said how the way we make houses is crazy, what with all the chemicals we put into things, so if you had MCS and you couldn't afford to build a safe house from the ground up, if you had to buy an old house and make it safe, what you did was you painted corn starch on the walls and then stuck the Reynolds Wrap over it all, and that seals everything bad inside, behind the foil, and keeps it away from the canary.

And then, finally, finally, she told me that Bly had a deal of MCS but was okay with electrics and he was okay if he was careful and stuck to the rules, and I said, "Like the mask?" and she nodded and said, "You know, you could crack open a book. Wouldn't kill ya. I got one or two that explain things." And then she got up and pulled that very book I had been looking at off the shelf, and that finally was a real coincidence because there were a million books on that bookcase, easy. Maybe two.

She winked at me and said, "You can read, right?" and I nodded.

"I'll put a light on outside," she said, "on the porch. And maybe it's about time you need to be outside again and maybe we could think about eating something," and that sounded good because I suddenly realized I'd eaten nothing since I could not remember. So while she started fixing something in the kitchen, I went back out and set on a red plastic chair, with a light overhead of me. I flicked open the book like you do when you don't really want to read it, from the back to the front, and I saw a whole lot of things I didn't understand right off the bat, but I ended up at the front where the name of the person that wrote it was, and that turned out to be Mona Mochsky. I looked at her, through the back door, as she stood staring at the inside of the refrigerator with her hands on her hips as if everything inside was misbehaving itself. Then I looked back at the book she wrote, and right under her name it said, "For all my friends who lost their lives to environmental illness." And I thought "huh."

I went over to see Mona.

"Mona?" I said.

"What is it, kid?"

And I said, "Bly's really sick?"

"Uh-huh," she said.

"But he's gonna get better, right?"

Mona looked away from the mischievous food and peered at me.

"Sure," she said. "Depending on what you mean by 'better.'"

Then the door swung open and in came Bly. He'd been taking that fourth box of groceries out somewhere, and he was wet to the skin and looked out at me on the porch and nodded and said "Snowflake!" and grinned and then looked at Mona and said, "What's cooking?" and then we ate soup.

As we ate, Mona said, "You know, it only takes a straw to show which way the wind is blowing," and Bly nodded and said, "Ain't that the truth," and I sat there and thought "what?" and I also thought, "Please don't ask me what I think about that for I have no idea what you are all talking about."

Then Mona said, "What did we learn today?"

She looked at Bly, and before he said anything to her he looked at me and whispered, "This happens every evening," and he told me how every evening, anyone who was sitting on Mona's porch had to say something they learned during the day, and it didn't matter if it was a big thing or a small thing, you had to say something. She figured that a) we all oughta keep learning all our lives and b) we probably was anyway, but it didn't hurt to practice.

So then Bly stared out into the desert, which was getting hard to see. It had stopped raining again but the sky was dark and night was coming along at a good speed. He thought a while and then he said, "The most important thing I learned today is that the darned goat truly will eat anything." Mona snorted a laugh and then Bly added, "Plus, I learned that Ash really is a snowflake," and I said "hey!"

"A delicate child of life," said Mona, nodding, and I said "cut it out!" but they were only messing with me and somehow I didn't mind them saying what used to hurt real bad when the kids at school said that kinda thing. Except they would never have said anything fancy like "a delicate child of life"; they would have said something worse and way meaner.

Bly said to Mona, "What did you learn today?" because it turned out that she had to do it too. So then she stared out into the desert (because it seemed like that was part of it, like the desert was going to give you the answer) and said, "Well, today I was reading about epigenetics." So, well, then me and Bly looked at each other and both said "epi-whut?" at exactly the same time, and that made us laugh again.

Mona read a lot of science books. She said it started when she got sick and when the doctors couldn't find out was wrong with her. Just because they couldn't find nothing, well, that

don't make you well again, so she started reading herself to
try to figure stuff out. And when she lost her job because of
being sick, then she started to read even more. That's how she
ended up with a whole library. And today she'd been reading
about epigenetics. I knew what genetics was because I recalled
something from school about it. About DNA, and genes, and
chromosomes and what-have-you-got. They was what made you
who you were. But only up to a point, said Mona.

"That is to say," she said, "they was what made you up to
the second you were born, but from then on, well, you might
become one person or another person, depending on how you
was raised. You heard of nature versus nurture, right?"

And Bly nodded and I did too, though I hadn't. But what she
meant was that your nature was in your genes and then how
you was nurtured, how you was raised, that had a big effect on
you too.

But then Mona went on and said that still ain't all there is to
it. And what's left is epigenetics. Which, she said, is how things
that happen to you, things like diseases, and stress, and toxins
can actually *change* your genes. Like, some trauma can alter the
way a gene is behaving. Turn some version of a gene off and
another version of it on. That could change who you are. That
if you got too stressed, it could make you sick. And she said
epigenetics was kinda new and no one knew much about it.

She said it was sad, thinking about little kids getting trauma-
tized from terrible things before they'd even set out in life, and
how that could make 'em sick or even change their personality,

like it could make them mean when they weren't mean before. And how then maybe that might make them make their kids mean, and so on, and the world would get worse.

"You know, Ash," she said, "never mind a straw. It only takes a snowflake to show which way the wind is blowing," and never had I felt lighter and lonelier in my whole life than sitting on that porch in the darkness with the whole dang desert in front of me than when I realized that both my names, my real name and my nickname, meant almost nothing. Nothing but something light, something so light and so fragile as to almost not exist.

"So?" said Mona and she was looking at me, and I said "what?" so she said, "Which way is the world blowing?" and I recall for a fact that she said "world" and not "wind." Because that was the exact moment that I started to understand, I'm sure of it, though I know I didn't look like I was understanding nothing.

Then she said, "Snowflake, what did you learn?"

I looked out into the desert (because I wanted to do things right) and I looked for a long time and then I gave up and said, "I guess I learned a lot of things," and there was no need to say more, because everyone had seen me learning a whole bunch of stuff. About MCS, and EHS, and off-gassing, and German automobiles from the 1980s, and fainting goats.

"Not bad for your first day," said Bly, and I looked at him like my eyes was going to pop out and I said, "What? Is it still the first damn day?" and that I found hard to believe because it felt like I'd been in Snowflake for years. That sounds dumb, but that's how it was.

"You only got here this morning," said Bly. "But you did already have one sleep."

"Tiring learning stuff, ain't it?" said Mona, and off she went like the Pez dispenser. But when she said "tiring" then my good God did I feel tired again, and I said, "Are you sure you're okay with me staying, Mona? It's kind of you," and Mona said it was nothing and that she'd had hundreds of waifs and strays and not just Cooper and that it was her pleasure and a whole bunch of kind things like that.

Then I said, "So where can I sleep? I'm kinda done," and she said, "Right here!" and I looked into the house and I must've looked stupid to her because she said, "Right here" again but slower and then I started to get the feeling that what she meant was "right here."

As in, on the porch. Which she did.

Then she went inside to find some blankets and things and while she was gone, I looked at Bly and I guess I looked spooked. I said, "Can't I stay with you?" and he laughed and nodded over past the sheds and said "there?" and I said, "Yes, at your place," and he laughed and pointed past the sheds and said, "That is my place," and then I started to get the feeling he wasn't pointing *past* the sheds. He was pointing *at* the sheds.

Bly had been living in a pair of sheds. And I wondered what the heck happened to people to make 'em think it was normal to live in a wooden shed.

Then I said, ". . . Mary?" with a quiet voice, and Bly explained how she slept in the back of her truck and anyway, I was venting too bad to be anywhere near her.

"Venting?" I said, because I know I'd heard it earlier on but still didn't really get it, and Bly said that it was normal and nothing to worry about, but they'd seen it enough, when someone comes out of flatland, and they're still pumping out all the chemicals and perfumes and what-you-got. Like how the human body is kinda like a sponge, and it soaks up everything it comes into contact with. And then vents it back out again. Once I'd been here a few days, or maybe a few weeks, and finished venting, then I'd be fit for civilized company once more. He was funning me when he said that, I could tell, but right then I wasn't feeling in the mood for jokes.

Then Mona came out with a load of stuff. There was a folding metal bed, and a sleeping bag, and a bunch of blankets, and she rolled one up for a pillow and Bly started to go.

I said, "Bly?"

He stopped and came back and said "yeah, what?"

And I said, "You're gonna go back to the academy, right?"

" 'Course," he said. " 'Course I am. It's what I wanna be. Why?"

"Nothing," I said, so then he said goodnight, but then he stopped again and turned around and said, "It's good to see you, Ash."

Then he went off into the dark, with a flashlight to find his way to his shed.

I felt a bit less lonely then, but and because I was happy to see Bly again. And Mona was real kind, though she did say some stuff from time to time. Such as, I was just taking my clown boots off when she poked her head back out of the house and looked at the boots and said, "Kid, you might wanna check inside your boots every time you put 'em back on," and I didn't know what she meant but then she said "scorpions."

Then she added, "maybe rattlers."

Then she went back into the house. And I was just about getting into the sleeping bag when she came bustling back out of the house and said, "Darn, I think your dumb brother forgot to close the yard gate." She went over to the gate that led out from the bit of desert that she called "the yard" and into the bit of the desert that was called "the desert."

Then she came back and started giggling and said, "Because we wouldn't want a coyote to come in here and, you know, eat your face."

Then she said goodnight.

FLUOXETINE

You may not wonder too greatly when and if I tell you I didn't get much in the way of sleep. The only good thing about the storm was that I figured the coyotes might stay home. And I wasn't going to leave my bed for one second with that rain hammering down, so at least I didn't get to worry about scorpions and rattlers in my boots neither. I don't suppose there was never a storm like it, not in the history of creation since God made the world, or anyhow, not since last monsoon season, that's what Mona told me later.

They'd put the bed right up against the back wall of the house, as far under the porch as could be, but still sometimes when the rain got turned up real high, I felt it splash all the way over onto my face. The first couple times I set up straight thinking "rattler!" but I soon got tired of that.

Somewhere in the middle of the dark, and the middle of the roar of the rain on the porch roof, I figured I wasn't going to get no sleep, so I might as well give up trying. Kneeling, I worked my fingers up onto the metal shelves where my (and I mean Bly's) clothes and my bag were, and felt around and then the lightning flashed and I saw my bag so I said "thank you" and pulled my bag off the shelf and under my blanket.

First I got my phone and lit up the screen. It still had a mite of juice, just a tad. But no signal. Not one bit. I pulled out the postcard. I set there under my blanket, looking at it, hoping Mona didn't know I had my phone switched on because her bed was just the other side of the wall.

I guess I'd never really looked at the picture on the postcard before. I guess I'd just been more overly concerned about what was writ on the back. It was from Bly, to Jack, and all it said was "this is where I am really" and he gave the address, Mona's address, and then he'd put, "I'm real sorry. I love you Dad." And that was that.

I'd looked at those words a thousand times and a thousand more. And now finally I had started to learn the other stuff, about how Bly had dropped out of cadet school but had pretended to Jack he was still there. Because he was ashamed. And how Jack had pretended to me that Bly was still there. Because he was ashamed. And no one had told me my damn mother had paid Bly a visit. Probably because everyone was ashamed of her too, but she was still my damn mother. My family. And with all of that, I'd never really looked at the picture on the front.

It was of a building. And it was a real big building. The building was the color of the desert in which it was set, and I mean red as rust, aside from one or two scrubby-looking plants, and they was dirty green. And the building was put right on top of a hill, and behind it was a sky as blue as the day it was made, with nothing in it but wonder. The building was kinda made of blocks, it had this square look about it, but on top was another block, like a tower, and on top of that was a man of gold, with one arm to the side and the other out front, like he was pointing at something.

It was hard in the dark, under that blanket, with the light from my phone, but I turned the card over and read the tiny letters printed at the bottom where it said: The Church of Jesus Christ of Latter-day Saints, Snowflake, Arizona. You know, I guess I had figured it would all make sense when I got there. It didn't. But there was no time for any more wonder, because the battery went and my phone went with it.

You always think you ain't ever gonna sleep, but you do. No matter what. And that storm must've kept up through half the night or more and I lay in the dark with my eyes wide thinking over and over *Bly, are you really sick?* but somewhere and somehow I slept.

First thing I knew was a buzzing, before I even opened my eyes. No roar of the storm, that was gone, just this gentle buzzing nearby. I opened my eyes and saw something flittering around, hovering no more'n a foot above my head, and at first I thought it was a moth or a big bee and then I saw it was the smallest bird you ever saw. A hummingbird, and now I knew why they call 'em that because the wings just hum away as they flit about. And boy, it was about the prettiest thing I ever saw in my whole darned life. It was about the size of your thumb, and when you looked real close, its feathers had more colors than the rainbow and stranger ones too.

The sun was shining and then I saw there were more like six hummingbirds, coming and going to a glass ball that was dangling off of a string at the edge of the porch. They was sucking at a tube that came out of the ball and inside was the thing they was getting after, but I didn't know then it was sugar water.

I watched the hummingbirds for a time, and I wondered how late it was and was about to look at my phone when I recalled it was dead. The sun was low in the sky, and I had no idea what that meant, but there was no sound from the house, from Mona or Cooper, so I guessed it was early.

It wasn't like the storm never happened, because there were pools of rainwater here and there, and everything was wet, but the sun was coming up fast and it was already hot and I started to see Arizona like I thought it would be. As soon as the sun set to work on the wet, things began to steam, like they was on fire. Steam coming off of clothes on the washing line and from the ground, and the tops of fence posts and gateposts, and from the sheds where Bly was keeping. Never seen anything like that, the steam, and the hot sun, and the buzzing little birds, and if I looked in one direction, it was like I was sleeping inside somewhere, with two walls and a ceiling, but if I looked the other direction I was outside in the whole damn state of Arizona, with red desert and blue, blue sky and I realized right there that I had never slept outside in my life, not before, not once. It made me kinda happy to think that I finally had. And been woke by the prettiest thing in the world. I guess it ain't so long since we all slept out, most every night. Just a few thousands of years ago, which Mona most likely would have called "recently."

Then from somewhere I heard her screaming.

"Socrates! You . . . goat!" and I knew the Capricorn was in a whole heap of trouble for something.

So, two things happened when Socrates ate something bad. First was something physical. By which I mean that *he* might've liked the taste of my sneakers, but his insides didn't. So there was a whole heap of mess right by the dang door when Mona went outside and she'd gone and stepped plumb into it. The second was something mental. By which I mean he became the meanest, sorest goat on God's earth. He was in a real bad mood, for that day and most of the next few too. Mona told me to keep clear of him and that I was happy to do, because there's something crazed about the eyes of a goat at the best of times and these wasn't the best of times.

Did you ever look at a goat? Up close, I mean. Then you'll know how their eyes are the darndest things. Because goats are a lot like people, that's something else you'll know if you've hung out with 'em, but the one way they ain't like people is their eyes. They got square pupils, well, to be exact about it, what they got is rectangles. While what we got is circles. So that's funny, but it's not funny when a goat gets sore, because Socrates started butting stuff with those big horns of his. He was butting the side of the house and then he was butting the front door and then he started on Mona's little Antarctic car and then he started butting Cooper. Which made Cooper turn from a sweet dog into a real mad mutt and they started going at each other till Mona ran over waving her arms at Socrates and he fell over with his legs straight up.

Like he was dead. And that morning everyone wished he was, because when Bly came over he stepped in the mess too, and then went about saying "darned goat" a lot, acting like he wasn't mad with Mona for not cleaning it right up, but I knew Bly and I knew he was. Mona seemed a little grouchy too, and said how her head felt fuzzy like when she's spent too long near a cell phone that's switched on and then she looked at me and said, "But I know that can't be, right?" and I looked away and didn't say anything but I felt bad.

Then Mona did her "I wonder what will happen next" thing and what happened next was she made some tea and we sat on the back porch, which had become my bedroom (and I saw how no one looked at my bed), and we drank the tea.

Bly had been around the side of the house, washing his sneakers under the standpipe, and when he came back Mona made a gun shape with her fingers and pointed 'em at me and said "shoes" and we looked at her and she said, "Ash, I've been phoning around," which was strange because it must've been later than I thought and I must've slept right through it all because she'd been phoning around and she said she'd found some shoes in my size, so maybe Bly and I wanted to go pick 'em up.

That sounded good, so I went into the bathroom and took Bly's clothes off and had a shower and put Bly's clothes on again, even his underpants (which was funny). I went outside again and found my toothbrush in my bag. I fished out a tube of toothpaste I'd brought with me and was heading back to the bathroom when Mona saw it and said "uh-oh!" She took one look at the ingredients in it and said, "I thought so! Triclosan!" and set it straight in the outside garbage bin.

Then we went through all the stuff in my bag. She said "aluminum," so my deodorant went in the garbage too. Then she found me a tube of toothpaste that was okay and she said, "This won't destroy you from the inside out and it won't upset me neither," so I went back into the bathroom and brushed my teeth. I did not stare at myself in the mirror the way some folks did, the way a lot of folks still do, because there wasn't so much to see that I wanted to see. So I was staring into space, kinda, wondering what was wrong with aluminum and triclosan and what the heck was that anyway and then I saw a little cardboard packet of pills on the top of the cabinet, and it had a name on it that I sorta recalled, but could not.

Bly and I wandered over to his truck and I saw his sheds—there was a small one he slept in and a small one where he kept his stuff, which was near enough not much. He had a lot of bottles of pills and he looked at me looking at them and said how they helped him to detoxify. In the other shed I saw his bed, which was unmade, and it was a sleeping bag on a mattress set on three wooden pallets, like they deliver things on, laid end to end. He explained how he always aired everything every morning, kept the door open for a while, but how a) it was only safe to do that when he was around, to stop the goat eating his stuff, and b) he figured it might rain again before we was back today, so he shut the door and that was that.

Bly was in a good mood. He was smiling and laughing a lot with me and he said, "You'll like Finch," and I said, "Who's Finch?" and Bly said, "He's the guy with little tiny feet like you."

I said I did not have tiny feet but I didn't tell Bly that he had giant feet, so I said nothing but I recalled the pills in Mona's cabinet and I said "fluoxetine" and he said "what?"

I said, "Mona's got something called fluoxetine in her bathroom," but of course then I felt bad for snooping, but Bly shrugged. I said, "I know it, don't I? Ain't it what Mom took one time?"

Bly nodded and said, "Uh-huh. Prozac."

And then I was about to say that Mona didn't look depressed. In fact, I was about to say that Mona seemed like she was one of the most un-depressed people I had ever set eyes on, but I was glad I didn't, because before I even said it I could imagine Bly saying, "Well, I guess that's for why she's taking it, dumbass," and so instead I said nothing. Nothing at all. And as the years have gone by, I have come to appreciate that that is more times than not the right thing to do.

CHAPTER 5

GLYPHOSATE

I dunno, maybe it was what Bly said. About how I was gonna like Finch. But I did like him, straightaway.

You ever had that happen to you? Like we got out of Bly's truck and by the way it wasn't far to Finch's but we figured the monsoon wasn't done with Arizona yet so we drove, and as soon as we got out of the truck, we saw this guy heading towards us with an easy way about him and a short and tidy beard and a smile for free. And I thought, I am gonna like you, and I don't know how but I knew he was thinking the same darned thing. So then he said, "Morning Bly, morning Ash," like we'd done it a thousand times already and we stood there, with our hands on our hips, like three musketeers with all the time in the world and nothing planned for it.

I opened my mouth to say something about how we came for the shoes, but then that seemed rude to make that the first stuff I said, so I shut it again.

Finch said "coffee?" and we nodded because tea is fine and all but it don't get your engine ticking in the same way.

We set down on Finch's porch and his house was kinda like the others I'd seen, one story, metal sidings, painted tin roof, wide porches, which are as good for the sun as for the rain. Bly and I just set there while Finch went about on the porch.

He had everything: one of those gas stoves you take when you go and camp, and pots of coffee and what-you-got and a barrel of water, and the more I looked the more I got the feeling it was a whole damn kitchen, right there. And Bly and I set and watched the desert and said nothing and that was nice and then a jackrabbit with the longest ears appeared right in front of us, between two scrubby bushes. It stared at us, one two three, and then it vanished as fast as it came.

"Big, huh?" said Bly, and Finch came over with coffee and said "what?" and we told him about the bunny which he said was either called the American desert hare or the blacktailed jackrabbit and we could take our pick, both were good for him.

It wasn't the jackrabbit that got me looking, though, the stuff that got me looking and thinking was Finch's clothesline. Now, most of us, you got a clothesline, you put clothes on it. Not Finch. He had sheets of paper hung on his. There was a pole about twenty feet out into the desert and from there to the corner of the porch was a line, and on the line was pegged sheets of paper, just like they was his socks.

"What you reading?" Bly said, and Finch said something I didn't hear but I didn't want to come across as rude so I said, "Did it get wet? Some rain, huh?" and Finch shook his head and said, no, it didn't get wet, and how he keeps his books dry and then he nodded and along the porch I saw all these clear plastic boxes and in them were books and papers and stuff. I was just starting to wonder why they was all outside on the porch and not inside his house when he smiled and started explaining about ink.

"Printing ink gets to me. Bad," he said. "At least, when it's fresh. So I have to off-gas the papers first. A few days is good. Hard when it's raining all the time."

I nodded and he said, "See, I'm pretty bad with electrical stuff. I can only read for a little while on the Net. So I email what I want to the copy shop in town and they print it and I collect it. Trouble is the ink, right? But if I off-gas it, well then it's okay to read. Trouble is, I want to read stuff right away, and I end up reading it on the line."

I nodded again, but I was thinking, "You are kidding me," and then Bly said, "What's with this . . . glypho . . . ?" and Finch said "glyphosate" and then he said "come have a look," so we did.

Finch put a mask on and I looked at Bly but he said he was okay with ink so we went and peered at the papers like we was inspecting a bunch of new recruits. Now, you gotta understand that Finch was wearing a mask. So it was kinda hard to hear the stuff he said, and what he did say came out kinda funny. So when he said "Monsanto" it sounded kinda like "moh-han-ho" and when he said "shitheads" it sounded like "shih-heh." And so on. What I'm setting out now is more or less what I think he said.

"This," said Finch, "is an article about Monsanto. You know about them, right?" and I didn't, but then he said, "Vietnam, Agent Orange . . . ? Real nice guys . . ."

I had heard of Agent Orange. I just never thought that someone actually made it. But Finch was running along.

"Back in the seventies," he said, "they started making this

chemical called glyphosate and it's about the most widely used herbicide in the world. You know Roundup? That's glyphosate. And it ain't just your folks using it in their gardens. Farmers use it. They use tons of it on their crops. On cotton, corn, wheat, sugar beet, you name it. Kills the weeds. And to make sure it don't affect the crops, well, Monsanto got that covered too, because they've genetically modified the crops to be resistant to glyphosate. Smart, huh?"

I nodded and Finch said, "Yeah, but we're not done yet. What this article here says," and he pointed at the papers on the line with his chin, but it was in a mask, so it was like he was pointing his mask at it, "is that the World Health Organization has stated that glyphosate *probably* causes cancer."

He said how it was banned in a bunch of other countries that were smarter than we were.

"And it ain't just a matter of cancer," he said, "it's been linked to birth defects and infertility and kidney damage and autism."

He said he had another article by a doctor at MIT that said that very soon, one in two babies would be born autistic. On account of glyphosate.

"And do you know what the stupidest part is?" he said.

So here I shook my head because it was kinda hard to understand much of anything at all, though I got the gist, as they say.

"The stupidest part is, they don't even have to prove it's safe. If they were making a drug, they'd have to prove it's safe. But it's *only something* that's going on all our food, so they don't have to."

That much I understood, so I said, "But that's stupid. They

don't have to prove it's safe?" and over the top of his mask Finch raised his eyebrows and said, "Shih-heh, righ?" but I don't know if he meant the EPA, or the United States government, or Monsanto. Or the rest of us dumb idiots for letting it all happen. Shih-heh.

Then Finch said "shoo!" and we left the ink on the line to keep off-gassing while we went back to the house and Finch pulled his mask off and said "uff" and then "shoes" again.

While I tried to imagine a world where every other person was autistic, Finch rummaged around some more of his boxes and in the end pulled out a pair of old red sneakers.

He held 'em up to me.

"They're yours if you want them," and I pointed down at my clown boots and he laughed and said "sold!"

Then I couldn't help myself because I had been seeing that everything Finch needed and wanted and used and spoke about was right there on the porch. And I had noticed a sleeping bag rolled up under a chair. And I had taken a peek through the back door and seen that there was not much of anything inside.

So I said, "This is your house, Finch?" and he nodded and guessed what I meant and smiled but there weren't too much happiness in that smile when he said, "Yep, it's my house. Can't live in it, but it's my house."

And then he explained how he'd bought the house a few months before but how it hadn't been built to be safe for EI people so it needed a heap of work done to it to make it safe, and

I said, "Like Reynolds Wrap?" and he nodded and said, "Yeah, and a bunch of other things."

He told me how he'd been living in the open, or sleeping in tents, or on other people's porches since he got sick, and how that was about twelve years, and that finally, after those twelve years, he'd got a porch of his own to sleep on, and that felt pretty darn good. And I was thinking, well, if this guy is faking being ill, he's doing a damn fine job, sleeping in the open for over ten years. Then I looked up and Finch was talking about his house. He smiled real happy and something I didn't understand made me want to cry and never stop. It came up out of nowhere like when you're gonna be sick. But then it went again just as quick, and I was okay.

We stayed a while at Finch's, that day. He told us what he was planning on doing with his house, and Bly said that it was gonna be great. I did a lot of nodding. He told me how you couldn't off-gas a book the same way you could hang a sheet of paper on the clothesline, so he showed me how he read books, and he did a lot of reading.

He had this special plastic box. It was a couple feet wide and a few inches deep, made of clear plastic, so you could see through it, more or less. In one side of it, he'd cut himself two holes, and he'd attached a rubber glove to each hole and sealed them up, so the gloves reached inside the box. Then, when he got a book to read, what he did was he put the book inside, and put the lid back on, and read the book through the lid, and turned the pages with his hands in the rubber gloves. Only sometimes the pages were too thin to pick up with the gloves, so he showed me how he used the eraser on the end of the pencil to turn the pages and he was real good at that, because I thought it looked kinda hard.

"I do a lot of reading," he said, looking at his plastic box and smiling. "You do a lot of reading, Ash?" and I shrugged and said "a little," which was not the exact truth back then, but it is now, so maybe that's okay.

Then Cooper showed up.

He came trotting around the porch like he and Finch was old friends, which I guess they was, because Finch was glad to see the mutt, and the mutt seemed just as happy, his tail all wagging, and Finch found him something to eat and said, "Don't tell Mona," and I don't know if he was talking to the dog or me and Bly.

"I guess Socrates won the argument," Bly said and I nodded, because he sure was one mean goat that morning, at least till someone scared the legs off of him. "Come to visit?" Bly said then, and that last part was to Cooper.

Finch tickled him under the chin and stroked his beard and said how his beard was getting to be as white as the beard that Socrates had, but I didn't know if he meant the philosopher or the goat.

We figured we oughta take Cooper home.

I thanked Finch for the sneakers and Bly and me and the old

dog went back in the truck and I was glad the sneakers were good ones, maybe even a little cool. And as we went I thought about owning a house you couldn't live in or it would make you sick and wondered what that was like and then I thought, well, if somewhere was making you sick you could move on and maybe you could always find somewhere else safe to go. Then I wondered what would happen if you couldn't. I mean, if you kept running and running across the whole damn face of the world until, finally, there was nowhere safe left to go. Nowhere. What then.

Like I said, I never did read too much, 'less I had to. But that was before what happened. (I mean what happened to me, not What Happened.)

After, I read a lot, everything I could get my hands on. Not just stuff about getting sick, but other stuff too. Like I might read anything. Like there was one time early on when I was sitting in Dr. Behrens' waiting room in Snowflake and the only darned thing to read in there was the book that's like the Bible to those guys, the Latter-day Saints. The Book of Mormon. So I read that. I can't say I understood a deal of it, but I will say this: whoever said you never start a sentence with "And" had never read the Book of Mormon. Or maybe they had.

Later, I read the Bible some too, and I found out where that whole "And" at the start of a sentence game got started. People say you shouldn't do it. But why should they go around judging what other people say?

Like, some people say, "I wonder what will happen next." I used to know someone who said it a lot, like it was a story she was living in. I wonder what will happen next. As if something is *always* gonna happen next. Stories always have something happening next; that's something I found out when I started reading. There's always a whole heap of stuff. This thing and that thing, then another. Some business and a how-d'ye-do from time to time. But real life ain't a story, so sometimes what happens next is nothing. And when I got to thinking about that, and about stories, I wondered to myself if you could write a book where nothing happens next. Not ever. I guess people must've tried to write books like that. I guess they ain't no fun to read. And that's why I'm skipping whole bits of this. My story. Days here and weeks there. And later, a year or five. Because in those bits, *nothing* happened.

But I was talking about real life, and what happened next to me was nothing. I mean, *something* happened, but it led to a whole bunch of nothing.

So here's the last that I recall from before I got sick.

Just after we'd got back from Finch's, I was sitting on the porch with Bly and Mona, and the desert was out there, yonder, and Mona had tied Socrates up somewhere on account of his still feeling sore about life, and Cooper was curled around Mona's feet and she was saying how we all gotta learn to think for ourselves. She said how Blake had said that, and I thought she was talking about one of the canaries, but then she added, "and that was two hunnered years ago!" so I knew she wasn't talking about one of the canaries. Especially as she fixed me with a look and said, "William Blake. Him that was 1757 to 1827."

I mentioned to her what Finch had been reading about. It just didn't seem right to me. Right or fair, and she said, "See, we can blame the government, or the companies, or the capitalist system, or men, or the Man, or we could even blame God though no one seemed to do that before when they believed in him and they sure don't do it now, now that they don't. And we could blame any blessed one of these folks, but you know who's really to blame? We are! We set around and let all this crap happen."

Bly was nodding his head like he agreed but somehow like he disagreed too, and I got caught up for a time thinking about that, how we can think two different things at the same time and how that might seem confusing but how most everyone can do it, if only they knew they could. And Mona went on and said how we got all this stuff about chemicals wrong.

"Think about it. Tobacco, asbestos, vinyl chloride, hormone replacement, thalidomide, radiation, heavy metals, chlorofluorocarbons, exhaust gases, chlorinated solvents, and oh I could go on. Well, we got it backwards. We were so eager to have all the wonderful stuff, we didn't like to think too much if it made us sick, and we didn't wait around to find out. What you don't know can't hurt you. Right?"

I could tell from her voice and her look that she was setting Bly up to reply and he knew it too, because he said "wrong!" And then he said, "Sure, but people don't know no different," and he said he didn't know nothing till he came to Snowflake and Mona started explaining stuff and telling him stuff and showing him stuff and then she said, "The truth is, people don't wanna know. It's too hard and takes too much thinking about."

And then I opened my mouth, because there was something I wanted to say, but then I shut it again, because like I said, I was already learning that sometimes it's better to keep your mouth shut. Then I thought: darn it, I wanna say something. So out loud I said, "The limits of my language are the limits of my world," and Bly looked at me and said, "Snowflake, are you feeling all right?" and Mona looked at me and said, "God-dang, Ash."

Then she thought for a time and said, "You sure are one fascinating biped."

She made guns with the fingers of both her hands and pointed 'em at me and said, "Ludwig Wittgenstein. 1889 to 1951," and then started saying how that was exactly the point. How you couldn't know nothing, or understand nothing, or talk about nothing, 'less you had the words to do it with.

"How do you know Wittgenstein?" Mona said to me, and I guess I shrugged and said how Mr. French (which I always found funny because he was our English teacher) was always saying it, but I had no idea what he meant or who Ludwig Wittgenstein was until we were sitting on Mona's porch, looking at the desert.

I don't recall exactly what happened next. I know Bly looked at me again and said, "Are you feeling all right?" again because this time I answered, "Well, no, I guess I caught a cold in the rain there yesterday." I was feeling kinda muzzy. And I had one hell of a headache, right in the front of my head, and then Bly said, "What's that?" and I saw they was both looking at my arms.

So I said, "That's just a rash I get," and they was looking at the red spots and red patches down my arms because I was only wearing a T-shirt. Then they both looked at each other and I said, "What? It's just a rash I get. Sometimes. I had it before. The doctor said it's nothing. Like maybe it's stress. He said." And then I went and got up and went to the bathroom and washed my face because I thought that might help but I still felt kinda muzzy and on the way back from the bathroom, heading back to the porch, my legs stopped working.

I don't know what else to say. Even after all this time. Never quite figured it out. But my legs kinda seized up. Just like the dang goat. Well, not exactly, because I was still standing and I could still move 'em, but only just, like when you're walking at the seashore and you walk into the waves and the water makes it hard to move your legs. It was like that, only if the seawater was made of molasses, then that's how it felt.

I just about made it to the porch and Bly took one look at my face and said "shoot" and that is the last thing I recall because I passed out again.

I guess everything I have told you so far, everything about Snowflake, and Mona, and Bly, and the canaries, and Finch, and everyone, all of that was more or less my first three half days out there in the Forties. And I ask myself if you'll wonder some if I won't spend more'n two minutes talking about the next three weeks. Because that's what it was. Three weeks. Three weeks I spent in my bed, right there on Mona's back porch. And I was sick.

I had that rash, and my headache, that would come and go, but the most of it was I was tired. I don't know if I can explain that word. Tired. Like I slept almost all the time, but when I say tired, I'm not talking about being sleepy. I mean something else, something about how I had no energy. Not for nothing. I was a rag. Limp. I was a shell, just lying there, and I don't recall eating and I don't recall even going to the bathroom though they told me later they'd helped me do both. Because when I say tired, I mean I could just about lift an arm, if I had to. Mostly I didn't.

And I know I kept asking "what's going on?" or "what's wrong with me?" but no one would say anything and I know once or twice I said something about how I had to see a doctor but I don't recall what happened about that 'cept I didn't go. Not then.

What I do recall is Bly standing over me and looking down, and sometimes there was rain behind him and sometimes there was blue sky and then he seemed like the man in gold from the roof of the temple. And sometimes Mona would sit with me for hours, and sometimes she would talk to me and sometimes she would read to me and sometimes she was quiet, real quiet and for the longest time.

The weeks went by, and there ain't no point talking about it anymore, because you wouldn't learn nothing from it. See, when you first get someplace new, there's a lot to tell, because it's all new. But when you been somewhere for a times, well, then you pretty quick get to the point where there's no new tale to tell. And if you spend three weeks in bed, then every day is the goddamn same, and suddenly what happens is time speeds up. When every day is the same, time whistles right on by.

So here we are now. Three weeks came and went. By the end of which I started to come out of it. I spent more time awake, though I never left my bed, 'cept I needed the bathroom, and when I did that, they set me in a wheelchair that was Mona's from when she was first sick and real bad with it. She told me she'd kept it for years, because you never knew what was going to happen next, and I nodded, even though that was something I hadn't started to learn yet, not really.

Mona and Bly spent a lot of time with me. Bly would come and stand over my bed and talk. He'd talk about how he was gonna go back to the academy when he got better, and I looked at him and tried to imagine him as a police officer. Not just a cadet, but the real thing. Sometimes I could, but other times he reminded me of the guy on the postcard again and I could not get that picture out of my mind.

I had other visitors. Mary came over, and Finch, and Detlef too, who grinned and said, "I got you some popcorn" like we was going to the movies. I was a regular celebrity, lying there in my bed, with my bedroom that was half house and half desert, and Cooper under the bed, sleeping. Even Socrates wandered over once in a while and tried to chew my blankets till Mona dragged him off. And people said a lot of things to me as I lay there and I didn't understand a lot of it, so then when they were gone, I would ask Mona and Mona would explain. She explained how they'd seen this before, and probably would again, and how I was venting. She said how the body can cope with so much for so long and then sooner or later it all has to come out. She asked me about the rashes and if I had had headaches before, and I said sure they was just stress, and she shook her head and said sure it was stress but *what kind* of stress? And why?

She said how I had been keeping a lid on my MCS and that just like clothes or books or stuff that needed off-gassing, my body did too. That the rashes showed I had been sick before and was on the verge of breaking. That now I had come to a safe place, my body was letting it all out, and that my blood was full of toxins and I would go on feeling bad until I could get rid of 'em. Or most of 'em. And then I asked how long that would be, and she said "well, we'll see," and then I said that maybe I oughta go to the doctor in town, and she said "well, we'll see" to that too. I thought "what?" because I was sick, and I knew I needed a doctor. But I was too weak to argue.

Mona said my body was venting. Off-gassing. And, boy, was I gassed-off. I lay there and wondered what the heck was happening to me. It felt like the end of something, though I couldn't have given you a good reason for why, or what it was the end of.

HAWTHORNE EFFECT

I said before how I didn't never read until I got sick, and then, when I had, how I started to read everything I could lay my hands on. That started there, in my little bed, on that porch out back of Mona's house. I don't really know why, but maybe it felt like the end of the world. I mean, it felt like the end of *my* world.

One day, way early on, I took my phone out. I checked to see that Mona wasn't around, then I plugged it in and charged it up, and as soon as it had some charge I turned it on. I knew it was no good as a phone. Not unless someone had built a cellphone tower overnight, just for me, and I doubted that. But it had pictures on it. Pictures of my friends, Malik and Ximeno and Mary-Beth, pictures of the guys at the shoe store, who were okay, pictures of Jack. One picture of Bly. Pictures of my long-lost parent, my mom, who I had not seen in forever. I didn't know what that meant anymore. I mean, what it meant to me. And when I looked at the photos, somehow I knew they belonged to a different life, and a different world, and I knew that something had changed. Then I turned the phone off and put it away. And I started reading instead.

And now? Later on, so much later on, all these years later? What about reading now? And writing? After What Happened, maybe it's all the more reason to read, and keep reading. Or maybe there ain't no point in that anymore. Maybe we're done. Still, I'm gonna keep telling this story.

The days go by, and they take no notice of you. Not one bit. You might lie in bed for three weeks, dead to the world, but the days go on and roll by anyhow. So by the time I sat up in bed, rubbing my eyes, and felt like I was waking out of a dream, the monsoon was over and the sun was here to stay.

I told you some parts from when I was lying there dead, but all of that is unclear in my mind. The first thing I recall with any surety, I opened my eyes one morning, there in my open-air bedroom, and I saw the pope, in the desert, dancing. I was lying on my side, and it did not escape my attention that there was a whole bunch of people standing there in my bedroom too. They was just off the porch, but when your bedroom includes the whole of Arizona it's kinda dumb to split hairs. There was Mona, of course, and Bly, and Mary, and Finch. And there was a lady I hadn't met before. But they weren't looking at me; they were looking the other way at a two-inch-high plastic pope, dancing from side to side. I found out later he was solar-powered, so he would never stop jiggling till the monsoon came back, or nighttime, whichever was first.

All five of 'em, Mona and everyone, they was all standing with their hands on their hips, shaking their heads, and chuckling, like they'd never seen the pope dancing before. Because who has? He could swing his plastic hips, though, that's for sure.

I sat up. I didn't feel right, but I felt a whole lot better than I had. I swung my legs out, without checking for rattlers since I figured the pope would've scared 'em off anyhow, like Saint Pat did in Ireland, then Mona turned around and said, "Snowflake! You're awake!" and then they all turned to look at me, and they still had their hands on their hips.

"How you feeling?" said Bly, and he came and sat by me on the bed and put an arm around me and I knew he was the kindest stepbrother in the whole damn world. And what's the step got to do with it, anyhow?

Mona turned to the lady I didn't know and said, "Jenny, this is Snowflake," and I was already opening my mouth to say, "My name's Ash and I'm pleased to meet you."

Jenny smiled. She was a sweet lady, I could tell that. Gentle. She was about forty or fifty I guess and kinda pretty just because her eyes were always smiling. I mean, almost always. There was something about her that was way different from the others I'd met so far. Took me a few weeks to figure out what it was. When I did, it was three things. First thing was, she had money. Lots of it. Second thing was, she wasn't sick. Which meant, the third thing was, she was the only darn one of 'em who actually wanted to live in the desert. Imagine that. She liked it. She said it was beautiful and peaceful.

Jenny smiled at me with her eyes and she looked concerned and said, "You're not well, so they tell me," and I guess I shrugged. I recall that I never shrugged much before I came to Snowflake. Just like Bly didn't. Seemed it was catching, and maybe not the only thing.

Then I tried to stand up but I didn't do a whole great job of that, and Jenny said to Mona, "You've taken Ash to a doctor, haven't you?" and Mona stared through the air and shrugged. Then Jenny said, "Mona you have to take this kid to see Dr. Behrens. This minute," and I didn't really get it but it was like Jenny was kinda telling Mona off, even though Mona was twice her age. Not exactly, but you know what I mean. I found out about that later too. Jenny was a good woman, and if Mona had helped a zillion folks with EI, then Jenny had too, in a different way.

Turned out she owned four or five houses in the Twenties, as well as her own in the Forties. Like, she owned Sally and Dolly's houses. She'd had them built as safe for EI folks as can be, and she rented them out as cheap as cheap. And I'll say this. She had money, but it took you a while to notice. Not like with some rich folks who wanted you to know it all the damn time. Building them houses, she said it was down to Mona, that Mona had talked her into helping the canaries. And Mona, to tell it right, Mona said it was all down to Jenny helping, with her money. They would both laugh it off, and they was gentle women, but I saw right there that when Jenny told Mona to take me to the doctor, then Mona took me to the doctor.

Later that day we climbed into Mona's Japanese circus car and she was real quiet as we headed on in. I didn't know what I'd done. And maybe I hadn't done nothing.

"Jack, Bly's dad?" I said. "He used to have a little car too."

Mona said nothing.

"Yeah," I said. "It wasn't exactly the same as yours. His was called a Lada."

Mona stared through the windshield.

"He used to say, 'She may be little, but she's a whole Lada fun.'"

I slapped the dash and pulled a goofy face and that was me trying to make her laugh and what I got back was precisely nothing.

"Yeah, it was a joke he had," I said. "*Super* funny. Bly and me, we laughed every time."

Mona blinked a couple times, so then I tried to get her to do the speaking instead, and I asked her what was with the wobbling pope and then she smiled a tiny bit and said it was something she'd promised Jenny. She'd ordered one for her and Jenny had come over to pick it up. Said it was to go with the rest of 'em, so I asked, "The rest of what?" but then we were pulling up outside the doctor's office in Snowflake.

Now, you will recall how I said I started to learn things when I started to read. And how I started to read when I started to get sick? Well, here's one of the things I read about. It was in some book on Mona's shelves, I mean, in Mona's library, and I can't tell you when I read it, but whenever it was, it reminded me of that afternoon when we rode into town to see the doctor for the first time.

So there's this thing called the Hawthorne effect, and what this says is that when you go to the doctor, you feel better before you've even seen her. Just the idea of seeing her makes you feel better. You've heard of the placebo effect, well, it's kinda like that. Just the thought that you're gonna have someone look after you and take care of you is enough to make you feel better for real.

And I did, riding there in Mona's car, that afternoon. I felt ill, but I felt better than I had in three weeks; I even wondered whether I actually needed to go see the doctor. Another week, I figured, and I'd be fine.

But the funny thing was that Mona seemed as sick as I'd ever seen her. I mean, she was okay, she was driving, but she was real quiet, and she wore a mask, and she looked real tired.

When we got outside the doctor's office she said, "Ash, you're gonna have to go in by yourself," and I said, "Okay, sure," and so I went in alone. And waited.

And I waited. And what happened then, well, it sure weren't the Hawthorne effect. First thing was, I felt my headache coming back, and I started to feel muzzy again. You know the smell of lilies? Those big white lilies with the huge orange stalks covered in pollen. You know how they make some people react, like it gets hard to breathe, and your nose starts running, and your eyes start watering. Well, it was like that for me in the waiting room, only there weren't no lilies. There was just me, the "and-how-will-you-be-paying" lady behind the desk who'd signed me in glaring at me from time to time though I did not know why. And the Book of Mormon. And all the time I was getting worse, feeling sicker and sicker, so by the time they called me in to meet Dr. Behrens, I was ready to meet my Maker instead.

Dr. B did not smile much. I'll guess she was around Mona's

age, and she had gray hair kinda like Mona's but short, and that's where the similarities ended. She had those little lines people get around their mouth from pursing their lips permanently since they was twelve. I started off by trying to tell her what was wrong with me and how I'd fallen sick, but she didn't seem too interested in any of that. What did seem to interest her was who I was living with, and where I had lived before, and how often I had been to the doctor.

Then she asked me if there was a history of mental illness in my family. She did that just like this: "Is there a history of mental illness in your family?" she said, pursing her lips, so I thought about Mom and the fluoxetine and then I thought about how my dad might've been Germany's craziest export for all I knew, so obviously what I did was I shrugged.

Things got worse after that. I kept trying to say, well, yeah but I feel real sick and maybe it's something I caught on Greyhound Lines, Incorporated, but she didn't wanna know. Before about six minutes was up, she held up a hand, and blinked at me, and pursed some more, and said, "What would you say if I told you there is nothing wrong with you?"

That sure stopped me good. Because I was thinking what do you mean there's nothing wrong with me? I'm dying right in front of you, so I did not understand what she meant. And then I did, because she said, "What would you say if I told you this is all in your head?"

And I said but there's rashes on my arms! You can see 'em! But she said I had made 'em happen with my mind and did I know that it was known that those folk called stigmatics whose palms bleed like they're Jesus on the cross could make it happen just by really wanting it to?

To be fair, I do not recall the rest of that interview. I remember thinking about what Bly had said, about how no one *wants* to be sick. And not to let anyone tell you different.

What I recall next is sitting in Mona's car in a daze thinking what just happened? Mona was quiet as she drove me home, and when I said how I was feeling worse after sitting in the waiting room she mumbled something about the carpet they had in there and the glues that were used to make it and then she said something about finding me a mask, an old one, a good one, that had been off-gassed so it was safe to use. Then we were back in the Forties. And yes, I was a bright and eager kid back then, and yes, up to that point I knew nothing but what was in front of my eyes, but them things were set to change and though it's a real long time ago now, I think I could already see that they was changing.

I said before, how when I woke up from my three weeks in bed, I was waking out of a dream, and into real life. Hard part is knowing which was the dream. The three weeks, or the part that came before that.

I CAN'T CURE YOU,
SO YOU MUST BE MAD

"**D**umb goat."

That's what I heard Mona saying, one dry and sunny day. She was staring off in the desert and I figured Socrates must be out there, up to some noteworthy goat business.

"He's one handsome buck, but he's sure not the smartest," she said, hands on her hips. Then I saw where she was looking and she wasn't looking at the goat, she was looking at Bly. He was fixing a new fence around Mona's yard, and sawing a piece off of a wooden rail he'd put up, only he was setting on the part he was sawing.

"You got the brains in your family, huh?" she said to me, and I said, "We ain't blood related, he's just my step," and then she looked at me funny.

Real quiet she said, "We're all related, Ash. Be better if some folks understood that."

I'll explain.

The night before, at what-did-you-learn-today time, she'd been talking about some tests she'd just had done. Genetic tests. What Mona said was, you spit in a tube, and put it in the US mail, and four to six weeks later you'd find out who you are. Everything, like medical stuff, as in, will you get Alzheimer's early or are you at risk of being celiac or is it more likely you'll have breast cancer (that one's mostly for women, I guess). And then there was other stuff. Weird stuff. Like whether you sneeze when you walk out into bright sunshine and is your back going to be hairy (that one's mostly for men, I guess) and whether you can smell asparagus or not. I am not funning you. God made a gene for that. Hardly seems worth Her time, don't it, but there you are.

And then there was the other stuff, that shows where you came from, like are you from Europe, or were you made in China, and how much of you is from where exactly, and it even tells you how much Neanderthal you got in you. So, the Neanderthals were these other people, like a whole other species of people, and once upon the time folks thought that we'd wiped them out. As in, Homo sapiens had wiped out the Neanderthals, because we're still here (more or less) whereas those other guys stopped existing around 40,000 years back. Which even Mona would probably not call recently. But now we know what we did was this: we didn't kill those guys, we had babies with them. It's called interbreeding, and it sounds a whole lot more fun than killing people. So, this means they became part of the gang. And Mona was super excited because she was 2.8 percent Neanderthal, and they say that's a heck of a lot. A heck of a lot.

Anyway, and I am getting to the point now, because then she waved the printouts around and said, but look, we all came out of Africa anyway, and told us that there was this theory that everyone alive on Earth today was descended from just one woman. One woman, and she lived about 200,000 years ago. One mother for the whole human race. Like all the other possible branches of the human race got killed off and maybe we were real close to extinction, way back then, 200,000 years ago. Maybe we were all little fragile critters, and about to snuff, but somehow we stuck together and we made it through. Till there's nigh on eight billion of us. But this one woman, they call her Eve for reasons I guess I don't need to explain, well, her offspring survived. And here we all are, with just one mother for all of us. Imagine that. Seems kinda stupid to argue about wars and religion and gender and the color of your damn skin when you know that. Don't it?

"I guess I'd kinda like to do that test," I told Mona and she said, "Good idea, Ash!" and then she told me it was $99 so I forgot all about that.

Then Mona said, "I guess I'll go save your brother's life," by which she meant she oughta tell Bly about the rail he was sawing, and she wandered off, and I thought, huh, he is one handsome goat, and maybe that was the first time I'd realized it, because up to then he was just my stepbrother. He was just Bly. The boy who wanted to be a police officer, more than anything in the world.

This was a week or two after I got back from that first visit with Dr. Behrens. Truth is, I was kinda in shock after that visit. Two days later, I made Mona take me back into Snowflake again, because I still felt sicker'n hell and I knew it wasn't all in my damn mind. I decided to get my shit together this time and have it out with Dr. B, but things did not work out as I intended. I made a big deal of it and kinda talked her into doing some tests, and she just told me I was wasting her time and my money, and truth is, I had precious little of that left. Not enough to waste on finding out whether I could smell asparagus, especially since I already knew that.

So they did one or two tests on my blood and what-have-you and they found less than nothing, which is just what Mona said they would find because they really don't have any clue about what's going on with MCS.

And then, one day, Dr. B tried to write me a script for some fluoxetine and I walked out and got in Mona's car and we went home.

Then I tried moaning some to see if it would help. It didn't, but I did it anyhow, till I guess Mona's ears must've quit working. Like I said to her, what the heck kinda doctor do you got in Snowflake, anyhow? Maybe there's a better one down the road, in Show Low?

Mona shook her head at that.

"There surely ain't," she said and when I said, "So where is there a good doctor?" she said nothing. Then I said *is there* a good doctor? and she nodded and said, "Well, there's this one guy helped a lot of us folks. Dr. Ray."

So I said, well, let's go see him and Mona said, "Yeah, thing is, Ash, he's in Texas," and since that may as well have been

Mars, well, that was more or less that. But she told me how some MCS folks had been to see him, and how he was one of the few doctors who believed in MCS and EI and even had some theories as to its whys and what-have-yous. He was important, Mona said, because he had argued for a lot of people against their health insurance companies. Like these insurance people, they sure didn't want to pay out on anything, never mind on some disease they don't believe exists. But Dr. Ray went to bat for a few folks and that's how they got their disability payout.

"Without Dr. Ray, some of us snowflakes would be living on the streets right now. Or maybe dying," Mona said, and when I asked who, she said, "Oh, Detlef, Finch, the Sick Birds. Most everyone. . . ." And then she jabbed a thumb at herself. "I told you before, Ash, we're the lucky ones."

And I wondered if she included me in that "we." Because I still did not believe in this EI thing, not really. And even less did I believe that I'd done gone and got a dose of it too. And I believed even less that, just by coincidence, I had gotten the same thing my stepbrother had gotten. I said that to Mona and she just shrugged.

"Wouldn't be the first time," she said, which was something else she was real fond of saying. "And maybe you two shared the same house for a while, someplace near a source of contamination."

She drove along and I was left thinking about all the crummy houses we'd lived in and the pollution here and there and, well, everywhere. But still I didn't buy it. There had to be something else the matter with me, and I wanted to know what the heck it was.

Now all that took some thinking about, so I did.

We trundled home and when we got there I asked Mona about something I didn't yet know.

"Mona," I said, and she said what?

"What did you do before you got sick?" And she told me how she'd been a teacher, and I asked what did she teach.

She said, "Stuff. I taught stuff," and then she said how she'd loved it but how that life was over. Then she shut up.

And I shut up too.

Still, Dr. B had made me sorer than a goat what'd eaten somebody's sneakers. Like I said, I couldn't believe a doctor could be like that. Just tell you you're crazy, and the more you try to tell her you ain't crazy, the more she purses her lips and the higher her eyebrows raise and the more she stabs her fingers on her computer keyboard, right in front of you.

I felt I must've missed something. I know I was missing a lot right then, because a) I couldn't think straight and b) I was in shock, like I said. Something felt different. But I kept thinking, well, I'll be better in a day or two. And then I made that a week. And then the weeks started to go by and started to become months, and they didn't care whether I was better or not, and I wasn't.

And like I said before, there is no point me telling you all about each of those days. What happened was this: I was sick,

I was tired, I could barely move, and I became the most miserable kid in Arizona. And what do you wanna know about that for? You ever been miserable? Maybe so miserable you thought it would be better if you didn't exist no more? Well then, you know what I'm talking about.

I don't remember so much from those early days. One thing: I recall I started writing a letter to my mom. I had no idea where to send it. But it was all I could do, to make me feel like I was doing something. I thought I oughta tell her I was sick. I don't know why; I hadn't seen her in the longest time, but I figured maybe she'd come and see me, even though I would never send it. You think I'm crazy, right?

It took me an age, first because I didn't know what to say. And second because my arm got tired from holding the pen for more than two minutes. But I put a few things down, like "How are you?" and "Bly's okay, more or less" and "Oh, I oughta tell you I'm sick." When it was done, I read it once and then set it aside someplace. It was a bad letter, but I just couldn't think of what to say that might be better. And anyway, it had nowhere to go, and neither did I.

Only other thing that comes back to me: that first afternoon, that very first afternoon when we got back from seeing Dr. B, I sat on the porch staring at the desert, while around me, Mona and Bly and Finch were having a discussion. They weren't discussing me, or being sick. I was no great news. They'd all been through what I'd been through, and not just once but hundreds of times.

Hundreds of people who'd doubted that they were sick. And I do mean hundreds. Doctors, friends, family.

Family. I had noticed, without really understanding, that there were no couples in Snowflake. Not in the Forties, I mean. No families. Everyone was alone. As the time went by, I got to learn why that was. Relationships don't survive having someone with MCS. They just don't.

So no, Mona and Bly and Finch weren't talking about me, they was talking about a film. They'd all watched it, over at Detlef's one evening. He had a TV set behind a glass wall, which he said made it safer to do.

I'd never heard of it, but it was some horror film, and they was talking about whether it was scary or not. Bly said it wasn't, and Finch said it was but he didn't know why for sure, and Mona said it was scary too, and she did know why. She said it went like this. She said whether you found it scary or not, well, it all came down to whether you was paying attention or not.

At the start of the film, she said, there's a whole lot of scenes of people talking about the legend of this witch, a witch that people say lived in the woods nearby. And at the very end of the film, when the horror finally comes along, the final scene, well, it's one of the things that somebody at the start was talking about. And it only makes sense if you remember that bit, so it's only scary if you was paying attention.

Then Finch said, "Yeah! that's it! That's right, Mona!" while Bly just set staring into space, and I guess he was feeling told off for not paying attention. But I could see he saw Mona had a point, because he said, "Maybe life's like that."

And everyone said "life's like what?" and he said, "Maybe life's only scary if you're paying attention."

Finch asked Bly what he meant and Bly said how maybe it was only when you started to learn about the world, like he had from Mona, that it got scary. Like before, all he had thought about was being a police officer. That made sense to him and it was all and everything he wanted. Then Mona got him thinking other stuff, such as maybe you could think about glyphosate giving everyone cancer or kidney problems or destroying people's guts. Or maybe you could think about antibiotic resistance, which is how all our wonderful antibiotics are starting to not work anymore, how bad bacteria are evolving faster than we can make new drugs that'll kill 'em, and how very soon we'll be back in the nineteenth century when simple things could kill you, like setting on damp grass, or wearing corsets. Or maybe you could think about those same antibiotics, the ones we're so precious about, and then read about how they don't only kill bad bacteria, but the good ones too, the ones we need to be healthy, that live in our gut and do good things for us, like help make serotonin which is what keeps you happy and what you don't got enough of if you're depressed. Or maybe you could think about all the plastic in the world's oceans, how they was saying now that every single fish that's caught has teeny-eeny particles of plastic in it, that you're eating, and then, come to that, how all the sea salt in the world has plastic in it too, and most of all the drinking water supplies too. Or maybe you could think about how all the insects were suddenly dying on account of pesticides used in farming and how insects were important for the whole chain of life on Earth. And heck, did he mention climate change yet? Did he mention that the climate was changing? And that we was all gonna fry?

Then everyone stared out into the desert for a long time, till Finch said, "Screwit. You got any beer, Mona? I sure could use a beer." And everyone laughed.

JENNY

That really gets my goat.

We sure do say some funny stuff with the English language. Because if you can tell me why getting someone's goat means they're feeling sore, you're doing better'n me. Maybe it has something to do with sneakers. Anyway, the point was this: the point was that my goat was truly got.

See, I am not gonna dwell on this for too long, but I was one unhappy kid. Day after day went by and I sat in my room, staring at the two walls that weren't there, staring at the red sand and the jackrabbits and I didn't even bother shouting when Socrates ate a pair of my socks or butted the end of my bed, which he had started to do in recent days. I was too busy being sick and wondering if this MCS thing was real.

Bly would come and talk to me sometimes. And then other times, he'd go missing for hours, even a whole day, and I wouldn't know where he was at. And every time he did that I got a bit sore at him for leaving me alone, but I always managed to not tell him I was sore.

Save one time, when Mona let the damn goat butt my bed almost the whole damn day, and I was too weak to stop him. And by the time Bly showed up in the evening, I snapped yeah, well, thanks for coming back and he just looked at me for a second and then he said, "Other folks got problems too, Ash" and went off to bed and I felt bad.

When I wasn't staring, and I wasn't moaning, I was frowning, and trying to figure stuff out. The fact that Dr. B had told me that this was all in my head? Well, I could not get that *out* of my head. And I would say that out loud sometimes, and Mona would say, yeah, but what does that even mean?

"All in your head," she said. "All in your mind. What does that mean? Because it's all in your mind, it's not real? Even if it is *all in your mind*, you're still suffering the same. And one day, doctors are gonna finally realize that there ain't no god-dang difference between the body and the mind anyhow. There ain't no mind without a body, right? And without a mind, a body is nothing. Right again?"

I nodded, but she wasn't finished. I guess I'd hit a nerve and I guess I knew why. Because although this was all new to me, she'd been through all this before, a long time ago, and I guess I was bringing it back.

"You know what Voltaire had to say about doctors?"

I shrugged. I guess I didn't. I guess I didn't know who Voltaire was either, and I guess that was obvious to Mona, because she told me.

"Voltaire was a French philosopher."

And I said, "Wait, I know this. *I think therefore I am*, right?" and Mona said no, that was René Descartes, 1596 to 1650.

"Voltaire. Only his real name was François-Marie Arouet.

1694 to 1778. Had a lot to say about a lot of things, and a lot to say about doctors in particular. Like this: he said the art of being a doctor consists in distracting the patient while nature gets him better."

And I said "huh" and then I said, "Yeah, but that was seventeen-something," but Mona said, "You thinking it's got any better?"

So I said, "Yeah, some. Like, we have modern medicines now, right? Drugs and what-you-got."

So then Mona said, "A doctor is someone who prescribes drugs about which he knows little for a body about which he knows even less."

And I said, "Voltaire again?" and Mona said, "Smart guy, right?" and I couldn't do much but nod. It was either that or shrug and I'd had enough of people shrugging, myself included. So I'd taken up nodding instead.

Then she said, "EI is just the latest in a long line of diseases that folks once thought were nonsense. One day they'll understand it. When enough folks have it and they start taking it seriously. Then they'll figure it out. The world is getting more'n more dangerous and more'n more folks are gonna get sick. We're the canaries in the coal mine, Ash, don't you forget that. We're just unlucky to be living now."

Then I thought about asking Mona whether we was lucky or unlucky as she couldn't seem to make her mind up. But I didn't, because I was a miserable snowflake back then.

At first I didn't want to believe I had MCS. Mona gave me an old off-gassed mask to use when we drove into town, but I was too dumb to use it. Or stubborn. Or something. Something like I was too scared to use it in case it turned out that Mona was right.

But when I didn't wear it, I'd come home sicker. And when I did, I'd come home not so sicker. Sooner or later, and I cannot say which, I finally started to realize that it was true. Mona had been right. What I was scared of was really true. I had been poisoned by the world. And what can I tell you about that? Nothing. It hurt. That's all I can tell you, but like Bly'd said to me, other folks got their own problems, right? So you can probably just figure out that I was feeling just like you do, when you go to bed one cold and miserable and lonely night and wish your world would end, just end, quietly, in your sleep.

Life had gone off the tracks. I'd set out into the world to find Bly, and I had. But then I'd hit a brick wall. I slept a big chunk of every day, and even when I was up, my legs were stiff and sore. I couldn't walk more than fifty yards at one time. I had headaches, I couldn't feel the ends of my fingers or toes, and sometimes that would spread as far as my elbows and knees. And I had them rashes like from before I was sick. Or, as Mona kept reminding me, from before I *knew* I was sick. And yet I still didn't believe this was happening. I didn't really believe in MCS. I didn't believe it was what was wrong with me, but the canaries wouldn't hear anything different, and neither, in her own way, would Dr. B. She said I was mentally deranged; the canaries told me I was physically assaulted by chemicals. And no one wanted to talk about nothing else.

I had run out of money paying that dumb doctor. I was living in a room that only had two walls, it was coming to the winter and already the nights were getting cold. Half the time I still couldn't accept what was happening to me, what they said was happening to me; it just didn't seem possible that one day you could be fine and the next you was sick for life. And the other half of the time it was plain that that was exactly what had happened. I mostly got about Mona's house in her wheelchair to use the bathroom, to roll up for suppertime, and so on and so forth. And I slept.

But there were some good things too, I know. I knew that even then. One of them was Mona.

The other was Bly.

He was real worried for me, I could tell. After that time when I was mean to him for leaving me alone all day, and even though he had jobs to do, he would find reasons to hang out at Mona's even more'n usual. He'd talk to me, and he even read to me when I was too tired to hold a book up, which was most of the time.

Another thing he did, he went out of his way to find things to talk about, like one day, when he went into town, he came back and said he'd been to the library to look something up.

I guess I didn't look too impressed. Because I was foolish back then, but maybe that's being hard on myself. I was young, and I was sick, and the world had fallen apart around me. So maybe I didn't want to hear about his trip to the library. But Bly, he went on anyway, smiling like I was being nice to him.

"You remember how I told you about Mr. Snow and Mr. Flake?" he said, and I nodded and said, "Yeah. You said what are the chances?" and Bly said, "Yeah, well, that's what I went to find out."

So he'd been to the library even though that meant folks staring at him wearing his mask. If he stuck to the places he usually went, like the store or the gas station, people knew who he was. But if he went someplace he didn't usually go, like the library, it would mean more people staring. Anyway, he'd done it. And then he'd looked up how many people were called Snow in America and how many people were called Flake. He said he could only find figures for 2003. He didn't know why that was, but anyhow he was only interested in the percentages. He said that there was a one in 20,000 chance you would be called Mr. Snow. And then he said there was a one in 250,000 chance you would be called Mr. Flake. So the chances of a Mr. Snow meeting a Mr. Flake would be one in five billion.

And I was wondering what the point of all this was, but I kinda knew already, and even before he said, "So that was pretty lucky, right?" I was already thinking how lucky I was a) to have Bly for a stepbrother in the first place and b) to have found him again when I kinda felt I'd lost him.

And he was staring at me and sorta smiling and then I said "nope" and he said "what?"

"I think you made a mistake with your math," and he looked

upset, so I put my hand on his arm and said, "No, you did the sums right, I'm sure. You always were better at sums than me. But you forgot something. I guess half of those Snows were women, and half of those Flakes were women too, right? So the chances of a mister Snow meeting a mister Flake must be a quarter what you said it was. Right? So the chances were actually one in twenty billion."

Then Bly blinked and said, "Yeah, I guess I forgot about women," and then I realized my hand was still on his arm and I took it away and he said, "Ash, Mona and me, we wanna take you out. You're just set here all the time."

I said I didn't wanna go anywhere, not till I was better, and Bly looked at me so hard I thought he would cry and then he said, real, real quiet, "That might be some whiles," and then Mona came out and said, "Well? we going on our trip, or whut? Cooper's ready. You ready, Ash?"

So we took our trip.

It wasn't far. Once upon a goddamn time, I could have walked it. And that made me feel miserable, that more or less recently, as Mona would have it, I could've walked to Jenny's house, but now they had to load me into Bly's truck to drive a half a mile.

There was Bly driving, and Mona, and her mutt sat on her lap, and Mary came too, and she had some new correspondence from her insurance company that she wanted to talk to Mona about. So there was the four of 'em and there was me, all squeezed in the cab one way and another. At least we left the goat at home, and I was glad not to see him for a spell. There was something about his dumb face that got to you in the end. Somehow it made you feel dumb too. Just like Socrates. The real one I mean, the original.

A half a mile don't take too long in a truck, even on a road made of nothing but desert, but while we rode I wanted to ask Mona something, and I figured she couldn't not answer me with the other guys in the truck, so I said, "Mona?" and she said, "Yes, dear?" and I said, "What did you teach?"

"Oh," she said. "Oh. Well, I guess I taught philosophy. And stuff."

So then that explained why she was always talking about philosophers, which was what I had been guessing.

"What was the other stuff?" I asked, and she waved a hand and said "stuff" again, so Mary chipped in and told me how Mona was being modest. Then she told me how Mona had taught linguistics too. She had been a professor of both philosophy and linguistics at UCLA and how she was a genuine big deal in that subject. How there was a theory named after her. Well, half a theory. The Mochsky-Lerner paradigm, it was called, and I had no idea who Lerner was or what any of this meant but I stared at Mona and she made a big point of staring out the window and then she said, "Look! Bunnies! Look, Cooper! Bunny rabbits!" on account of how she'd seen some of the jackrabbits skipping out in the sand.

"Wow," she added, "shoot!" like we'd just seen the most amazing thing in the world. "I wonder what will happen next."

We got to Jenny's house, and I pulled myself out of the truck and the others were nice. They waited for me to take my time but they didn't make a big deal out of it, but still, I wasn't feeling fun about life. Not one bit.

Mona and Mary went on ahead and Bly and Cooper and me came along after, and I whispered to Bly what are we doing here anyways? and he said wait and see.

So then I hit him in the ribs and he said, okay, well, we wanna show you something. Just wait.

Jenny came out of her house.

It was just like the Sick Birds' houses, I mean, the way it looked, but it was probably twice the size. They explained to me how since Jenny was building houses for sick people, she thought she ought to build her own so her sick friends could come visit, so her house was EI friendly too.

But anyways, what we had come to see wasn't inside the house, it was outside, around the back. In the yard, Jenny said, and it still made me wonder why these folks kept calling their backyards "yards" when they was the whole damn desert.

We came around the side of the house.

It was a little like being on drugs, 'cept I have never been on drugs. Life seems plenty interesting enough without making it more complicated, you know? But I'd heard stories about how people on drugs, they see things that aren't there, or they see things that are there but see them real weird. They hallucinate, is what I'm saying.

So the first thing Jenny said was, "You wanna see the pope?" In Jenny's own particular part of the desert there were people. They were tiny people, standing in the desert among the plants. They were all made of plastic, and they were all moving. Each one was about two inches high and they were all solar-powered, and they was jigging and dancing and wiggling from side to side. All at once, and there must have been a thousand of 'em. No, maybe ten thousand.

"Neat, huh?" said Mona, smiling, and I stared.

"What?" I said, and Jenny said how she'd been given one, years ago, and then she'd started collecting more and then people started giving them to her. And here she was now.

"What was the first one, Jenny?" Bly asked. He had a big dumb smile all over his face and I liked it.

"Elvis," said Jenny. "Wanna see?"

We did.

So she led the way. She'd put them in little groups of four or five, or sometimes ten and twenty. And on the way I saw aliens and presidents. I saw skeletons and I saw nuns. There was Michael Jackson, surrounded by a group of dinosaurs. There was even a dancing goat and for a second I felt bad we hadn't brought Socrates. Then she showed us Elvis, and he was dancing away, though Jenny said he was about ten years old.

"Even though he's dead," said Mona, and she began chuckling to herself like it was the funniest thing ever.

"I must have half the world's plastic here," Jenny said, and Mary said how it lasts forever but then she added, "Well, maybe it's better here than in the oceans" and Jenny said "amen" but I was thinking if half of it was here then the other half was on Sally's living room table. And a third half in Bly's shed.

Mona had a tight hold on Cooper, in case he decided to eat a president or something, but Jenny said it was okay. From time to time she'd lose one to a coyote or something. She showed us how she'd used Krazy Glue to stick a five-inch nail to the base of each and every one, so they didn't fall over in the wind or the monsoon or what-have-you.

I was looking at Bly. I remember just watching that big ol' smile of his and even as bad as I was feeling, something started smiling inside me too. Then he pointed.

"There's the pope!" he said and, yup, there he was.

He was surrounded by two strippers wearing nothing but sashes that said "Vegas" on them and a dancing donkey and some little balding guy with a beard in a gray suit who I didn't know until Mona said, "What's Lenin doing with the pope?" and Jenny shrugged and said, "I figured they could learn from each other."

And Mary said, "And what are the strippers learning?" and Jenny said, "Yeah, well, maybe they got as much to tell the boys as anyone else does. Maybe the donkey too. Who are we to judge?"

And I could see that Mona was looking at me and I also knew that the smart old nanny goat that she was, she could see what I was thinking, namely, what was it all for?

She said, "Even in the games of children there are things to interest the greatest mathematician," and everyone looked at her and we all said what? at the same time, so she said, "Gottfried Leibniz, 1646 to 1716."

"Oh," I said. "Right."

Then things went a little weird. Weird like awkward.

Mona tugged Jenny's arm and nodded to the house, and there was a man standing there. A real one, not a two-inch-high plastic one, wearing a hat against the sun and dark glasses. He weren't dancing neither. And then Jenny kinda changed. She'd been all silly and happy and then she changed and Mona started making noises about how it was time we was leaving and I thought that was weird since we'd only just got there.

Jenny turned to me and put a hand on each of my shoulders and said, "You come back anytime, Ash? You hear me?" and then we left.

We nodded at the man standing by Jenny's gate but we left and on the way back they explained who he was.

Jenny's boyfriend. He was a guy about the same age as her, maybe a little younger, and he had the hots for her. But she was in two minds. He wanted to get married but Jenny said she had never been married and what was the point of rushing into things.

"But she's fifty!" I said, and Mona said "yeah, well, ain't we all" and then some stuff about how she didn't wanna get tied down. That she kinda liked having Steve (that was his name) as a boyfriend but how she wasn't ready to get committed, not yet. As in get married, or something serious like that.

"So how long have they been seeing each other?" I asked, and Mona thought for a bit and then she said, "About fifteen years, I think," and I stared out into the desert.

Seems that Steve would turn up without asking sometimes and then Jenny would get mad (which I found hard to believe because of her smiling eyes but they told me it was true) and he'd tell her he loved her and why couldn't they get married and she'd send him away until she was ready to see him again.

And as we pulled up back at Mona's, Mona and Mary and me and Bly and Cooper, I thought it sucked that all of us sick people were alone when we might wanna be with someone, while the only person around here who was well had someone but didn't really care. That seemed to me to be not right.

We ate our dinner. It was dark early.

Mona asked what we had all learned today and for a long time no one said anything. Even Mona, who always had something to say. It seemed that everyone was in some kind of funk that night. Finally Bly said, "I found out what Jenny's boyfriend is called." And that was all anyone had to say.

I went to bed, and I was already using two more blankets than when I had first slept outside. The novelty of that was wearing thin, I can tell you. Sometimes I slept in my clothes too, but was still cold, and that was one of those nights when the temperature dropped to freezing even though the days were still warm. It does that when you're five, heck, almost six thousand feet up.

And I think I had just got to sleep when something knocked the end of my bed and I set straight up thinking "coyote!" but it wasn't a coyote.

It was Bly.

He was acting funny. I said, "What is it, Bly?"

He had a flashlight that he was waving around but he weren't speaking, until eventually he whispered, "Uh, you cold, Ash?" and I said "no kidding" and then he didn't say anything else.

He sat on the end of my bed and I could only just see him in the torchlight. He was pointing it at the floor now. We looked at each other there in the dark and I smiled real quick and looked away. Then no one said anything and then he mumbled something and I said "what?"

Then he said, "Uh, it's warmer in my shed."

And I said, "Oh, oh yeah?" and then he said, "Wanna come?"

I told him yes, I would like that, so we wandered over to his shed and he held my hand because it was dark and I might've fallen over a coyote or a goat or something and then we went into his little shed and actually it wasn't much warmer in there, but he was.

So we held each other, all night, and eventually we got into just one sleeping bag. And then I finally felt warm.

And I ain't gonna talk about that anymore, because a) it took me all by surprise, and b) because when I woke up in the morning, it was late, and I had slept in late too, maybe because I finally had gotten warm at night, and c) I can't talk about it because of what happened next. Which was that then I went out into the day and found Mona and as casual as I could I said, "Uh, Mona, where's Bly?" And Mona said that Bly had left, that he had gone. Bly had gone.

CHAPTER 6

KNIGHT OF THE HAPPY COUNTENANCE

Yeah. I still blame that god-danged goat. Socrates. I don't believe he ever liked me and I can't say I ever found a great liking for him, and if he hadn't eaten my darned sneakers, life might've been very different. Like Bly might have not left, because I wouldn't have been there more'n twenty-four hours, because I'd have left the day I rolled into Snowflake. Maybe the day after. And I'd've seen Bly but that would have been that. For now he had done gone and anyway I knew it weren't Socrates' fault, it was mine. It was on account of what had happened.

Mona huffed and puffed around the house and she must've said I wonder what will happen next a million times till I wanted to strangle her. I sat and stared at the desert, which is what you did in Snowflake if something went wrong, or even if it went right.

Mona said, "He didn't tell you nothing?" and I shook my head, and all I could think about was the night before and how much I wanted him back. I wanted him to come back and I wanted there not to be a little note on Mona's kitchen table saying, "Mona, thanks for everything. You're the best. I gotta go. B."

But there was.

Mona was getting on my nerves. Because we was both upset that Bly was gone without saying anything, but whereas I was showing I was upset, Mona wasn't. Sure, she huffed and puffed but she didn't appear too upset; she made a lot of tea and cuddled Cooper, and Mary came over to talk about her insurance problems and how she was gonna have to find a lawyer but a cheap one, and Mona said there was no such thing and it was fifteen minutes before she even told Mary that Bly had gone.

And finally I cracked and I snapped and said, "Dammit, Mona, Bly's gone! Don't you even care?"

Mary raised her eyebrows and Mona, she stomped off into the house and I hobbled in after her and then I saw she was crying and she wouldn't speak for hours. I mean for a long time.

And when she did, she said, "We all have different ways of coping," and I said I was sorry over and again and she shook her head and said it was okay. But I felt mean.

Mona went to blow her nose in the bathroom and when she came back she said, "He didn't even take his goddamn pills with him" and she had the box of fluoxetine in her hand, and I thought what?

"Those are his?" I said, which meant he'd lied to me about that, and then I said, "but he didn't seem depressed," so I guess I was getting stupider not smarter because of course Mona said, "Yeah, well, that's for why he was taking 'em. Like I said, we each have our own ways of coping."

"So what was they doing in your bathroom?" I asked, and she told me she'd made him promise to keep them there, so she could keep an eye on how he was using 'em. So then I had to worry what that meant too.

She asked me didn't I ever see that the more Bly appeared to be happy, the more he was hurting *underneath*, and I said nothing because I hadn't seen that at all. Maybe just that one time when he told me how other folks have problems too. And at the time I thought he meant other folks in Snowflake, who needed his help, but now I realized he was talking about himself.

And when Bly laughed, all I saw was Bly laughing. When he smiled, all I saw was him smiling. But now here was Mona telling me that the happier my step seemed, the worse he was.

"The Knight of the Happy Countenance," Mona said then and I had no idea what she was talking about. But she added, "In the book, the Don is called the Knight of the Sad Countenance. But actually he's happy with what he got in life. He just don't know it. Whereas our Bly looks happy, but isn't. It's the other way around."

So then I had even less idea what she was talking about. But she explained how it was some book I'd never heard of but it was a good book. It was about a crazy old Spanish guy who gets it into his head he's a knight and it was sad and funny at the same time, and she added, "And that's what life's like. So that's what makes it a good book."

I thought how happy Bly'd seemed the night before, and then I thought how he'd go missing from time to time, and wouldn't say where he'd been. And then I didn't know what to think anymore. Except that it was my fault. Because of what had happened, with him and with me.

Mona said, "You two didn't have a fight, now, did you?" and

at least I could say "no!" to that without lying, because that much was true. We hadn't had a fight. Far from it. The opposite. We'd had the opposite.

Mary was upset too, and when everyone else found out, they was upset: Detlef and Finch and Jenny. And the Sick Birds wondered where he'd got to and who was gonna do their groceries, but Mona told 'em not to worry and that she could take over like she had before Bly came along.

We kept hoping to hear something, some word from Bly, but none came. I started wondering about that box of pills, the fluoxetine, and I wandered out to Bly's shed a hundred times and all his other pills were there. And then I saw his mask. But it was the fluoxetine that had me worried and by the middle of the second day I said to Mona, "If he stops taking the antidepressants, what then?" and Mona didn't laugh or have a joke or anything else to say. She just shrugged and went to make tea, so I followed her and said, "But it will be okay, won't it, I mean, he'll be okay? He wouldn't do anything stupid. Would he?"

Mona stopped making tea and said gently, "You're all for having everything harmless, Snowflake, aren't you?" She held my chin with her dry old hand and smiled and it was one of the saddest smiles I will ever see. If I live to be a hundred, which ain't likely.

So I worried even more, but over tea she said, "Antidepressants. Like I said, we all got our own ways. Worked for Bly, and that's a good thing. Time was the doctors wanted me to take 'em, but they messed with my head real bad. Made me even worse. You know what? If you look at the little bit of paper that comes with 'em, in the box, it lists all the possible side effects. And one of the possible side effects is *suicidal tendencies*. This is something you're taking because you feel suicidal, you understand?"

I understood, but that didn't make me feel any better, and then Mona told me about not one, not two, now wait up, *three* of her friends who'd killed themselves while taking antidepressants, so then I thought Mona why the heck are you telling me that? And I guess she realized that too because she suddenly said, "But our Bly'll be okay. Trust me, Ash, he'll be okay," and she smiled but, heck, the damage was done.

So I worried and worried until that evening, when there was a phone call ringing on Mona's line, which happened from time to time, if not often. She went in to answer it and I heard her say "uh-huh" and "yeah" and "yes, sure, wait please" and then she came out and said the call was for me.

I went inside and I was on the phone for about a minute and then I came back out and set in the red plastic chair while Mona and Mary stared at me till Mona said are you gonna tell us or will I have to beat it out of you? And then I shook my head and told them it was Bly's father who was on the phone. It was Jack.

He said he'd heard from Bly. That he was well again and had gone back to finish his training to be a police officer.

So Mona stared at Mary and Mary stared at me and no one knew what to make of any of that, till finally Mona said, "He who has a *why* to live, can cope with almost any *how*" and then she said, "Friedrich Nietzsche. 1844 to 1900," and I wanted her to shut the hell up about philosophers for one damn minute. But I know what she meant. She meant that Bly wanted to do something with his life, and what he wanted to do was be a police officer. So he had gone to do that. And sickness be damned.

Cooper came up to me and climbed into my lap while I set there in the red plastic chair, and he seemed to know something was wrong. He weren't no Socrates, but he was a smart dog. He'd spent all day sniffing around Bly's shed and back and forth to the house and he knew something was wrong. Now he was just tired and he set in my lap and licked my hand, over and over.

The dark was coming on in and Mona said, "What did we learn today?" but so quiet I barely heard her, and if I hadn't heard her say it a hundred times before, I wouldn't have understood. But her heart wasn't in it and she didn't make anyone say anything, but it got me thinking anyway and what I was thinking I'd learned was this. That love between people is strange, and not simple, and sometimes it's downright complicated.

Then I recalled the last part of the phone call with Jack, so I told Mona and Mary.

"My stepdad says he's coming here," I said and Mona asked why, so I told her why. "He says he's gonna take me home."

"Oh," said Mona. And that was all she said, and I was feeling funny about that, and then after a long while she said, "But Snowflake, this is your home."

And I thought, huh. Yeah. So that's what I learned today.

LEARNING TO BE SOMEONE ELSE

Matters were fraught in Mona's house the day Jack came to take me back to flatland.

Before Jack even showed up, the cable guy came. Now, we weren't sure why but he came to fix the Internet. 'Course Mona didn't use Wi-Fi, but there was an old wired connection all sealed off in a tinfoil box in the room with the washing machine. And she hadn't had no problems with it, but the cable guy said he had to update the equipment and then he started asking what speed Mona had and Mona shrugged and I said, "She's got one meg" and the cable guy said, "Well, don't you want nine megs?" and Mona shrugged and went off to ask Mary if they wanted nine megs and though she'd told the cable guy to stay in that one room, he didn't, and then he was walking through the whole house and Mona and Mary started getting agitated on account of all the cologne this guy was pumping out. And I guess he was new to Snowflake, or at least to the Forties, and I tried to explain about MCS to him but then I felt kinda stupid because I still didn't believe it myself, not really, not a hundred percent, despite the evidence of my own body.

So that had been the first thing, and then there was the next thing. A good commotion.

I saw the start of it as I was moving my stuff. My clothes. A few books. That kinda stuff. After more or less three months I was leaving my room with only two walls, but I was not going far. The days were growing short, and the nights cold. And by the way, just because the temperatures were falling didn't mean that Mona closed any doors or windows. All through the day she'd leave every window and door open and just leave the screens closed to keep bugs out. It aired the house, she said, but what it meant was there was a gale always blowing through the place.

So then Mona and I decided to move me into Bly's shed, the one he'd slept in, and move all his stuff into the other. I said I could just about fit me and all my accoutrements and what-have-you in there, seeing as I was smaller than Bly. And had few accoutrements. But it didn't feel right, somehow, like I was taking his space. It felt like stealing. But it was that or freeze all to death, so I moved into the shed. Bit by bit I was shuffling between my old room and my new one, and I was coming back over to the back porch when I saw Socrates.

He was standing at the back door, and he was looking at something. He was acting kinda funny, and then two things happened at once. Cooper came trotting around from the far side of the house, and he trotted right over to where Socrates was fussing. And then Socrates rolled on his back with his legs pointing at the sky and Cooper started barking at something by the back-door step.

Somehow I knew it wasn't Cooper barking that had scared Socrates, and I shuffled over and by then Cooper was in the house going crazy at something under the refrigerator. He was snapping and snarling and barking, and Socrates had recovered some and come inside and was butting the side of the fridge for good measure.

So I stood there and wondered what all to hell and then Mona come out of nowhere and stood with her hands on her hips.

She said something I couldn't hear on account of all the racket, and so she said it again and it was one word and that was "rattler!"

I stepped back but Mona didn't seem too scared, she just pointed at her dog and her goat and said, "Well, isn't this a fine example of interspecies cooperation!" But then she started fretting about her goat damaging her icebox, and I shouted what are we gonna do and Mona pointed one finger at the sky like she'd had an idea cartoon-style and marched off somewhere. When she came back she had a snake-wrangling tool, which was a long stick with a loop of cord at the end that you could tighten from the end where you held it, nice and safely away from any snakes you had wrangled. She plopped down on her hands and knees and started fishing around under the refrigerator while Cooper ran around in circles like it was Christmas and Socrates alternated every two minutes between butting things and rolling on his back with his legs stuck in the air.

Mary came by and Finch was with her, and so then I was shouting "rattler!" at them and they nodded like it happened every day, which it didn't, and it was right in the middle of all of this with Mona wiggling her tiny little butt in the air that my stepfather arrived.

We didn't see he was there at first, but Cooper did. He was most often the friendliest resident of the Forties, and maybe the most observant too, and he was the first to notice Jack, because he was running in circles around the kitchen and on one of his circles he didn't come back.

I turned and saw Jack standing there with a funny look on his face and when I say funny I mean he was as confused as a pigeon, but Cooper was licking his hand, real friendly. I guess Jack was more confused when Socrates got bored of butting things and wandered past him and back outside into the yard, and then Mona shot upright shouting "yee-ha!" and she had a four-foot rattlesnake dangling from the end of her stick.

She took one look at Jack and said "oh" and went outside and after a few moments came back and said, "Who might you be?" So I explained who he was and everyone said hello and then Mona explained to Jack that they would require him to come and sit outside on the back porch since he was so fond of fabric conditioner. And you can imagine for yourselves what his face was like when Mona said that.

So Mary and Finch took him and I asked Mona what she'd done with the snake. She said she had a bin out back for folks like him and later on she'd drive him way into the desert and let him get on with his rattling. I was happy, because even though the snake was dangerous and had scared the hell outta me, and more besides outta Socrates, I didn't like the idea of killing it. That just seemed mean.

Then of course you know what Mona said, and after she'd said I wonder what will happen next she had me take glasses and a jug of ice water outside while she made the tea.

By the time we got outside, Jack had got well into business.

"What do you mean? Ash is sick?" he was saying and Finch was nodding in somber fashion and Mary started talking about venting and Jack's eyebrows were moving steadily up his forehead. Back in the day, Bly would often joke and say that Jack didn't have a forehead, he had a fivehead, so there was plenty of room for his eyebrows still to move into. It would be kind to say he had a receding hairline, but the truth is there wasn't much of anything left up on top.

I had a hard time not giggling. I will explain that Jack was tall, real tall and skinny. He was strong though, he was tough. He was a carpenter and worked on construction sites and everyone always said how he was tougher and worked harder than the big guys, the ones with big muscles, and he moved twice as fast as they did too. But now he was set in one of the red plastic chairs and the only thing moving was his eyebrows. Them chairs, they was real low to the ground. Like, they was good for lounging with old friends and staring at the desert but they were not designed to hold business meetings in or aid with the rescue of stepchildren from desert communities. So Jack was trying to perch on it, with his gangly old legs bent and his knees somewhere near his ears while he listened to Mary saying how sick I'd been but how I was a little better now.

The other thing about them plastic chairs was this: if you moved in 'em too much they built up static electricity. And though Jack was trying to perch on the edge of his seat, he kept sliding back into it because the chair very much preferred its customers to lounge around, just like old friends. And each time Jack slid himself back up to the edge of his seat, he rubbed up a tad more static. So now, little by little, the remaining hair on his head was standing on end.

And that was why I had to stop myself giggling, because after ten minutes of this with his eyebrows all raised and his hair standing on end, it looked like Jack had seen a ghost, or at least a rattler under a refrigerator, and all he could manage to say was "what?" or "I beg your . . . ?" or "do you mean to say that . . . ?" before someone would chip in with something else they thought he needed to know about poor little Ash.

Finally Jack turned to me and said, "Well, have you been to see a doctor, Ash?" and I thought uh-oh, let's not speak about the snow that fell in the fall, but I nodded and of course he asked "and what did he say?"

So I said she told me there's nothing wrong with me and anyway it's all in my mind.

He started saying, "But look, if the doctor says you ain't ill . . ." and then Mona was near enough the maddest I'd ever seen her because she just said, "If the doctor says you ain't ill, that makes you feel better, right?"

Then she shut up and stared into the desert, but Finch chipped in and started explaining to Jack again about MCS.

He told him how it was only just starting to be understood, and that there was some recent research into negative programming of the amygdala, which is in the brain, and that perhaps the role of infection of the vagus nerve and a collapse of tolerance for certain pollutants was about to be understood.

So you can imagine then that Jack's eyebrows finished raising. He made a big effort and lowered them and looked at Finch. He said, real polite (because he was always real polite), "That all sounds grand but with respect, Mr. Finch, Ash has been told by a doctor that this sickness ain't real and, with respect I mean, you are not a doctor."

'Cept then Finch went and told Jack that actually and as a matter of fact he was a doctor. Leastways, he had been until he'd got sick and had to give it up. And that was news to me. I stared at old Finch with new eyes, and then he explained to my stepfather how he had been a "tenured professor of immunobiology" at a certain medical school and when Jack asked where, Finch said oh, Boston, and when Jack asked where in Boston, Finch said, real quiet, Harvard.

"Harvard, sir," he said, and then Mona turned and smiled at Finch and it was the saddest and at the same time the sweetest smile you could see, and it meant a whole lot of things and some of 'em I could work out and some of 'em I could only guess.

Then there was silence for a good amount of time.

Everyone stared into the desert, even Jack, who was getting the hang of things quick. The silence was complete, and the only sound was when Cooper went up to the bin the rattler was in and started growling and Mona said "hush, sweet mutt" and he climbed up into her lap instead.

As she tickled Cooper under the chin, she turned to Jack and spoke to him. She smiled and she spoke gentle and what she said was about having EI. She said it was no easy ride, and that I was setting out into a new world. She said I was gonna have to stay here a while, maybe longer'n a while. She said I was gonna have to learn to be someone else. And I listened to Mona speak on my behalf and maybe you think I oughta have spoken for myself. And I guess maybe I could have, if I'd really needed to, but right then, I just let Mona roll right on, and it felt good to have someone on my side.

"At first you're afraid you're gonna die," Mona was saying to Jack. "Then you're afraid you won't. I think I can say that goes for all of us." And she nodded at Finch and Mary and they both looked at the ground like it had suddenly got real interesting, and there was a tear on Mary's cheek that just appeared.

"So your Ash here," said Mona, "well . . ."

She turned to me.

"You've done the easy part," she said. "You got yourself sick. Now comes the part that's much harder. Getting well again."

And she explained how I had to stay in Snowflake, out here, away from flatland, till I got better, or at least till I could cope with it my own way.

"But you got no money," Jack said to me. "You can't—"

"Sir," said Mona, "that's okay. Ash don't need money. We look after each other here and those of us that can help those of us that can't. I ain't just talking about money."

Jack tried to say how he didn't like the sound of charity for his family and Mona asked him if he was a religious man and he said, "Yes ma'am." So then Mona said, "Faith, Hope, and Charity. And the greatest of these is Charity," and Jack was fresh out of arguments.

Mona asked him if he'd like to stay for lunch and he mumbled yes. Then Mary started asking him about where he worked and the construction sites and if he'd ever heard of EI-friendly houses and did he know how they used Reynolds Wrap to make their homes safe if they couldn't build new ones and did he know what kind of chemicals was on the construction sites he worked on?

Finch leant over real quick and before Jack knew what was happening, Finch pulled his lower eyelid down and inspected it. Then he looked at Mary and nodded and Mary shrugged and Jack said what?

"You could maybe wear a mask when you're working," Finch said, and Jack said what? and Mary said, "You don't wanna end up like your son, now? Or Ash? You wanna keep working, right? So you gotta protect yourself. And you might wanna quit using that fabric conditioner too."

By the time Mona came out back again with lunch, Jack said actually thank you very much but he had changed his mind about eating and he oughta get on the road.

I walked with him around front to his truck.

He climbed in and wound the window down.

"Listen, Ash," he said. "You ain't said nothing. You let them do all the talking for you, you think I didn't notice?"

I raised my shoulders a tad.

Jack looked at me again, harder.

"You're sure about this?"

I nodded and asked him how Bly was doing, and he put a smile on his face that didn't really belong and said, "He's gonna make it. He's doing good. Phones every week to tell me so."

Then he said, "Listen, I heard some news," and he told me about my mom. Seems the trucker from Nashua, New Hampshire, was a Mormon, which is what he was doing stopping in on Snowflake in the first place, visiting that big place of worship with the man on top in gold. Jack explained how my mother had become a Mormon too, and when I asked Jack how he knew all this, he said how she'd written him to forgive him.

"Forgive you for what?" I asked, and he said "search me" and shrugged, which it seemed was infectious in Snowflake, even after as little as forty-five minutes of being there.

So now I was thinking "and she couldn't write to me?" but I didn't say it. Anyway, I guess it was obvious because Jack put his hand out the window and on my shoulder and said, "She loves you, Ash. I know she does. She just has a real funny way of showing it."

Yup, I thought. Like not at all.

Then he cracked a smile.

"Maybe she didn't write to you because you have nothing to forgive."

And then he drove away.

METRONIDAZOLE, GOD OF PHARMA

For three billion years, Mona told me, there was only bacteria.

"Imagine that!" she said, one evening, at what-did-you-learn-today time. So I tried, but I gave up because I didn't know whether I was supposed to be imagining three billion years or there only being bacteria on the whole face of the Earth—the only living thing, she meant. Or maybe I was supposed to do both, but that seemed to me impossible. For one thing, I don't believe you can imagine three billion years, any more'n you can imagine one billion, or even just a plain old million. It all starts to get meaningless pretty darn quick. Time, that is.

When you think about time it never works out in any logical way. For example, the evening that Mona told me that the only living thing on Earth for three billion years was bacteria, I had been living in the Forties for about three months. But it felt like three years. To say the truth, I was having a hard time remembering life before Snowflake, and the whole of my life before, all eighteen years of it, seemed to me to have lasted about as long as the three months. And then, at exactly one and the same time, I felt like I'd only just arrived at Mona's. So that makes little sense, and then when someone asks you to imagine three billion years, well, that makes none, don't it?

A few days before, Mona had started going on about bacteria.

She'd ordered a couple books on the subject and no one had seen her face since they arrived. Bacteria was her new favorite subject, and I'll say this for Mona, it didn't matter how old she was, she kept on learning. There's always something more to know, she would say, almost as often as I-wonder-what-will-heck-you-know-the-rest. That is not to say, however, that it didn't get a mite tiresome at times, like when she had a new favorite subject, and right now her new favorite subject was bacteria.

After we'd eaten, Mary stopped by. She had a whole bunch of letters in her hand, as usual, and she'd come to ask Mona something, as if Mona was some kind of legal expert. And I guess Mona kind of was, because she'd been through it herself, and had helped a whole bunch of people. The problem was that after years of paying out, Mary's insurance company had said they were reviewing her case and it looked like she was going to lose her benefits.

But this evening, Mary didn't even get her letters out before Mona was telling her everything she'd already told me about bacteria, and some more for free. Bacteria were simple, she said. They were just one single cell, whereas we had zillions of cells in our body, but that shouldn't make us go getting all superior, she said.

"Guess how many cells are in your body!" she said, so I mumbled "twenty-five" under my breath, while Mary had a real guess.

"I dunno, maybe ten million? No, a hundred million!" she said, and this is what I mean about numbers that don't mean anything after a time, because Mona told us the actual answer was about ten trillion. Ten trillion. But before we got a chance to figure out what that meant, she said, "Now guess how many bacteria you are carrying in your body," but she couldn't wait to tell us.

"One hundred trillion," she said. "One hun-der-ed tri-llion! That means there are ten times as many bacteria in you as you have cells in your body. So who's the boss, huh? If only ten percent of you is you, then who's really in charge here?"

I said that must be a misprint or something, and she said no, and explained how you had 900 different *species* of bacteria living in just your nose, and other powerfully tedious facts like that.

Then she told us how human beings have 21,000 genes, while the combined number of genes of all the bacteria living on your skin and inside of you came to about four and a half *million*. And that meant that of all the genetic programming going on in your body, only a half percent of it was human. Only a half a percent of you was you.

Then she said there was even a theory that these guys called mitochondria, which are tiny things inside our body's cells that make energy, were originally bacteria. So they'd got themselves a permanent hitchhike through time by becoming part of us.

So I said, "Well, just because these bacteria are along for the ride doesn't mean they affect us much, does it?" and I can tell you what that got me. What that got me was a long *discussion*, and when I say *discussion* I mean Mona talking at me about how bacteria can control our behavior.

"There's the one called toxoplasma," and she started giggling before she even got any further. "This one's great. See, if you're infected with it, well, what happens next depends on what sex you are. If you're a man it makes you more risk-taking. It makes you less pleasant, and less moral too. And it'll make you do things that aren't so safe. For example, it's proven to make you three times more likely to have a car accident. If you're a man, that is. Whereas if you're a woman, it makes you more trusting and more easygoing. It makes you wanna play house, make nests, have babies, and be generally nurturing. Toxoplasma! It's a gender-stereotype-reinforcing bug! A sexist bacteria!"

And off she went again like her head might fall off.

"Well, why would it do that?" Mary asked, so Mona said that the book said that say you was a toxoplasma bacterium and you infected a male rat. Now that male rat is gonna take more risks, maybe not stay away from the cat that's been snooping about. So the rat gets eaten and you've managed to pass yourself into a new host. And then, say you infect a female rat and you make it have more babies, and you can infect them too, then you've found yourself a whole bunch of new hosts.

"Pretty cool, huh?" she said.

"Yeah, but that's real rare, ain't it? That bacteria," I said. "Toxo-what-have-you? That must be real rare."

"Oh, sure," said Mona, "only about one in four people have it."

"One in four?" I said, like I was dumb, which *was* dumb because here was a number I could understand.

"Unless you're a woman who lives in Paris, France," Mona added. "In Paris, France, four out of every five women have it."

Four out of every five.

Then Mona told us about an experiment in Berlin, Germany, where they proved that women are most attracted to men who have the greatest difference in bacteria in their gut from what they got. They did this using identical T-shirts that ten guys had slept in. And when they got ten girls to rank the T-shirts (just the T-shirts, mind) in order of how attractive the owner must be, they found out that it was the bacteria being different that made 'em attractive.

"Well, why would the bacteria do that?" I asked.

"Make you diversify your colonies of bacteria, I guess," Mona said. "I always told you diversity was good. Right? Right!"

And I thought about that. Did you only take a shine to someone because of the bugs in their gut? Not because they had nice square shoulders, or an old faded red T-shirt that does something special for 'em?

Or was that T-shirt only attractive because of freaking bacteria?

"Not so smart now, are we?" Mona said, and started giggling again. "Bacteria have been around for longer'n we have. And maybe they're controlling a bunch of what we do and think. There are far more of 'em than us, and when we've wiped ourselves out and all the fancy tigers and lemurs and what-have-you too, you know who'll be left? Right?"

"Yeah," I said, "but these bacteria. The ones living in us. They're not all bad, right?"

I said that partially to reassure myself, because whenever Mona started talking about bacteria, I started feeling all itchy and scratchy and would want to go have a shower and not come out. Mona had already told us that some bacteria were good for us, in fact, how we actually need some bacteria, like the ones in our gut, to help us digest food and so on.

"Yeah," said Mona, "but here's the rub. There are good bacteria and bad ones. And we take antibiotics to kill the bad ones, like when we get some infection or other. Trouble is, these antibiotics, they kill the good ones too. The book says that if you take this thing called metronidazole, it's real bad news."

"Metro-what?" I said, and Mona said, yeah, don't they give drugs weird names.

She told us that the book said it was proven fact that the use of antibiotics was being linked to all sorts of woes and illnesses and syndromes. Obvious things like irritable bowel syndrome and celiac disease. And then things that were less obvious, like autism and ADHD. And then things that were just way out there. Like obesity, like depression.

So then I remembered that even Bly had talked about that— about how you needed the good bacteria in your gut to help you make serotonin or you'd get depressed and then I remembered that Bly wasn't here anymore and I felt real depressed myself.

I wondered where he was and if he was a police officer yet, and I wondered how smart he'd look in his uniform and how he'd have women falling at his feet and some of the men too, no doubt. Then I felt sick, and I don't mean with MCS, I mean something turned over inside of me and it hurt and I wanted him to come home. To Snowflake.

And the point was, shouldn't they have to prove these things are safe first, before they get used all across the planet? Before millions of people have used 'em and swallowed 'em and before they have ended up in our rivers and waterways?

Something occurred to me and so I said it. "These drugs. They sound like gods in a third-rate role-playing game," I said, so then Mona looked at me like "whut?" and I said, "Metronidazole."

I said they must've been made up by a bunch of jerks sitting in a boardroom with a set of Czechoslovakian Scrabble tiles and a bottle of whiskey.

Mary laughed and said uh-huh, or gods from ancient Sparta, and Mona put her head in her hands and said they weren't the gods of Sparta, they were the gods of Pharma. Big Pharma.

So then Mary and me, we played our last guessing game of the evening.

"There are fifty thousand chemicals in use in the Western world," Mona said. "Guess how many of 'em have been shown to be safe."

And we both guessed, but we was both wrong. The actual answer, by the way, is about three hundred. Three hundred out of fifty freaking thousand.

"That's . . ." I said, but I couldn't think what it was.

"Dumb?" said Mona. "Irritating? Outrageous? And you know why it is, don't you? You know why they're used before we know they're safe?"

And yes, I did by now, for I had spent long enough with Mona.

I knew she was setting me up for the answer, just like she used to do with Bly. And I told her.

"Money," I said. "That's why. People wanna make money first, and maybe wonder how after. Maybe."

Mona did her fingers into guns thing at me.

"Gotcha. People think Big Pharma is there to make 'em better, but it ain't. It ain't. It's there to make money, and if they get away without killing anyone in the process, well, that's a neat little bonus."

Mona nodded, and I knew I had become Bly. I had stolen his bed and I had stolen his life and I had stolen his answers to Mona. I had even stolen his sickness. But he'd stolen something of mine in return when he went wandering off back down to flatland. And that, in case you didn't know, was my heart.

And maybe it was just the bacteria that made me feel that way. And maybe it was just the bacteria that made Bly do what he'd gone and done too. But that didn't matter none, it all hurt just the same.

NOCEBO

"So that's what your face looks like," Mary said to Mona one day and cracked one of her tiny smiles. It was somewhere in November, and it was coming on cold. The nights were a little below freezing, and the days didn't show much on the thermometer that was stuck by the back door. The days were warm still, long as you was in the sun. That was one of the things about being up at five, well, heck, six thousand feet. It's warmer. I mean, actually it's colder, but it *feels* warmer if you're in the sunshine. Not because you're closer to the fiery orb, but because the air is so darn thin. There ain't so much air to stop the sun's rays, and that warms you up.

Mary had called around again with a file of letters and documents to go over, and Mona had finally read everything there was to read about bacteria. Now that her face was no longer hid by a book, we simple folk could try to speak to her about something other than how bacteria are gonna rule the world, if they ain't already, and that was surely open to discussion, at least as far as Mona saw it. Mona seemed a little weird for a few days after the bacteria thing. Like she was seeing everything different, and I guess, maybe I was too, because while what she had to say about bacteria was mightily tiresome, it was also, if I tell it right, quite a thing. It sorta did change your mind about things. About what we're all so fussed about, when the bacteria have been here for four billion years and we've only been here for twenty minutes. And will be real damn lucky, as now we know, to get to twenty-five.

Anyway, at last Mary got her chance to show us what was eating at her.

She pulled out a bunch of letters from her health insurer, and then a bunch of letters she'd been getting from some lawyer she'd found. Then the three of us stood with our hands on our hips and Mary said, well, whaddya think? And Mona and me thought for a bit and then at the same time we both said about what?

"That!" said Mary, and she jabbed a finger at one of the letters from her lawyer.

Now, the thing is, it had taken Mary about a hundred years to find a lawyer who took her seriously about EI and who'd agreed to help her in her case with the insurance company. She'd told me one time how three folks had laughed down the phone at her. How one guy had just said "fruitcake" and hung up. And about how finally she'd found this one guy in Flagstaff who'd listened for a real long time and then how he'd agreed to do it.

Even then, Mary said, it had not been easy, because he didn't understand things.

So Mary had had to educate her lawyer all about environmental illness and she was finally happy that they was good to go up against the insurance company, and then he sent through a letter of agreement between them about a week ago and on that was written a list of terms.

"So?" said Mona, and Mary said, "Look at item 26."

So we did.

Item 26: client to confirm if tinfoil hats are to be worn in court.

"Oh," said Mona.

"Gee," I said.

"Yuh," said Mary. "I spent two months getting this guy to the point where he's ready to defend me, and now he's yanking my chain."

It sure did seem that way. Like this guy thought it was funny to ask if they all had to wear little tinfoil hats like those crazies who think the government is fooling with their brainwaves. The government or aliens. You take your pick. Because everyone knows those guys are crazy, though I guess, thinking about it for a moment, I guess they don't think they're crazy. I guess they think they have darn good reasons for wearing tinfoil hats and I also guess they think their thinking is logical.

"So whaddya gonna do?" asked Mona.

"Well, that's what I'm asking you," said Mary. She looked real worried, more'n I had ever seen. "Do I tell this guy to get lost?"

And I thought, yeah, tell him to get lost, but Mary's point was she'd spent so long getting this far, and she'd already paid some time already and that money would be in the trash if she started off again with someone else. Even if she could find a someone else.

"Well," said Mona, "I guess he has a sense of humor," and

that could not be denied, but my point was a) yeah, but what kind of sense of humor and b) do you really want a clown representing you in court anyways?

And Mary did not know what to do.

A few days later I was hanging out with Finch. Mona had started up on deliveries again since Bly had left, and she made me come with her, just to get me out of the house. I was still tired all the time, and I had the headaches come and go, and I couldn't walk more'n fifty yards without falling over, near enough. So we had been buzzing this way and that in her little Japanese car, and sometimes I'd go to every drop, and sometimes she'd leave me to talk a while with someone or other and pick me up on the way home.

Finch was still camping outside his house. He'd made some progress on stripping out things that didn't oughta be in there, but there was still more to do and it was getting colder every day.

I told him about Mary and the lawyer and the tinfoil hats and what did he think she should do?

He shook his head and he looked mad. Angry for Mary, because she needed help with her case and she'd been sleeping in the back of a pickup truck for seven years and wasn't that bad enough? He was lucky, he said.

"Screwit," he said. "Insurance companies. You pay them for years and the second you need something back they do everything they can to avoid paying out. They think it's all in our heads."

And he was mad, like I said.

So then I was thinking about Dr. B and what she'd said to me. It's all in your head. It's all in your mind. You ain't truly sick. It's all in your mind.

So I said to Finch, "What do they mean by that anyway?"

And he said "what?" so I said, "I mean, do they think we're imagining it? Or do they think we're pretending it? Or what?"

Finch huffed around his porch for a bit and it was always funny to see him mad, because he was, 99 percent of the time, so calm, so calm, always *so* calm like he was a Zen master and had medals to prove it. And then every once in a little while something would rile him and he'd say "screwit."

When he'd finished making coffee, he'd calmed down.

He said, "Yeah, I guess some folks think we're pretending." And he told me about how he'd had to go before some kind of committee that the insurance company set on him, to prove he was ill, or else he wouldn't have been getting his payout. And he said there was one guy on the panel who tried to rile him, who told him to his face that he was just putting it all on.

"There are folks like that. I don't think Dr. B is one of those guys. Most doctors, they mean something a little different. When they say it's all in our heads, they're talking about something else. They believe that *we* believe we're sick, and they also believe that we really *are* sick, but that the sickness is a product of the mind, not the body."

So what I said was "huh?"

So then Finch took a deep breath.

And then he said, "You heard of the placebo effect, right?" and I nodded because everyone knows about the placebo effect. You go to the doctor and take some pill and it makes you better and all the while your doctor is chuckling away to his- or herself because actually the pill was made of nothing but baking soda and/or sugar. And Big Pharma is chuckling away twice as hard because they just charged somebody a small fortune for a tiny little dollop of baking soda and/or sugar. And baking soda and/or sugar don't make you better. Least, they shouldn't, but they can.

So Finch said, "Yeah, that's about right, but there's more to it than that." And then he told me about some of the really weird things about the placebo effect.

Like, thing number one, you can be *told* that the pill you're taking is only a placebo pill, and it can still work anyhow.

Or thing number two, that the more expensive you think a placebo pill is, the better it works.

And then there's thing number three, the placebo effect is so powerful that it gives real drugs a run for their money. Finch told me how the drug companies have a mighty hard time proving that the shiny new drug they just made is better than the placebo effect, which is to say, better than nothing but the human mind telling itself everything's gonna be fine.

Then I thought about someone I knew, and something that someone was taking. *Had been* taking.

"Yeah, but something like Prozac, that works for real, doesn't it?"

So then Finch told me how the results for fluoxetine, for

instance, were debatable. How maybe it shouldn't be sold, because according to some tests, it ain't no better than the placebo. So then I was thinking about Bly, and the pills he'd been taking, the pills he didn't take with him when he left, and how they could mess with your head so much they made your depression worse. And now here was Finch telling me maybe they weren't even better than taking baking soda and/or sugar pills. That they was just the placebo, with side effects.

Then Finch told me what I thought was the weirdest thing of all: that how well you responded to a placebo wasn't random. It was down to your genes. You inherited it from your ma and pa. And 25 percent of people respond real well to it. And 25 percent of people don't really respond to it that much at all. And then there's the 50 percent of people in the middle. Finch said it was down to one little gene with a real long fancy science name that I didn't catch. Depending on which version of this guy you ended up with, well, that was how much you'd get outta them fake pills. That and how much you thought they cost.

Now, just as I was thinking, yeah, but what does all this have to do with us sick folks, Finch says, "So that's the placebo. But the thing is, where there's light, there's always dark too, right?"

And Finch told me all about this thing called nocebo. And nocebo does the exact opposite of placebo. By which I mean that if placebo can make you better when you're sick, then nocebo can make you sick when you're well.

"I don't get it," I said to Finch. "You can't think yourself sick. Can you?"

So Finch gave me a good old Snowflake shrug and said, "If I told you that chair you're sat in was covered in maggots this morning and I had to scrape 'em all off before you got here, what would you think?"

And I said, "What? This chair was covered in maggots?" and Finch said, no, it wasn't but he reckoned that even telling me that might make me start feeling itchy and then two seconds later I was telling Finch about how I felt whenever Mona started talking about bacteria. There you go, that's the power of the human mind. That's nocebo, Finch said.

"Maybe," Finch said, "maybe you know those stories you hear about an old couple, and they've been living with each other for decades and then one of 'em dies. And then the other dies a few days later?"

And I said "kinda, yeah" and Finch said that the statistics showed that was more than chance. You really can die of a broken heart. So one guess gets you the name of who I was thinking about then. And Finch was talking on and it sounded like it might be real interesting but I wasn't listening no more. I was thinking about cold nights and my shed that had been Bly's shed and a few other matters like that. Things like faded red T-shirts. But finally I noticed that Finch was asking me something and what it was was this.

"So, do you think your MCS is all in your head?" he asked.

"No," I said. Right off. "No. Least . . ."

"Least what?"

"No," I said. "It's just that durned doctor put the thought in my mind."

Finch nodded.

"And the mind is a powerful thing."

"But haven't you ever wondered that?" I asked. "Haven't you wondered whether you being sick is all just in your mind?" And Finch told me, yes, he had thought about it, because he was a scientist, after all. Or he had been once, anyhow. But no, he did not think it was in his mind.

"If it was," he said, "it'd be a damn sight easier to fix than sleeping on porches for ten years and pulling houses to pieces."

Huh. That's for sure, I thought.

"No," he said. "I don't think it is. The history of medicine is full of diseases that were once thought to be nothing, or nonsense, or all in the mind. Until some smart aleck found out what was really wrong, and from then on people took them seriously. And MCS is just another one of those things. I told you that already, didn't I, Snowflake? We are filling the world full of chemicals that we have precisely no idea about, and one not-so-fine day the chickens will come home to roost. With the canaries."

And he smiled at me and I felt smiled at, but it didn't warm my innards like when somebody else I knew did it, and a little while later Mona swung by to take me home and I rode in the little Japanese car thinking about folks who died of a broken heart.

OBVIOUSLY YOU KNOW WHAT SEX A GOAT IS WHEN YOU BUY HIM. OR HER. OR HIM.

Christmas was coming and I knew that because Snowflake was white. I mean, I woke up one morning in my shed, and even with all my blankets and everything that had been Bly's, I was cold, and when I pushed the door open, it had snowed.

Now, this being Arizona, and at five-heck-six, all sorts of weird stuff could happen with the weather. And that was not the last time I saw snow in the desert, but it was the first, and it did not look right at all.

Mona made me a hot breakfast of her best buckwheat porridge that morning and for once we sat inside her house staring at the desert, not on the porch. But by the afternoon, the sun was out and the thermometer climbed right back up and it was hot enough to set in a T-shirt and watch the snow melt before your very eyes.

That afternoon, Mona and me put our masks on and rode into town in her little yellow car. And though I was still sick, by this time I was walking a little farther, and Mona wanted me to keep her company, even if I couldn't do much else of anything.

On the way, in the car, she told me she was worrying about Socrates.

So I asked her what was wrong with the old goat and she said, well, I wonder if he oughtn't have some company.

"He's got us," I said. "And the mutt."

And Mona said, yeah, but none of us was getting any younger. "Specially not Cooper," she said. "He's one real old hound now. Real old." And I didn't want to think none about that, because I did not like the thought of Cooper not being around.

"But no," said Mona, "that's not the thing. The thing is, I wonder if he oughta have some company of his own kind."

"You mean another goat?" I said, and Mona looked over at me as she drove and said, "That's what I mean. That's exactly it. See, I always wanted to have more'n one. But someone said I oughta see how I get on with one, because goats can be a handful."

She had that right. I had lost track of the things that dumb goat had eaten that he weren't supposed to. And when he wasn't eating sneakers or socks or what-have-you, he was eating a vast amount of regulation goat food. Mona had a deal with the animal supply place on the edge of town and she picked up a bundle of hay every few days, and that was one place we were heading that afternoon, to get Socrates his hay and his treat of a salt lick, which was a big lump of salt on a stick. It's kinda like crack cocaine for goats.

"So what happened?"

"Well," Mona said, "I guess one goat is a lot of work for an old girl like me. And then I got one, and you know that business about how I thought I was buying a nanny and then when I got him home I realized I'd made a mistake?"

And so then I thought, how do you mistake a big something like that? I mean, it's obvious what sex everyone is, ain't it. Ain't it? And then I thought, maybe it ain't. Maybe we make a lot of what they call assumptions, and maybe we all can be a bit more complicated. Animals, and people too.

Mona was yakking.

"So when I got him home, and I realized he was a he and not a she, I took him back to the farmer I bought him from and he said fine I could have another one but if so he'd be sending the little boy off to be dog meat, because he only needed one buck to do his breeding and he had one already and then he told me how boy goats were a lot of trouble and how they stank worse than the girls and how they were meaner and more aggressive than the girls too."

"That so?" I said, and I wondered if goats could get toxoplasma too. But Mona was telling me how she couldn't let him go off to be killed, because by then she already had fallen in love with him, on account of how he was so cute, so she told the farmer she'd keep him. And I said, "Cute? Socrates was cute?"

That was hard to believe.

"You have to remember, Snowflake, he was just a few weeks old. He was so sweet! So I kept him. But, I have to say . . ."

"What?"

"I feel kinda bad."

"You do?"

"Uh-huh."

"Why? You saved his life!"

"Uh-huh, but the thing about boy goats is, unless you're gonna use 'em to breed with, you have to take their . . . you know . . . you have to have 'em done."

"Done?"

"Seen to."

"Seen to?"

And I still wasn't getting it, till Mona said, "Heck Ash, you have to cut their nuts off!"

"Oh, yeah, sure," I said. "I know that."

'Cept until I came to think about it, I hadn't realized that there was something missing from Socrates' rear view.

"Time to suit up," Mona said, which meant it was time to put our masks on as we were near into town, and that was good because we couldn't talk when we had our masks on and I had heard all I needed to about that subject for the time being.

I remember too, that day, the first time I saw snow in Snowflake, and we rode into town in the afternoon, because something happened in town that I will not forget. And it wasn't the first time and it wasn't the last time this kinda thing had happened. But it's the one that's stuck with me.

We did our errands and went to Socrates' dealer to buy him his fix, and on the way home we stopped for gas. And all this time we'd had our masks on and even though I had stayed in the car I'd learned that just being in and around town was bad for me, would set me back for a day or so. So Mona was pumping the gas into her little yellow car and wearing her mask and then she went inside to pay and I was staring into space thinking about imagine how funny it would be if you couldn't tell boys from girls, not ever, and then I was thinking maybe it wouldn't just be funny. Maybe it would be good, and weren't there some species, like of insect or whatever, or maybe it's worms, where they didn't have two different sexes. And maybe that saved a whole heap of trouble. And my last thought maybe on this subject was that, if you can't tell the difference, like, you can't tell what sex someone is, then does it really matter?

So I was thinking all this and then there was a bang on the window but it weren't Mona come back, it was these four guys, like more or less my age, and they were laughing and pointing at me and one of 'em started miming like how he was dying, suffocating or something, with his hands around his throat and his friends were falling about laughing.

I stared at 'em and then I stared back ahead of me through the windshield with my cheeks burning but they did not stop, not until Mona came out and though she was half the size they were and though she was wearing her mask she started telling 'em off real good, and though all I could hear was "shih-hehs" that seemed to be enough and they slunk off but still funning me behind Mona's back.

We drove home.

At the town limits we pulled off our masks. Usually I kinda liked that bit: a) because it meant you could breathe again, which is always good, and b) because it made me feel like we was bank robbers and we had just completed an advantageous raid on a financial institution, and c) because it meant you could talk again too. But I did not feel like talking.

"Don't mind it," said Mona. "They're just morons and don't know no better. But one day they might, so we oughta feel sorry for 'em."

Feeling sorry for 'em was a step too far for me, though I saw what Mona meant.

"Out of towners, probably. I'm sorry, Ash."

I gave a good Snowflake shrug and said, "Right. Like, can they help it if they're untelligent?"

And Mona saw what I said and said "untelligent?"

Then I saw and said "un-intelligent."

But Mona said no, she liked untelligent better and she was never gonna use the word unintelligent again. From now on, it would be untelligent.

And already I was feeling better and that was what Mona Mochsky could do for you.

"Mona," I said then. "Mona, Snowflake sure is white."

There was a little snow still left on some of the roofs and on the sidewalks, but that ain't what I was talking about, and Mona knew it. I had lived in many a state and many a town, but I had never seen a place that was just so much of one color.

"Yuh, well, there's a Nigerian family live somewhere in town. They're something to do with the church. Then there's the Indian reservations either end of the county. And that's it. Otherwise it's all white. All white and all right."

All white and all right, she said. And when she said right, what she meant was Right.

"That ain't so diverse, is it?" I said.

"It surely ain't," said Mona. "Of all the right-wing-voting places in Arizona, Snowflake is right up there. But the funny thing is, out in the Forties, we're the biggest bunch of hippies you could imagine, more or less. I've sometimes wondered if being EI makes you a hippie, or being a hippie makes you EI."

"And?"

"I have no idea, but that's how it seems to have worked out."

Then Mona said, "Hey! You know, I think Socrates is fine. I ain't gonna get another goat."

And I saw what she meant. She meant there we were: a bunch of humans of all sorts of sizes, an old dog and a grumpy goat, and we was diverse and we all got along just fine.

Then Mona said, "Huh. Untelligent," and we both started laughing like crazy and that was good. There was still laughter then, even in the middle of it all, even as I learned to become someone else. And I won't blame us for it, even now when I know we was laughing on the side of the volcano, on the side of the volcano.

POLLEUX

How was I doing with learning to be someone else? Well, I was learning, but the thing about learning is, you never stop. As Mona always said. But there were signs and symbols of my evolution. For one, my dreams changed. To start with, when I dreamt, I was well again. I would be the Ash before I got sick. I could walk and run and take little things like standing for granted. But after a while I was sick even in my dreams and then I knew I had passed a turning point of some kind.

I could see how smug I had been, being well. How complacent. Never thinking anything really bad could happen to me, like I was immortal. I'd had never a thing wrong in my life till the headaches and the rashes come along, and they hadn't been much to write home about. So I never had. And now even the little joy of standing on my own two feet for more'n three minutes was gone, and I realized how dumb I'd been up to that point, because we're none of us immortal, never was one of us that was immune from disease, and surely not from death. And now all I was fit for was setting on the porch in a red plastic chair with my hair standing on end if I moved too much, or on Mona's couch. So what did I do? I read. There was nothing else for it. And I swear that reading saved my life, and if being sick was changing me, then reading changed me every bit as much.

I read everything. I read stuff about being sick, but I soon got bored of that and then I started reading books, real ones I mean. Stories. Thin ones and fat ones and good ones and bad ones. I did not care. Not at first. But the more I read, the more I came to like some things and dislike others, and the more I could tell a smart book from a dumb one. At least to my way of thinking, and that's important, because no two of us are alike. Not exactly. And like Mona, and like Finch, I began to read the news. Not the news from the *Silver Creek Herald*. I mean the news of the world. I would challenge myself to find an article or a story about something interesting that Mona or Finch hadn't heard already. And so I learned.

The single most important thing I learned was this: people are weird. But like I said before, the weirdest thing of all is, they think they're normal. And I guess the real truth of that remark is that it applies to all of us. Every god-dang one of us, as Mona might say.

Now, one day, Cooper went missing. It was the middle of December more or less. Mona didn't seem too vexed. She said, well, it looks like he's gone on his rounds, and I said what?

Mona said that every once in a blue moon Cooper would get a mite bored and go off to pay visits to some of the other folks. She called it going on his rounds, and it was just a matter of getting in her little yellow car and going to find him before he outlived his welcome.

I thought that would be hard, he was the nicest dog anyone ever knew. I couldn't see how anyone would get tired of him, but he was Mona's dog and she wanted him back. So we climbed into the car and started off.

We drove past Mary's truck, and there she was as usual setting on the tailgate with her letters.

"Seen the dog?" Mona called from the window and Mary shook her head. Then Mona said "well?" because Mary was still deciding whether to use the tinfoil lawyer or not, and Mary shrugged.

We drove past Finch's and the Sick Birds and then over to Jenny. And there was Steve, Jenny's boyfriend, standing at the gate, and her not letting him in because she said he had to learn when was appropriate to call, but none of 'em had seen Cooper. And we even rode all the way out to see Detlef, but Detlef had seen no one for days, unless you counted jackrabbits and we didn't.

"Where is that durned dog?" Mona said as she made a U-turn on Detlef's front yard, by which I mean the bit of the desert he'd put a fence around.

So I asked if he always went the same places and she said yuh. And then she said, "I'll bet I know where he's at," and she said it like she was cross with him. And that was where Cooper was, hanging out at some place Mona didn't want him to hang out. In case bad thinking rubbed off on him. That and the fact that Harry would feed Cooper too much beef jerky, which was why he liked to hang out there.

So we set off to Harry's place.

Harry was the last of the canaries I hadn't met yet. (No, not quite, because there's what's coming later.) I soon figured out that Mona had kind of been keeping that from happening, because Harry was a Bible-humping gun-thumping loon. What Mona had said about how everyone with MCS in Snowflake was a liberal lefty? Well, Harry was the exception that proved the rule.

Mona explained all this on the way over, so I wouldn't get a shock when I got there. As it fell out, I did get a surprise, but for a different reason. Mona forgot to explain probably the most important thing about Harry.

So anyway, we got there, and there was Cooper chewing stick after stick of jerky, and slobbering like only a happy dog can slobber. He was sat by the side of the woman feeding it to him. She was lounging in an aluminum chair, staring at the desert. No sign of any Harry, but then the woman gets up and Mona says, "Hey Harry," and the woman waved a hand and that's why I got a surprise because it turned out Harry was short for Harriet. Mona forgot to explain that part, and I guess I just felt like an idiot. For making an assumption about someone just on account of their name, I mean.

So, maybe diseases don't have no politics; they ain't choosy who they choose to infect, and Cooper, it seemed he had no politics neither, because he was hunkered down at Harry's place, and seemed he would be as long as the dried cow lasted.

Still, Harry was as sick as anyone in Snowflake. She was real tall, maybe even six foot now she'd stood up, and skinny, and her cheeks were sunk in, but she wasn't pale like the Sick Birds. She was more kinda gray. Seems she had everything wrong with her: MCS, EI, and then she had some of them long-term infectious things, Bartonella, I think.

And she read too. But the things she read were different from the things Mona read. Not ten minutes had passed before she started in on Mona about some nonsense she'd read about how *the coloreds* commit more violent crime than white folks, and Mona was sticking it back at her. She was saying she didn't suppose it was a watertight piece of research she'd read and asking her which lunatic website she found that on and how you could believe *anything* if you only read the things that told you what you wanted to believe in the first place. Cooper was chewing jerky and I sat in a blue plastic chair on Harry's porch the way we sat on red plastic chairs over at Mona's, and watched 'em go to it.

By now somehow they'd stopped talking about Harry's racist delusions and had moved through immigrants and had now got onto climate change and I couldn't even work out how.

So now, the thing is you probably don't like Harry, and that's all down to me, because of how I told you about her. Like, I could have started out with how we got there and how Harry said hello and was polite and asked all about me, and asked about Bly, and got me a drink and said did I want anything to eat. I didn't tell you that she was quietly spoke and listened to what Mona had to say without interrupting her. But I didn't, although she did do all those things. I told you about what a loon she was, even before you met her, and now you know these bad things about her, well, there ain't no way back for Harry, there surely ain't. And why, you ask me, why should there be, when you've told me how she was a racist-sexist-gun-loving wildebeest? And if you asked me that I don't know that I would have a good answer.

On the way home, after we'd rescued the mutt from eating his own weight in dried cow, Mona huffed and puffed about Harry. She was real sore. And she moaned about how dumb you had to be not to believe the world's climate was sorely screwed.

But then she said, "But I'm the god-danged nut" and when I asked her for why, she said because every time she went to Harry's place, which was not often, she fell for it and got sucked into some dumb argument. Like the one about climate change.

"Half the world knows about climate change, and don't need convincing. And the other half of the world don't believe in it, and it seems like nothing you can say or do or show 'em will change their minds."

"But people must be changing, somewhere, mustn't they," I said, because once upon a time hardly no one believed in it, and now plenty did.

And Mona said that was down to young people, people like me and Bly, thank God. And she actually said "thank God" though I might not have told you that I never met a bigger atheist than Mona.

"You young folks. You ain't so stupid. It's as you get older that you get stupider. That's how it seems to me. That's why you gotta keep on learning. You gotta keep from being untelligent."

So then we laughed and then Mona said, "You know what Harry's problem is?" and I said "she's a regular piece of work?" and Mona said "no, well yeah, but no."

Then she said how Harry's problem was that she was scared.

"Why doesn't she wanna believe in climate change? Because she's scared."

And I thought about that. I thought about that not just for a while, but for a good few weeks, I believe. But right there in the car, I said, "Yeah, maybe, but that don't excuse her for being a racist, does it?"

And Mona said, no, it didn't but maybe it showed where the answers were.

So by now I had precisely no idea what she was talking about and I told her so.

And she said, "Look. Climate change is terrifying, right, if you stop to think about it. And part of the problem is us. Like, we know how scary and real it's gonna be."

"I guess," I said. "But what do you do?"

"You gotta do two things. Yeh, you have to tell people how scary and real it is. But at the same time you gotta give them some hope. You gotta give them some serious practical things they can do and support and believe in, while there's still time to do something about it."

And I thought that sounded good in theory, but what could you actually do for real?

"Well, here's one thing," she said. "I was reading the paper the other day, and it said that as a matter of god-dang fact, we know who's to blame for climate change. Some smart-ass has actually done the sums. Turns out that just one hundred companies are responsible for two-thirds of the total emissions of carbon in all of history."

So I said, yeah, but what use was it knowing, and Mona said the use in knowing was that you could take 'em to court. And sue 'em. And, yes, people were already doing that, and if they won, that might start to change things. And she had already explained the power of grabbing a capitalist by his bank balance.

"Just one hundred companies. That's not unknowable. You can tell who these people are and make 'em pay."

"But what's the use of making 'em pay," I said. "That don't bring the planet back."

"No, it don't, but it stops 'em doing what they've been doing and it might still be enough to save our necks."

We was home. And Cooper went away to sleep it off, while Mona made some tea.

"Soon be Christmas," she said, "and now you've met everyone, for better or worse."

And I told her for better. Even counting Harry, it was still for better.

I was tired after our trip, and Mona said I could nap on her couch, save me going out to the cold, for the days were not so warm now. As I took my tea, I said, "Wait, you said I met everyone, but there's still one more," and Mona looked kinda confused and asked me "who?"

I told her that Bly had told me about the guy who lived real far out. In the deep. The guy who Bly had told me was the first canary.

So Mona said huh, yeah. There's him. The very final guy I hadn't yet met. And there was something funny about the way she said that, so I said what's the deal?

"No deal, Snowflake," she said. "We don't see much of him anymore, that's all. He's waaay out. His name's Polleux. The Great and Terrible."

And I said what? and Mona said nothing, ignore me, and I could see she was joking about something though I did not know what.

"John Polleux," she said. "That's him."

It was the first time I heard that name, and at the time I thought no more about it. Those days were ahead of me still, but they were coming fast.

QUIS ME LIBERABIT DE CORPORE MORTIS HUIUS?

I was looking in a book at Mona's place. This was a few days before Christmas. It was a kinda different book from every other one she had in her library. Every other book in there was either a book about being sick and how to get well, or a storybook. And all those kinds of books were full of words, and they weren't so handsome. But there was this one book that was different. It was large and square and it was full of photographs and there were hardly any words in it, and it was beautiful.

It took me a while to figure out what the book was. The photos was mostly of people, though there was some that was just buildings or the empty countryside. But the ones of people were strange. The second picture in was of a woman, least I think it was a woman but it could have been a man, set in a car. She had hair cropped short, and she was set in this beat-up old Nissan, yellow like Mona's Suzuki, but covered in rust and dust. And she, if I was right about that but I guess it don't matter, she was setting in the car with a telephone in her hands. She was wearing white rubber gloves and she was holding the telephone a little way away from her head and then I saw there was a white cable, the phone line, sneaking out of the car door and off somewhere, into some house I guess. And she had this look on her face. This look that I can't describe, less I say she looked terrified. That's all I can say. And I flicked on through the book and there was all kinds of folks, and after a minute I realized that more'n one of 'em looked sick and then there was a picture of Finch in there and I knew for sure what I was looking at. It was a book of pictures of canaries, though not just from Snowflake but from all across the great nation.

Later, I asked Mona about the book and she said how a photographer had come by a few years back and made the book. She took it from me and showed the pages where there was pictures of Detlef and of Mary too.

It was funny looking at pictures of people you knew in a book. They looked the same, but somehow they looked different too, 'cept I can't tell you how. Maybe it's because people don't move in pictures, they don't talk. You just see a single moment, frozen. And that's not what people are. People are moving and speaking things. And there's something that ain't real about a photograph. Something that's a mite disturbing, maybe, though don't ask me how.

"Listen, Snowflake," Mona said to me. "We got to get you better."

"Better?" I said. "You mean well?"

"I mean better," she said, and that was when I realized what a stupid word *better* is. See, what does it really mean? Does it mean *better* as in not so sick, or does it mean *better* as in not sick at all?

Then she started telling me I oughta take some things to help me recover. Now, this wasn't the first time we had had this conversation. And she wasn't the only one I had had it with. Most everyone in the Forties had some advice for me. Do this, don't do that. Take this, don't eat that. Mary had told me she could write out a list of vitamins and minerals I oughta take to help with being fatigued. Even Harry had offered to look at my blood under her microscope because she could see if there was Lyme in there, or Bartonella. And I said, you can do that? Not because I didn't believe her, but because I didn't know you could do that sort of thing yourself.

And she said, "Blood under a microscope is blood under a microscope" and how you didn't need a white coat and a certificate to tell you what to look for. You just had to learn it someplace, like from a book or the Internet. I didn't know if that was true, but Mona said that when you got sick with something like MCS, you had to learn to be your own doctor, because the normal doctors a) didn't know nothing about it and b) were too busy getting bribed by Big Pharma to dole out their expensive tablets to spend any time reading about emerging illnesses.

Then Mona said, "'As long as men die but want to live, doctors will be derided, and well paid.' Jean de la Bruyère. 1645 to 1696. Another French fella. You gotta take matters into your own hands."

So then, one night, when I was feeling pretty low about being tired all the damn time and having headaches for no reason, I thought that either I could go on being mad at Dr. B for doing nothing or I could be my own doctor. So I gave in.

I was wrapped up tighter'n a caterpillar in blankets and a sleeping bag and Mona had run a cable out of her house so I could plug in this little electric heater at the foot of the shed. It was just a single white metal tube and it was on real low but it was enough to keep me from freezing.

But then I put on the flashlight and went out of my sleeping shed and into the other one where I had put all Bly's stuff. And there was all his pills and tablets and what-have-you and I grabbed a bunch of 'em and took 'em into my sleeping shed.

I didn't know what some of 'em were, but I thought I'd just keep it simple to start with, so I took anything that said vitamin on it. Just one of each, and then I put my flashlight out and waited to wake up in the morning, cured and all.

That didn't happen.

What did happen was that fifteen minutes later, I suddenly felt my face get real hot. Now, I can tell you that I hadn't felt hot for some durned time. Not sleeping in a shed at five-wait-six thousand feet up, no matter how many blankets I had.

So I said to myself, that's kinda funny, because my cheeks were burning like when someone calls you something like Snowflake and you hate being called it. Then my elbows got hot. My *elbows*, and just when I was thinking it's not really my elbows, it's the joints at my elbows, no wait, it's *both*, my knees started to burn too.

Then my chest, then my forehead was burning and itching

and then my whole skin was the same, feeling like when you get sunburned, and it's tight and hot and itching all over. Then my heart started thumping away, and ten seconds later I was banging on the back door shouting "Mona, I'm dying" and making a general kind of din.

There was some fuss then while Mona said what's going on and Cooper ran around in circles a bit and I said I took some pills and she screamed and said what!? So I said it was just some vitamins and she said what? again and I said I don't know.

So we went to the shed and found the ones I took and she grabbed one bottle and said, "You took one of these?" and I looked at it in the dark and it said Vitamin B3 and I nodded and said, "But it's just a vitamin."

Then Mona started laughing. Then she said I wonder what will happen next and I said what's gonna happen next is I'm gonna die and she laughed some more and said, "Snowflake, you ain't gonna die. What you got is the niacin flush."

So of course I said the what? and she took me back indoors and gave me a big glass of cold water and put a wet cloth on the back of my neck and I sat there while she talked to me and told me I'd be fine and I didn't have to worry. She said how some vitamins you could take as much as you liked, and they would do you no harm.

"Your B12," she said, "the only way you could kill yourself with B12 is if you fell in a vat of the stuff and got drownded. But B3, that's niacin, you gotta give niacin some respect."

She showed me the bottle and it said Vitamin B3, 100 mg, and that meant each capsule was 100 milligrams of niacin, B3.

And she said that most people only took a little bit. Like 15 or 20 or something. But some people took more, and if you was gonna take more, you had to work your way up to it, bit by bit, and give your body time to adjust. Otherwise, you got what I had right then, which was a classic case of the niacin flush.

"So now you know how middle-aged ladies feel when they get the hot flashes," she said, and off she went giggling again like her feet was loose.

What happened next wasn't so funny. I got a little mad. Well, I got more'n a little mad. I was cross and I shouted and I said some mean things because they'd all told me to start taking stuff but no one said it was dangerous and what kind of quacks were they anyway. And all Mona told me was that I was ungrateful and nothing more but she didn't have to. I could tell she was real mad at me too.

We didn't speak to each other for days, not really, we just hung out and got our own food by ourselves and not together and read a lot. And when folks came by it was kinda awkward. I saw people whispering what's wrong and what-have-you and Mona shrugging and no one asked me straight out and that was good because I was kinda mad at everyone for telling me to take stuff and not telling me it could be bad if I didn't get it right.

It went on like that for days, like we was an old married couple and not a damn kid and a fifty-what-have-you old lady, and on it went until two things changed it.

The first thing was that Christmas came.

It wasn't the holliest-jolliest Christmas of all time, and we didn't have presents for each other, but Detlef was throwing a big party out at his place for anyone that wanted to come and Mona asked me the morning of the party if I wanted to go and I shrugged and she said she'd like me to and anyway Cooper was coming and then I started crying and she put her arms around me and said, well, let's go then, Snowflake.

So we did, but things still weren't the same between us. I felt bad and tried to talk in the car on the way over to Detlef's, but it was hard going and we was silent a lot. It was dark already and we bumped through a tiny little bit of Arizona with the headlights on Mona's car just about making out the way. At the party, there was lots of folks there, most everyone in fact. No one gave anyone any presents. After a time, while I was setting with Mona by a wall watching folks talking and laughing, she leant over to me and said, "A man is a being that can get used to anything," and I took a guess at Nietzsche but she said, no, it was Fyodor Dostoyevsky, and though he was better known for being a writer he was also a little bit of a philosopher, and therefore it so happened she knew his dates and they was,

"1821 to 1881. Look at these folks. Imagine what every one of 'em been through to get to this room, this Christmas. They been through pain and sickness and fear and they've faced up doubt and disbelief and arguments on most every side. Yet here they are. And in the end they got used to it."

"I feel like we oughta have presents," I said to Mona. "You've been so good to me. I oughta give you something."

But Mona, she said I didn't have to, it wasn't why she was helping me and if I had the chance to help someone, wouldn't I do the same? And I thought about that and just while I was thinking about it Mona said, "Yeah, it's Christmas, and we got each other," and I didn't know if she meant she and me, or everyone and I guess, thinking about it, she meant both. We all had each other, the canaries, and even Jenny was there and even her boyfriend Steve and he was super nice and I liked talking to him a lot. Just like Jenny, he didn't doubt that the canaries was sick. He was a lawyer in San Francisco when he wasn't standing at Jenny's gate trying to get let in. Where Jenny smiled with her eyes all the time, Steve was kinda serious looking. When you spoke with Steve, you had the feeling that he was worrying about something, only he never said what. When he was talking he would often reach for the back of his head, which was a shave-or-be-bald kinda deal. It was like he was checking his hair was really missing. Still, I liked him a lot.

And Cooper had a fine old time at the party too and ran around in circles till Mona laughed and said how he was gonna sleep well that night, for sure. She dug her elbow into my ribs, gentle.

"Just think about the journey everyone in this room took to get here tonight, to a house owned by a giant German in the middle of the Arizona desert at Christmas."

She nodded over at Sally and Dolly and told me a thing or two that made my hair stand on end, about how at one time they was homeless for a year or more, how they lost the house they owned trying to pay for medical bills. Or Mary, who'd as of now been living out of the back of her truck for seven years. How she kept a gun under her cot after what happened to her one night when she was parked up in New Mexico. Or Finch, who'd been high-flying away at Harvard till he got MCS, on account of the vent from some lab being next to his office window, he reckoned. How his wife left him on account of she couldn't cope with it. She told me everyone's story, more or less, everyone's story, and none of 'em would make you wanna sing. And she asked if it wasn't some kind of miracle that we'd all made it this far, to Detlef's house, that Christmas. When she'd done, she leant in to me and said, "Look at 'em. We don't need presents. Not when we can give each other something, just by being here."

And I knew that was true and then I turned to Mona and I said, "Hey, you know what?"

"What?" she said.

And I said, "So Dolly finally had something to put on her calendar."

And Mona said "what?"

And I said, "Something to look forward to."

She looked at me.

"You are one fascinating biped, Ash," she said and finally I felt she liked me again.

So that was the first thing that made things better between Mona and me. And the second thing was this: that something happened that made us forget all about ever being mad with each other. Something way more important than her and me and our little fight about a vitamin. And that was that Bly came home.

It was just a few days after Christmas, and I got the best present I could ever have gotten. I was wrapped up tight in my shed one morning. A few weeks back, Detlef had come over and put a piece of glass in the roof so I could sit in there and read by daylight and stare up at blue sky if I wanted. Why he didn't put it in the side so I could see out, I guess you'd have to ask him that one. But that morning I was reading and from time to time staring at the blue sky when I heard a truck pull up in the yard and I knew Mona was home and, anyway, her little car didn't sound like that.

I was reading a book about how back in the day they sent people with tuberculosis to the desert, to Tucson and other places in Arizona and other places besides, because the dry air was good for 'em. And just as I was reading that, the truck pulled up and I stuck my head out of the door and there was Bly, climbing down from the cab, but real slow. If I had doubted he was sick when I first saw him again, there was no doubting it now. He was gray like Harry, but grayer, and he looked like he'd aged ten years in the couple months he'd been gone. He was hunched over and he moved real slow and he saw me and I scrambled out to him and he mumbled something about driving all night and he fell into my arms and I couldn't hold him, he always was bigger'n me, but somehow I got him into my bed. I mean the bed that was really his, back in his shed and he was in a daze and he didn't even seem to know it was my stuff in there and not his. And then he fell asleep just after saying "hello, Snowflake" and smiling a sleepy smile.

I closed the door and I went to find Mona and we stood with our hands on our hips looking at the shed, inside of which Bly was resting.

Neither of us had nothing to say, till after a long while Mona said, "Well, now where you gonna sleep?" and shook her head and I realized she meant me.

Cooper came wandering over and sniffed at the wheels of Bly's truck and Mona said, yeah, we're wondering that too. Where's our Bly been, that's what she meant, and Cooper left the wheels alone and sniffed about the door of the shed for a bit till Mona said, "You'll see him soon enough, mutt. Let him rest a while."

So we took Cooper inside and Mona made tea and we stared at the desert for a couple hours till we were done with that.

We was all full of questions and from time to time one of us would say, "D'you think . . . ?" or "what if he . . . ?" or "why do you suppose . . . ?" but we never finished them questions because we knew the only one who had the answers was lying in his shed, dreaming. Yeah, dreaming, without a doubt. But dreaming of what?

And in the end, we didn't have to ask no more questions, because just when we started wondering if we'd imagined Bly coming home and I even went to the front door to see if his truck was really there, the door to the shed opened and out he came. So I rushed as fast as I could back into the living room with Mona and said "shush, he's comin" like we was guilty about something though I don't know what.

In he came and sat himself in a chair and it was just like he'd never been away, 'cept it was obvious he had. There was the way he looked, for one, and for another, he was quiet, quieter than he'd been before.

Mona poured him some fresh tea and said, "You hungry, Bly?" and Bly said thanks but maybe later and then no one said anything for a long time and the desert wasn't helping. The best thing was Cooper who climbed up into Bly's lap and that gave us all something to do. Watch Bly tickle Cooper under the chin, just how he liked it.

Finally Mona said, "You stopping a while, or . . . ?" and Bly smiled and nodded his head and somehow shook it at the same time and said "I guess" which was a tad better than a shrug but not much.

"And the police academy . . . ?" she said next and that did get her a shrug. But Bly also said, "Yeah, I guess that didn't work out" and it didn't need saying why. He was not well. He'd tried to ignore the fact that he was sick. He'd tried to do a Dr. B and tell himself it was all in his head and all he had to do was go back to flatland and carry on just like before and then everything would be fine. 'Cept, it wasn't. He'd ignored his sickness but it did not ignore him, in fact, it took very good care of him and he was laid real low on account of it.

He told us how he'd kept trying with the physical training

but how he kept having to take days off and how they'd keep sending him to the medical center at the academy and when they couldn't find nothing wrong with him they started laying into him about faking it and was he really sure he wanted to be a police officer or did he just like the idea of it. Heck, you can probably work out the rest, and now here he was back home.

News always traveled fast in the Forties. So the first to show up was Mary who came in saying, "Yeah, I said to myself that's Bly's truck. I gotta go see, and here he is!" And she had about the biggest smile I ever saw her give anything or anyone.

Mary was the first but not the only one. Before long there was Finch and Jenny came by too. Harry set a chair opposite Bly and started asking him questions about the academy and saying dumb things like "I guess it's like the military, huh? Boot camp? Am I right?" and all the while not thinking once that here was Bly back because he didn't make the grade. Even Detlef rolled up in his Mercedes in the afternoon, and each time someone came Bly had to go through the whole story till Mona and me started taking over, speaking for him.

All the while we could see Bly getting more'n more tired till finally Mona shooed everyone out of her house, save me and Cooper. Socrates was nowhere to be seen and we was all glad about that though I still wouldn't have said it to his dumb-looking face.

So then Mona started wondering about where I was gonna sleep and I said I can go back to the porch though I was actually thinking about how I knew that two people could just about squeeze into that little shed. If those two people liked each other. And about how cozy it was if you did. But Mona said, "You are crazy, Snowflake. You cannot sleep outside now. It's way too cold. No, we'll figure something out."

And what she figured out for that night was that I was gonna sleep on the bathroom floor, after everyone had done in there.

It was the end of December, and it was dark real early.

Everyone was tired. Not just Bly, but all of us, it had all been too much for one day, and it hadn't been helped by Socrates showing up just at sundown in a real mean mood and butting the side of the house for half an hour till Mona ran outside and yelled "gah!" so he rolled over and pointed his hooves at the stars, which was just coming out.

"Dumb goat," Mona said and we all got ready to sleep.

Mona went into the bathroom first and got washed up and came out in her old robe, purple and quilted. Then Bly went and got himself ready and came out wearing just a T-shirt and his shorts and I saw how thin he looked and how he'd lost all his muscles in just a couple months.

There was this funny little thing. We just stopped and looked at each other and looked away but didn't move. Mona was over by the kitchen, fussing with Cooper, and there was this little moment when Bly didn't look at me and I didn't look at Bly, but I wanted to say something so I said, "Bly, I am happy you're home and all."

Then he shot a quick look at me and said, "O my Lord. Why am

I not strong?" and I said what? and at first he didn't reply but then he said, "Nothing. Nothing. I'm happy to see you again, Ash."

He leant down at me and we kissed real quick, like his lips just brushed me, and then he pulled away without looking any more or saying any more and he went to bed, and I rolled out the mat Mona had given me on the bathroom floor and turned the light off and thought about what he'd said and how I was lying on the bathroom floor and there was Bly, just about twenty yards away in the desert and how stupid that was.

But there seemed not a thing I could do to change it. All I wanted to do was get up and go out there but it was like there was some giant barrier, an invisible force, holding me back and keeping me on that bathroom floor. And you know, to this day, if you asked me what that thing was, I still couldn't give you an answer. Not one that makes any kind of sense, anyhow. Because that thing about how often it's best to say nothing? Well, that idea was about to get a real kicking.

Anyway, I said to myself, I kept saying to myself, the main thing, the main thing is that Bly is home. And as for the sleeping questions, well, we could sort that out. Maybe they would sort themselves out, somehow, and I got myself to sleep by thinking about that and it made me warm inside like the niacin flush only way better.

Things did work out. With the matter of the sleeping accommodations. It worked out because as things fell, Bly wasn't staying, nor ever had intended to, it seemed.

He was always the best kid, we knew that. Everyone in the Forties, and beyond. Bly was just the best. He was kind and he was honorable, never said a bad word about anyone, and never fell out with anyone neither. All he wanted to do was what he thought was right, and, like Mona said that Nietzsche said, he who has a why to live can cope with almost any *how*. But what if you don't have that why? What if that *why* is taken away from you, and no matter how much you scream and fight, no matter what you do, nothing can bring it back? What then?

What then, is that it turned out that Fyodor Dostoyevsky, 1821 to 1881, was wrong; sometimes a man cannot get used to anything. No matter how much he might want to, no matter how much he might try. And it seems that Bly was one of those men, because somewhere a little ahead of midnight, as Mona and Cooper was sleeping and as I was dreaming, we was all woken up by a loud noise, and that noise was Bly shooting himself in the head with a police revolver he'd stolen from the academy.

A noise like that, in the open desert at night, you get out of your sleep real quick and your brain is struggling to work out what it heard and what it was but I didn't need my brain to work it out, because my body already knew, even before Mona and I grabbed our flashlights while Cooper ran around in circles like it was the Christmas party all over again, even before we got outside, even before we opened the door to the shed and saw what Bly had done to himself with that gun.

Before all of that, my heart already knew that Bly was gone, and this time he was gone for good.

The police arrived and there were questions and questions and more questions and an ambulance and all I recall was the flashing lights in the night, flashing out across the desert and Bly's bloody body going into a bag and up onto a stretcher and he was gone forever, and by then it was way, way early in the morning and Mona stared out into the desert like she was seeing something, like she was hearing something, but I guess she wasn't. I know she wasn't because as we went back into the house, and everyone had gone, and we was all alone, just her a middle-aged lady and me a dumb young kid, with our Bly all gone and all gone in horror, I heard her whisper something to herself.

And I couldn't have made it out, save for I'd heard her say it ten hundred thousand times before.

I wonder what will happen next.

ROLE OF THE COMT VAL158MET POLYMORPHISM

There ain't no point in saying more.

No, I don't mean that. What I mean is, I don't know what to say, or how I should say it. You ever lost somebody? Of course you have, we all have, now. And so you know that when somebody goes, it's just a bad, bad time. And Time did what it always does when somebody dies, which is to say, it stood still and it kept right on moving, both things together. And because it did that, somehow I found myself stuck over and over again in the middle of a late December night staring at the body of my brother Bly with his beautiful head all a mess, while at the same time I was getting up each morning and eating and talking to Mona and feeding Cooper his chow and avoiding Socrates because I thought I might kill him if he pestered me right then.

And people came and people went and I was sleeping on the bathroom floor because although the shed was empty again there was no way on earth I was ever going back in there, never mind to sleep.

From time to time, bits and pieces would come back to me from that night. Like I thought I remembered how, when we opened the shed, Mona sank to the ground and started to howl. How Cooper came over to her and lay down next to her, quietly. Stuff like that. But what can you say? And what's the point? It felt like the world had ended. No, it felt like the world *should* have ended, but it didn't. It just kept right on going and Bly was still gone. He was still dead, and the worst of it was how. How he had done it, to himself. That was the real horror. That, and the fact that I had not just walked out there to his shed that night and lain down next to him. That I maybe could have stopped him.

That was the real pain. Still is.

So the days ticked off till one morning there was a phone call to Mona's house and she picked it up and said "oh, hi" and "I'm so sorry" and "yes, yes, I know" and "yes, of course," and when she hung up it had been Jack and the date was set for Bly's funeral and it was gonna be at Jack's church the day after tomorrow.

"We better get going," said Mona and I looked over at her all surprised because I didn't think there was any way in hell we was going to go.

"But that's two states away," I said and Mona told me it was three in point of fact and I said "oh, yeah" and "but how are we gonna—" but Mona just held a hand up and said, "Ash, do you wanna go?" and I told her that it was the only thing in the world I wanted and she said, "Well, then leave it to me."

So the following morning we set off.

There was Mona and Mary and me set in the back of Detlef's

Mercedes and Detlef and Finch up front, taking turns in driving. Then when both of them got tired, Mona did a spell and then Mary and I even did an hour or so but I couldn't do much more'n that before I was exhausted. And we headed east. East and a little north.

During other times, it might've been a real swell road trip, but these were not other times. These were the times when we was heading to Bly's funeral and no one had much to say but stare out the window and watch the great nation roll by and I will say this: America was big.

The plan was we would drive all day and through the night and if we stuck to the schedule, we'd roll up with an hour or so to spare before the funeral, which was ten in the following morning.

Once or twice, people would try to speak. Mostly it didn't go too well, and we all fell silent again real quick, but I recall Finch talking about some article he'd read the day before on his news line.

He said, "Ash, you remember I was telling you about placebo?" and he rattled off the name of that gene that meant you was more likely to get on well with the placebo effect. So I said, yeah, what about it? and he said he'd just read another paper and how it explained that the very same gene was also responsible for how kind folks are.

"Kindness," he said. "That same little fellow is responsible for it. And he can exist in one of two different forms. That's called a polymorphism. One's called val and one's called met."

Now I gotta confess I was already lost, but he went on and on and on about it across half of America until I started to get it. And a bit of me wondered why he thought anyone wanted to know about this, but I guessed he was just trying to find something to say. So we didn't think about Bly all the time. There was no danger of that not happening, but I guessed Finch was just trying to be kind, the only way he could think of.

"You know that genes exist in pairs, right? So you got two copies of the gene, one from your father and one from your mother, and that's four different combinations. So you can be val/val, or val/met, or met/val, or met/met. Four combinations, see?"

Then Finch explained how the val part made you more altruistic, which is to say, you do good things for other people without wanting something back. So if you was val/val you was real generous and if you was met/met, well, you probably know people like that, right? And then there was everyone else in the middle.

"Here's the thing. The val/val people, the ones who don't get no help from placebo, they're the altruistic ones. Whereas the met/met, they get all that placebo's got to offer. And they're selfish too! How is that fair?"

And I didn't say anything to that and neither did anyone else, because, well, what can you say to that? But I do remember thinking that if all we are is down to what our programming says and what the bacteria have in mind for us, then what does that leave for us? Does it give us any choice? Maybe it leaves us with just the choice of putting a stolen police revolver to your head. Or maybe even that ain't no choice you're making. You just think it is, but really it's on account of the bacteria and what-have-you.

But we made our way. And all we did was stop for food and the restroom from time to time, and that caused some problems. In the car, no one wore their masks, but when we stopped some-place, all five of us would put our masks on and head right into a diner. Some places, the waitresses looked like we was about to do that bank job I was telling you about before, and some places we got yelled at and others it was ok.

For lunch we was lucky and found a vegan café and they didn't bat a lash at the way we looked, but then later we was set in a diner and stared at the menu for a long time till Mona said, "There ain't nothing on here that ain't gonna kill ya" and made us drive off schedule to a whole food store to get something to eat that wasn't full of chemicals and in the whole food store someone got suspicious that we were terrorists and called the manager and we had to explain why we was wearing masks and he said he was gonna call the police and we said well, yeah, but do we look like terrorists, and even if we were, would we start our campaign of terror by blowing up mung beans? It all took forever to explain, but in the end we just about bought our food and left. And in this one gas station, Detlef went to the restroom and came straight back. He'd gone without his mask and there was one of them automatic fragrance dispensers in there, so he had to come back for his mask. Or get gassed.

So we made our way.

On account of Mona's detour to find organic falafels, we was a mite behind schedule. We'd been meaning to pull into a truck stop and sleep a while, but in the end we kept on driving and everyone slept when they wanted, and I was lucky, because as night came on, I was set on the outside, with Mary on the other and Mona in the middle and it was near impossible to get any sleep in the middle.

Detlef was driving and Finch was map-reading by a little flashlight like a pen because Detlef had taken all the lights out of the inside of the car.

"Makes the vehicle thirty pounds lighter," he said, talking about all the unnecessary stuff he'd pulled out of it when he'd bought it. That included the AC, and I was glad it was January that we was driving for sixteen hours across the southern United States.

I was dog-tired again as the night wore on, and Detlef didn't have a radio left in the car, or nothing, so I just stared into the dark, waiting for sleep to come and in the end it came. Then I was out cold. At one point, something woke me and I was only half awake but I saw that Mona had fallen asleep on my shoulder and I thought what-the-heck but then I also thought, what-the-heck, she's just a tired lady so I let her be.

On and off we dozed and it started to get light and we pulled into a gas station someplace to fill up. Finch took over driving and we'd only driven another fifty feet when there was a howl like the world was ending and blue lights flashing all behind us and Finch looked in the mirror and said "cops" and pulled over.

There was two of 'em. One stayed set in the police car, and I turned around and could see him, just the outline of him in the dawn light and he was on the radio. And the other cop strolled up to the driver's window like he was real bored and tapped on the window even though Finch had wound it almost all the way down.

Finch was real polite.

"Yes, officer?" he said and the cop bent down and looked in the window and looked at all of us and said "going someplace?" which had to be just about the stupidest thing anyone ever said in the whole history of the planet and I mean untelligent, real untelligent.

As soon as he opened his mouth I knew we was in for trouble. I saw him checking out our masks which were set on the back shelf and wondering what the heck that was all for. You could more or less hear his brain whirring.

"I'm asking myself," he said, "is this vehicle roadworthy?"

Detlef leant across Finch and said "roadworthy?" and I thought uh-oh, because Detlef started saying how it was not only legal and roadworthy but how Mr. Police Officer wouldn't find as much as a taillight out because he checked them every single time he got in the car, and I promise you that is true. Every single time. Every single god-danged time we stopped and started that Mercedes in sixteen hours, Detlef had made a full inspection of it first.

So I thought uh-oh, because Detlef was now explaining all this to the cop and more besides, like how his car wouldn't make no one sick, either, and could he say the same about his prowler?

The cop was not impressed and he leant in the window and said, "Sir, I'm asking you to be quiet. I am speaking to the driver of the car," so Detlef started to explain that he was the owner of the vehicle, not Finch, so then the cop said, "Right, both of you get out of the vehicle. And I wanna see some licenses."

Then Finch put his arm on Detlef's to say "easy, cowboy" and Detlef was getting huffy but I was hoping that Finch wouldn't get to the point where he was mad enough to say "screwit" because I figured that wouldn't do us no good.

So now the cop was acting like he could read and staring at Detlef's license and then Finch's and then Detlef's again and meanwhile his pal had shown up and had gotten Finch and Detlef to please put their hands on the hood of the car, gentlemen, with their legs out and back and three feet apart. All this time, Mona was set between me and Mary and she was like a volcano setting there, ready to boil. And when she came to the boil, she was out of the car without even waiting for Mary to move and the second cop said "whoa-now" and then "ma'am-get-back-in-the-car" and then he pulled his gun and Mona looked at him and said "don't be ridiculous" which kind of took him by surprise to have this little fifty-something-year-old lady look up at him.

Then she turned to the first cop and she let rip.

"You know where we are headed?" she barked, like she was addressing Socrates on a bad day.

"Ma'am, I do not—" the cop was saying but Mona wasn't in a mood for listening. She was in a mood for telling.

"We are heading to a funeral. And we are almost there but due to matters of force majeure (she was referring to the falafels) we are a tad behind schedule. And do you know whose funeral this is? (once again, she wasn't really asking) No? Well, we are heading to the funeral of a police officer. A young police officer, and he was the friend of all of us here and the brother of young Ash there."

And she pointed at me in the back seat, and I gave the cop a little wave and mouthed "hellooo" and then felt kinda dumb. But no one cared about that, because Mona was explaining how Bly had died tragically in the line of duty and all we wanted to do was be there for him to say goodbye.

And then, oh boy, then she took one mighty big risk and she said how in her life she had come across two types of cops and there was those that became a cop for others and there was those that became cops for themselves. And how Bly was one of the first kind.

Then she stared real hard at the cop and he said nothing and meanwhile the other cop was putting his gun away and looking like he was a gawky twelve-year-old kid and the darndest thing happened. The cop, the first one, he put his fingers to his cap and said, "Ma'am, I'm real sorry for your loss," and that was how we got a police escort to the state line, breaking speed limits, getting us back on schedule and arriving at the church with time to spare.

So we was in the middle of Mormon country again, but Jack's church was one of the few that weren't. We showed up at the Aurora Methodist in Detlef's old Mercedes and it was set in its grounds in a quiet neighborhood of streets of people's ordinary homes. The kind where their grass just runs up to the asphalt of the road and no one minds about fences too much.

Even with our police escort, we were not the first to arrive. Fact is, most everyone else had showed up already and there was a lot of people. A lot. People liked Bly, they always did. There was Jack and Suzanne, the new woman in his life, and I was pleased to see them both, and they was holding hands, even though they were about to bury Jack's boy, and I thought that was a good thing.

There was the rest of Jack's family, and I knew some of 'em, but none well. And there were a lot I didn't know at all because while Jack might've wanted to adopt me, there were those in his family who had wondered, and had wondered out loud, what he was doing adopting a little cuckoo like me, Jamie's kid, into his own family.

Then there was some friends of Bly's from school and there was even two cadets from the academy where Bly had been trying to learn to be a police officer. And I realized I hadn't seen so many people in one place in months.

We got out of the 1984 gold but rusting Mercedes and I suppose we looked like something. None of us had funeral clothes, but we'd all done our best to look smart. I was wearing my best pair of jeans that I got at the thrift store in Show Low one time, and a black hoodie. Mona was wearing a long dark blue dress and had a red raincoat on top because it was not warm. Mary was in her boots and shirts as always. Finch had on some slacks and a shirt and he looked the best of us, I guess, and Detlef was sporting a suit of some kind but it had seen better days, and he was wearing sneakers. And Mary was carrying a plastic bag with all our masks in it, in case we needed 'em, but all of us without saying figured we wouldn't put 'em on unless we really had to.

No one said anything to us as we made our way into the church with the other folks, aside from Jack who gave me a hug and I gave him one back while his Suzanne smiled at me and I smiled back at her.

The sermon was about running.

The priest, he went on and on about how people run through life and are always seeking something. That's what he said. Seeking. And they run and they run but they don't never find what they want, because (and it was kinda obvious this was where he was headed) what they're actually missing is God.

Well, so he explained that even if you don't find God during your life, it's okay, because when you die, well, God's there and He's just been waiting for you to quit running all the while anyhow. He's kinda patient like that, he's got all the time in the world. And then some.

Then he read this weird poem about a dog, and that went on for about a week.

And I thought some things like what a lot of bull it was and how it had nothing to do with Bly, or dying, and how this guy had probably never even met Bly and then we went outside and they put Bly's coffin in the ground, and he was in it, of course. It was real cold.

Afterward we went back to Jack's.

He and Suzanne had moved into some new place and it weren't big so it was full of all the people from the service and that was kinda bad because I started to feel worse almost immediately and it was also kinda good because you can get lost in a crowd, and I would estimate that 95 percent of the people there had no idea who I was, nor that I had just watched my stepbrother go into the ground, and so no one knew that I was wondering how it had come to be that we were all inside in the warm in Jack's place while Bly was lying in a cold dark hole outside.

We was all tired, us canaries, and I was feeling crappier by the minute. By this point I had turned into a machine for spotting places to set. I was a real hound, I mean. Whenever I went somewhere new, I was always scoping out the place I could get myself set down as soon as possible, and what's more I had given up waiting for people to invite you to set. When you can't stand more'n two minutes you have to take matters into your own hands, because no one says "would you care to sit down?" no more, so if you don't do something about it, you end up falling over in strangers' homes.

So I needed to find a place to set and as I headed on through the people in the living room, I saw a photo of me and Bly on the sideboard. And one of just me, and I looked around to see Jack and I wanted to say thanks for, well, I don't know for what exactly, but I couldn't see him.

Then I set in a big sofa next to two women I didn't know who were yakking away and I watched matters go by and one thing I saw was Detlef talking to this woman. She was a bit younger than him and he was looking awkward but smiling little smiles sometimes and she didn't seem to mind that his suit was as old as his Mercedes and after a while I saw that she was hitting on him. Well not quite hitting, because this was a funeral and you don't do that at funerals but I saw her handing him a piece of paper and she'd written something on it and I guessed that was her number. And I wondered if he'd ever pick up his phone and call her and if he did would she have any idea he was speaking to her on a wooden thing with plastic tubes attached to the real phone.

There was a tapping on the window just behind my head and I saw Mary waving at me. She pulled a face and I could see she was doing bad. She held her mask up and jiggled it and pointed at the car and I knew she had had enough of people and their fragrances. I nodded and mouthed "I'll tell Mona" and she looked like she didn't understand but she went off anyway and set in the car.

Then outta nowhere there was this woman, standing in front of me and just like with the cop, I knew I was in trouble. You can just tell, before someone opens their mouth, sometimes.

She was this mad aunt. An aunt of Jack's, I mean. She was called Zelda. And, well, I don't know what her motivation was, unless it was to be mean. She told me we'd met before and didn't I remember and I thought oh yeah now I got it, you're the damn bitch who said Jack was mad to adopt me. Then she laid into me about living with crazy people and for letting Bly stay there and how I was to blame for him going crazy too and not coming back to flatland. She didn't call it flatland. She called it "the real world" but I could debate you about that.

"And just what is supposed to be wrong with you? You look perfectly fine to me. Decided to drop out, have we? Is that your little game? Well, don't you think this family is going to pick up the pieces when it all goes wrong. You hear?"

On she went, like that. And some more.

Then Mona and Finch saw what was happening and as one we canaries decided it was time to leave so I found Jack and gave him another hug and he gave me one back though he looked kinda in shock, which I guess he still was. And all the time his new Suzanne held his hand and smiled at me real sad, but kind all at once. And while I did that, Finch was speaking quietly to the mad aunt and as we left I heard him telling her that if she knew what was good for her she'd start buying shares in Reynolds Wrap and good day to her.

We made our way home, bowling down the freeway, across them two or three states, back west to Snowflake, and I'll say this about America: it was beautiful, at times. Yes, it was.

There were no incidents on the way home. No one arrested us, no one thought we was terrorists or aliens. But two days after we got back, I was coming out of the bathroom one morning and I saw Mona looking at something, and when she heard me coming she put it back in her drawer, real fast.

Now I am not proud of what I did next but there was something about the way she acted that got me curious. And later that day, when she was outside giving Socrates an earful about something, I snuck over to the drawer she'd shut so quick.

Inside was a box of photos. At the very top was one of a young girl in running clothes. She was dressed for a race, with a number pinned to her chest, and the photo was in color but in that old-fashioned way, like in the seventies. And there were lots of people behind her in the photo, coming and going getting ready for some race or just finished one and just as I recognized the eyes and knew it was Mona, she'd snuck up on me and said, "I won, that day."

And I felt bad and Mona waved her hand and said "forget it" and I kinda got the feeling she'd been looking for a chance to talk about it anyway.

"It was what that priest said."

"What?" I said.

"What he said about running. It got me remembering. See that photo, I was fourteen. I just won the cross-country race. Five miles and I won and the next person came in more'n four minutes after. Man, I could run."

And she smiled but I could see a ton of stuff behind that smile. She told me how she'd kept running, into high school, at the university, and even when she started work and met her husband, Mr. Lerner, and she'd kept running.

"And that priest has no god-dang idea what running means," she said. "No god-dang idea. Running is freedom."

Then she was silent for a while and then I remembered something and said "Lerner?" and she nodded and said "yup."

"He was my husband. We met at college but it was when we started working in the same department that we got together. We spent six years on that thing. The Mochsky-Lerner paradigm they call it now. Even though there ain't no more Mochsky-Lerner."

"That must've hurt," I said, because I didn't know what else to say, but Mona said "whut? the divorce?" and I said yeah and she said "uh-huh."

"Yeah, that hurt. That was one of the last things to go, when I got sick. I'll give him this, he hung in there for a few years before he couldn't take it. I mean, things was real bad back then. The wheelchair an' all. And the running, that was bad too, and that was one of the first things to go. I remember, even at the start of being sick, trying to go for a run, and then another and then another because I just could not god-darn believe I couldn't do it anymore. And of course all I did was make myself sicker.

"But," she said, "you know, none of that hurt the most. You know what hurt the most?" so of course I shook my head and she rummaged in the box in the drawer and handed me another photo. It was of another girl and I was just thinking was it Mona or what, when she said, "The worst thing was my daughter."

So I said, "What? You have a daughter?" because in all this time I never once heard her mention any kids, and Mona nodded while I looked at the girl in the photo. I guess you could see she was Mona's. The eyes, beautiful they were, and they were just the same as Mona's. There was that same look in 'em too. Like iron.

"You know what hurt the most, was when my own daughter came to see me in the hospital for the last time and looked me in the eye and said, 'Ma, there ain't nothing the matter with you.' That was what hurt the most."

So I asked when that was and Mona said, "Well, oh, let me see. That would be eleven years ago."

Eleven years. And I thought "huh" and then I wondered how much of Finch's little polymorphism Mona's daughter had in her. And I guess I didn't like to think it was more than a little.

SELFISH GENE

I had a dream as I slept on the bathroom floor one night. It was still winter but spring was nearly come. In the dream, I was with Bly and we were at the wake at Jack's place, right after we'd put him in the ground. But he weren't in the ground, he was with me; he was at his own wake. In the dream, no one seemed to see him but me, and I wasn't surprised that he was with me and not in the ground, even though I'd just seen the coffin go into the earth not a half hour before. But that's how things are in dreams, right? All mixed up but you just take it all as it is.

And I was set with Bly on that big sofa instead of the two yakking ladies and suddenly we both had a glass of whiskey in our hands, which is funny because neither of us liked it.

Then I spoke.

"Yes," I said to Bly, "I've just buried my brother in point of fact." And then we drank the whiskey and he cried and I cried and we both cried and there was soil on our shoes from the graveside still. And it was the full moon and I argued in my head about asking Bly what he'd meant that night about O-my-Lord, but he had just died so I let it be and I let him mourn himself his own way.

That was the dream. I have no idea what it means.

When I woke up, Mona didn't give me two seconds before she was fussing over me and around me and what I understood in the end was that she had a surprise for me. Now that explained some things. Because she had been acting kinda funny for days, a couple weeks or more, and more'n once I found her on the phone but when I come in she'd hung up.

So now I found out what it all was.

By this time, I was walking a little farther. I didn't use the chair 'cept on real bad days, and on a good day I could walk a couple hundred yards at once without stopping, as long as I was careful. Still not telling you I enjoyed any of this. But do you wanna hear all that, about how I raged and fought? I guess you do not. It's not so interesting. My raging and fighting probably looks a lot like yours.

Anyway, Mona was looking concerned, she was looking like she was worried about something, as she asked, "So can you go for a little walk?" and I shrugged and said I guess we can find out.

So we went for that walk. We went away from Mona's place, in the other direction from Bly's sheds, in the direction of Jenny's. Just a little way there was a rise in the ground and then Mona's property fell away a bit and that was where we was going. It was only a hundred yards from the house, but on the far side there was my surprise.

There was Finch and Detlef and Harry, and they was standing outside a little cabin, like a little log cabin. And it wasn't big, but maybe two or three times the size of Bly's shed, and it had a little window next to the door and another one in the short end, and across the door someone had painted a sign that said "Welcome home, Ash." I looked at Mona and her smile was so wide I thought maybe she'd lost her mind, but she hadn't and she said, "It's for you, Snowflake."

I put my hand to my mouth and I knew I oughta say something about "what?" or "no, I couldn't" or "but I don't got no money" or just something like that, but all I could do was hug Mona and then I hugged Finch and Detlef and dammit I even had to hug Harry then, so I did.

Detlef started explaining things to me.

"Go on in," he said and I did, and it was tiny but after a shed and a bathroom floor it was a palace. There was a bed built across the end of one short wall, and there was a little place to sit and a table and the two windows and it even had a tiny wood stove to keep it warm in the winter.

Finally I managed to say thank you and I told Mona I didn't understand, but Mona said it was all their idea on the way back from the funeral. And when Harry had heard about it, she offered to help Finch and Detlef build it because she'd worked in construction before she got sick, and Mary had designed it and Jenny had paid for it all, the timber and the roof and even the tiny little stove. So when Jenny came over I hugged her hardest of all and I couldn't say anything but feel tears coming and she said, "Hush, Snowflake. We just wanted to help. Kid your age shouldn't have to go through so much."

And she smiled, but she left again soon after, which seemed

odd, because everyone else was in real good spirits and joking and all. It was a funny thing. This I mean, this that I am about to tell you.

Now Detlef explained that it, the cabin, wasn't quite finished. There were some little things left to do but they'd be done by tomorrow at the latest, and I could move in today.

"Besides," said Mona, "I want my bathroom floor back."

So what happened was Mona brought two red plastic chairs down from her porch and we set outside my cabin while Detlef and Finch and Harry did the last things. It was great to watch them work and the thing was, I saw how happy everyone was. Mona and Mary, the three folks working on it, all because of this thing they'd done for me.

And that got me thinking.

"Mona?" I said. We was out of earshot, so it was safe to speak and she said what? and I said, "Mona, I understand you helping me, and Finch and Detlef. And Mary. And Jenny is a real generous lady with her money. Ain't she?"

"Yuh," Mona said. "What of it?"

"Well, Harry. There she is, helping build my cabin. But she don't seem the generous type. I mean, she's always ranting about how people oughta do stuff for themselves, not rely on handouts and what-have-you."

Mona gave one short laugh that was like a branch breaking.

"Yeah," said Mona, "well, here's the thing. You're part of her in-group."

"Her what?"

"In-group. You're in it, Detlef and Finch are in it. But the rest of the world? Well, they're in her out-group. It's a psychological thing."

And Mona said that people divided everyone they knew into Ins and Outs. And if you was In, then you was fine and they'd be kind and generous to you. But if you was Out, then you were not popular. In fact, she said, sometimes you were almost not even human. To them. That's what she said.

"They done research," she said. "I am not making this up. They put people in a brain scanner, done a bunch of tests. They found out, if you think someone is in your out-group, well, the parts of the brain that deal with normal human-type interaction don't even light up. Someone is in your out-group, your brain literally don't see 'em as human."

Then I sat there for about three hours and we said nothing, just watched the guys, and then after about three and a half hours I said, "Well, that explains a lot."

"Don't it?" said Mona. "Ever wondered how the Nazis could gas people? They weren't all psychopaths. Not possible. Psychopaths are real rare. Ever wondered how people can walk past a starving person begging in the street and not give 'em even a dime, not even look at 'em?"

I thought about that all for another eternity and I was thinking about people I knew. Like that mad aunt of Jack's. Now she was real mean to me, but to everyone in her family she was a real sweetheart. Everyone said so. And she went to the United Church every weekend. But I knew for a fact she said it would be a good thing if all the starving people in Africa died because we shouldn't have to send 'em food. And then I knew other people who treated the whole world like they was their in-group, and I was set next to one of 'em, right then.

"Just depends where you draw the line," Mona said. "Between your own personal Ins and Outs. Like you might love your own family, but not someone else's. And you might think your own country is the greatest on Earth. And not any other place. But here's the thing. Why not?"

So that started me thinking.

First, ain't it funny how most folks think the country they're born in is the greatest? Instead of some other place? Ain't that a remarkable coincidence? I guess because most people never get the chance to see anywhere else, so they just buy the story about where they're from. Saves a whole lotta thinking and a whole lot of enviousness.

And second, I got on to thinking about family and about parents and by that I mean my dad and my mom. One of 'em I didn't know, and the other I wanted to know, but she'd run off again. And I still had found no way of finding out where she was at.

Then I went on to ponder about why people thought it was better to love your country instead of your state, or your town, or your family. Maybe because it was bigger? But if size was what it was all about, then wouldn't it make more sense to love your continent? Or the whole damn world?

In the end, I said, "But people are born selfish, right?"

Mona looked at me like I had said the most surprising thing she ever heard.

"What makes you say that, Snowflake?"

"We read a book at school. Well, we was gonna read it for biology class, but then Mary-Beth's parents heard we was gonna study it and they complained and it got taken off. It was about that gene that makes us get born selfish."

"Ah," said Mona. "Ah! Oh yes, I know that book. I have a copy of it somewheres." She waved her hand back up towards her place. "Trouble is, that's not what it says. I think that book has a lot to answer for. Well, the title I mean. It has to be the worst title ever. I mean, it's catchy, right? But it's not what the book says."

"No?" I said and Mona said uh-uh. And then she said, "Not at all. What it says is that at the level of our genes, they want to survive, and they'll do anything to make that happen. But here's the thing: in order to survive the best, it turns out that the selfish little gene worked out that the best way to survive isn't to be selfish at all. It's to cooperate."

And at this point, she nodded over at the three workers putting up a little kind of gutter thing so I wouldn't get a shower when I came outside in the rain. Well, I still would, but not as bad.

So I said "huh?"

And Mona said, "Crazy, huh? What the book says is that being kind to each other was invented by genes acting selfishly."

"Ain't that kinda depressing?"

"I don't think so. I think if even Selfish decided that Kind was better, well, that says a lot about the power of Kind, don't it?

And here's another thing, what the book says, it says that yeah, people are born with the nature to be both kind and selfish, but you know what makes people different from every other single life-form on the planet?"

I thought about that, and in the end I said, "We have cell phones?" and Mona looked at me like she was mad but then she said, "The thing that makes us different from every other life-form is that we know all this stuff about being selfish and being kind. And if you know about it, that gives you the choice, right? A wolf, it don't got no choice but to be a wolf. And a lamb, well, its options are limited. Real limited."

"What about goats?" I asked, and Mona was about to get mad for real but then she saw I was just yanking her chain so she said, "Yeah and goats. They don't got no choice neither. But we do. We're the only species that knows this stuff. Kinda gives us some responsibility towards everything else, doncha think?"

I nodded and was thinking on that and then she said how it was a shame a few more people never make no choices.

And here she looked over at Harry and not for the first time I shook my head and I was kinda cross with myself for letting her help build my cabin when if I was a different kind of person, she'd have lifted not one finger. And yet, I could not say that it was not kind of her to help.

And that left me real confused.

Things were rolling along in our little corner of the world. I weren't no better. I had sorta reached a plateau. Like, if I was careful and didn't do too much, I could walk some. Like a few hundred yards, as long as there was somewhere to set for a time at the end of it. But no matter what I did and what I ate or what pills I took, I could see I was never getting better than I was. And Mona was Mona and the goat was the goat and my mom was still missing like always and Bly was still dead. And I was still ill. We were all paying attention to our own little corner of the world, and maybe we weren't paying attention where it needed to be paid.

Spring came and went in about three days and then it was the summer in Arizona and I saw what that truly meant for the first time. And being so high, well, the nights were still cool enough to make a pleasant sleep, but the daytime, the mercury was rising in Mona's little thermometer on the porch by the back door.

As the days got hotter it became real hot in my cabin. But I wanted to pass my days in there as much as I could. For one thing, I didn't wanna appear ungrateful to Mona and everyone for making it for me. For another thing, I wanted my own space. And I wanted to read. So I opened up my two windows and my door and Mona got me some big old beach umbrella from the thrift store in town and that was that.

I came up to the house to use the bathroom, to eat. There was no electricity in my cabin so I used a kerosene lamp, but I didn't use it much. I rose when the sun did and when it went to bed then I went to bed not long after. And that was how I passed my days, in thinking and reading and reading some more and trying not to think about Bly too much.

Ever since Mona had told me about why Harry was happy to help me when she wouldn't have lifted a finger if my skin was a different color, well, something had gotten into me. I read that book, the one we were meant to read in biology class, since Mona had a copy, just like she said. And when I'd finished it I read it again, just to make sure I got it. Then I started to read some of the stuff that was mentioned in that book, books by other people. Mona didn't have any of them books, so I ordered 'em in town. They knew me at the library by now, and every week I would make Mona drive me there, even if she weren't going herself.

The library was a little west and a little south, a block away from the fire department, two blocks from the Little League park. It was not an attractive building, not like that big old church with the man in gold on top, which was a few blocks farther to the west, on a hill. No, the library was a single-story thing that looked like it had been built to sell farm equipment from, but it was full of books and that was all I cared about.

It was bugging me, and I mean I was obsessed. How could people be loving to some folks and then go out and murder some other folks? Either you're bad and mean or you're not, right? That was how I saw it, but the more I read, the less I felt I knew that to be true.

As the summer went along, I kept reading and then chance came along and gave me someone I could really ask about this whole thing. We had a visitor, out in the Forties, I mean.

Mona put the phone down one day and she had on her face that she got when she weren't sure about something.

"Well," she said. "I guess we'll see." And at least she didn't say I wonder what will happen next and I noticed that since a certain night with flashing blue lights in the last days of December she didn't say that so very much anymore.

We was gonna have a visitor, us canaries. We had visitors from time to time. Like there was the photographer who made the book that Mona was in, before I came. And there had been a small-time TV crew once. A writer, with some journalist from a British newspaper. They was the worst. People would come and want to tell the story about the crazy folks living in the desert and Mona was always in two minds, because on the one hand she knew if folks with MCS were ever gonna get any help, they needed to be understood, and they weren't gonna be understood till the normies had heard about 'em and made up their own minds about it. But on the other hand, the folks that came most often would write the canaries up as just a bunch of crazy folk in the desert. End of. Something to raise your eyebrows at over the breakfast table, or snigger about at the end of the local news. Lookit the crazy people! Hah! And that didn't help the cause, not one bit.

But this visitor was a mite different. She was a psychologist, and she was doing research into MCS. Now this part was what had Mona concerned.

"If she's a psychologist," I asked Mona, "does that mean she thinks it's all in our heads?"

"That's what's worrying me. But we gotta keep trying folks. Spread the word, you know that. But listen, Snowflake, you don't have to speak to her. I can take her to meet Detlef. Everyone likes Detlef. And Finch. Everyone likes Finch too."

But I said to Mona that, no, I would be happy to talk to the psychologist, and I said that because I didn't care what she thought about MCS and whether it might all be in my head or not. Because I had some things I wanted to ask her.

Now, Mona was out when she arrived and I was the first one to meet her. I heard a commotion from up at Mona's place and when I got up there I found this young woman backed into a corner being faced down by a goat, namely our friend Socrates. He wasn't in a party mood and the young woman seemed fresh out of ideas. I gave Socrates the legs in the air treatment and took her down to my cabin, explaining about myotonic goats and Socratic irony on the way. And I could hear myself speaking and I guessed I probably already sounded a little crazy to her, but there weren't nothing I could do about that.

We set under the big umbrella thing from the thrift store, taking the shade, in a couple red plastic chairs.

Her name was Stephanie Krokowski. I always remembered that name. I liked it. It was a proper sounding kind of name, one that meant business. Unlike being called Ash. I liked her too and she was older than me of course but probably still only twenty something and that made her closer in age to me than anyone else in the Forties. She had these pale blue eyes, the palest I had ever seen in anyone's head. Like blue ice. You couldn't stop looking at 'em.

But I knew I had to, so I looked out into the desert and I thought I oughta explain to Stephanie about how what you did in Snowflake was stare out at the desert. All the dang time. Like there was answers there. So then I was thinking to myself "idiot" and how now she really would think I was crazy. But if she did, she didn't show it.

She was from some fancy university up north and she wanted to ask me about my experience of having MCS and how it came on and how long I had been sick, and I told her, well, it ain't even a year yet and she said "yet?"

And looked surprised.

"You don't think you're going to get better?" she asked me, and I gave her the shrug.

"Folks with MCS don't really get better. You just get better at dealing with it. Or not."

And I explained a lot of stuff, the stuff I had learned, about being ill. Learning to be someone else. That kinda stuff.

Then I said, "Do you think this is all in our heads?" and she looked surprised again.

But what she said was, "I think it's way more complicated than that. Would you like to tell me where the body ends and the mind begins?" and then I relaxed a bit more and I thought Mona was probably gonna be okay with her too. And she didn't even think it was weird that I lived in a log cabin in the desert, with a goat for company.

Now she said something funny. When I say funny, I mean peculiar.

"There was a time when people used to think differently about illness," she said. "That's what I'm writing my PhD about. About how society views illness and how that changes over time. Say in the Middle Ages, or a hundred years ago, and now. But of course we know much more about disease these days."

So I thought go meet Dr. B and then come back and tell me that, but Stephanie was going along.

"And because I want to compare like with like, I'm writing about diseases that weren't understood in the Middle Ages, or even a hundred years ago. So in the Middle Ages, that's basically everything. And a hundred years ago or so, that's still a lot of things, like tuberculosis, or epilepsy, for example. And so I needed a modern illness that's not understood and I heard about MCS, and here I am. I want to interview everyone, if I can."

And I said "even Socrates?" and I made her laugh with that. By this point I was really liking Stephanie Krokowski. She was interesting and there was this gentle sound to her voice that made me feel good. I coulda listened to her all day. Longer.

"Now," she was saying, "there was a time when people thought that the spirituality of Man was based in illness. To put it simply, the more ill a person was, the more human he or she was. The more dignified and noble."

I said nothing to that because Stephanie had got my mind in a whirl. But I had no time for that whirl, because there was more. She said how some people had argued that it was these sick people who thought more and did more and achieved more than the healthy ones. And that sounded wrong to me, because how can you achieve anything much set in a red plastic chair all day?

"In this view, there were people," Stephanie said, "who entered the worlds of illness, and madness, and they did so willingly, and they came back with knowledge. Knowledge that was of benefit to all. That was how progress was made. Through sickness. Because what do you learn from health?"

And then I started to understand. What do you learn from health? Nothing, that's what you learn. You stay in your smug little world where you can stand for more'n three minutes and never even have to think about it. But make a body sick and, boy, does life get interesting quick. And when I say interesting, I do mean it. Though I also mean it's a real pain in the ass.

Mona showed up then.

She wandered down the desert from her house to my cabin and to start with she was a little edgy and said perhaps Stephanie could park her car a little farther downwind because it smelt of the flatlands and had Stephanie followed the instructions about visiting? And these instructions were that she'd washed herself and her clothes for a week in nothing but bicarbonate of soda and only when Stephanie promised she had, and then changed into some clothes Mona found her anyway, did Mona settle down.

Stephanie stayed two days, on my old porch as a matter of fact, and she met most of the gang and she made us all complete these questionnaires about all sorts of things like mental health and physical health and what-have-you and then, if we agreed, we each spat in a little plastic tube, and she had one for everyone, and she said she was gonna "sequence our DNA" and see if that had anything to say about anything. So of course Mona told her that what that would say was that she was 2.8 percent Neanderthal, and I was excited because ever since Mona had done it I'd wanted to, but I never had close to that spare $99.

Just before Stephanie left I was set with her on Mona's porch and I suddenly had this awful feeling like I did not want her to go. She had been fun and hadn't said anything rude about MCS and everyone liked her and felt relaxed and Mona even said she thought her PhD was real interesting stuff. So I was finding anything I could think of to stop her from getting in her car and driving back north, and one thing I asked her finally was what I had been wanting to ask her.

"Do you know anything about in-groups and out-groups?" I said, and she said, well a little, but there was a professor in her department who was an expert. Wrote about it all the time.

So I had her tell me everything she knew and then I wrote down the professor's name so I could see if I could read some of his work.

"Did you go to a university, Ash?" she asked then and I said, "No, but that don't make me stupid. Does it? Necessarily?"

She looked real upset and said, "No, no, I'm sorry, that's not what I meant. What I meant was it's, well . . . I mean, most people don't bother finding out about stuff. And you read and read and read and I think it's really cool."

So I shrugged and said, "That's what being sick does for you, right? Like the folks in your research used to think? Anyway, I have good teachers," I said. And I told her about Finch and his news line and Mona's what-did-we-learn-today time and how I was desperate to find something to tell 'em they'd never heard of, and how I hadn't yet managed it.

She thought for a while and then she said, "You know what you were asking me? About tribes? You're either in the tribe or out of it?"

I nodded.

"So yeah, it seems we are born with the nature to be both selfish and to be kind. And this tribal stuff is pretty hard-wired too. So that seems pretty depressing. No chance of the human race ever all getting along if we all belong to some tribe or other, right?"

And I shrugged and said, "Yeah, I guess that's pretty depressing," but Stephanie smiled and said, "Well, there are smart things we could do. Next time you're at the library, see if they can get you something about the Great League of Peace and Power. You got that?"

And I wrote that down next to the name of the professor, ready for my next trip to the library.

Then Stephanie started making those I-better-hit-the-road noises and got up and I was desperate to find some other reason to have her stay so I said, "You can't go" and she said why and I said, "Because you ain't interviewed Socrates yet."

She smiled and said, "Well, I don't really have the time. But I'll tell you one thing for free: I think that goat has borderline personality disorder."

Then she left and I watched her go.

"I liked that kid," Mona said. "She was smart. Not untelligent at all. In fact, she was real un-untelligent."

That afternoon we rode out to the library and they had a book about the Great League of Peace and Power, and when I read that it turned out to be about a thing called the Iroquois Confederacy which was how some real un-untelligent guy called Deganawida worked out a system that brought peace to the Six Nations of Iroquois people, back in the day. He knew how people stuck to their in-groups and out-groups, so what he devised was a system where you belonged to more than one group. So maybe for your Nation, you was a Mohawk or a Seneca, but then you would also be in a clan, like a Bear or a Hawk or whatever. The clever part was that these two sets of groups intercut, and since you ended up being loyal to your Nation *and* your clan, it stopped anyone fighting with anyone, because how could you go to war with another Nation when a bunch of 'em would be in your clan too? And vice versa and so on. It all worked just fine until the American Revolution came along and they were all forced to choose between the Brits or the Americans and that was the end of the Great League of Peace.

Still, somebody showed how you could turn something

negative into a force for good. Just like the selfish little gene that invented kindness.

Later on, I asked Mona if she knew what borderline personality disorder was and her eyebrows raised up and then she asked why so I told her because Stephanie Krokowski thinks Socrates has it.

Mona looked cross for a split second and then she burst out laughing.

"Yeah, I guess," she said and then she explained that border-line personality disorder folks were people who, amongst other things, were real, real sensitive and easily hurt by the world and who had a bad temper that could switch in at any time they got scared by something.

So I laughed and said, "Yeah, that sounds a little bit like our goat," but at the same time I was thinking, yeah, and it sounds like a lot of other folks too. Don't it?

TIME

Turned out I didn't win my game with Mona and Finch. Not with that thing Stephanie told me about the Great League. They both knew it already, though they'd forgotten the details. But at least they was happy to talk about it again when I brought it up, so I felt good about that. But I went on searching for something they'd never heard of and that was hard, because they was the two best-read people I ever met. And they made me realize how much they knew that I didn't and yet they always said how they knew nothing or next to it, and then I realized just how much there is to know and how much no one will ever know. I still ain't worked out if that's a problem or not.

Meanwhile, time did its trick of standing still and hurrying right along at the same time. And it did both those things twice as fast (or maybe I mean slow?) as before, because after Stephanie left there was a long time in which nothing happened next, 'less you count me feeling sorry for myself and time passing as something and I surely don't.

Four to six weeks later, for example, happened about the only thing I remember happening. Stephanie had been as good as her word and had all our spit tested, which was good of her because if you had gone and done it yourself you had to pay that ninety-nine dollars. So, just like Mona, we all found out where we came from and who our ancestors was, and how much Neanderthal we was too. Mona made everyone come over to hers for a gene-discovery party, because Stephanie had sent all the results to her to save mailing everyone.

So then, person by person she made everyone open their envelope. First funny thing was that it turned out that Detlef had 12 percent Spaniard in him and for some reason that made Harry bust out laughing. Though Detlef didn't seem to mind. He thought it was cool. Then we opened Harry's and boy, was she in for a shock. Turned out she had one and one half percent "West African" in her, and then she looked way confused and was quiet for some noteworthy period of time. We all nudged each other and winked and tried not to make too much fuss when she said, "Well, I'm feeling a bit beat today, guess I'll go home."

And after she went no one had nothing to say, until I said, "I wonder what will happen next," and Mona hit me on the arm but only for fun.

What happened next was we found out how much cave-person there was in everybody and every time they was 0.5 percent or 1.6 percent Mona'd chuckle and stick a thumb at her chest and say 2.8 percent and grin, and that went on till we looked at mine and it was 4 percent and she shut up bragging.

"Four percent?" she said. "Four? Are you reading that right?" so I handed her the paper and she said, "Huh. Four percent. You cave-kid, you."

Along with my results, Stephanie had put in a little note. It weren't more than a postcard, I guess. But she said how she'd liked visiting with me and hoped she'd see me again some day and then I wondered what kind of life I was gonna have, and would I have people like Stephanie in it and then I was thinking about Bly again so I told Mona I was tired and went to sleep it off in my cabin.

I read Stephanie's note again. She ended it like this: "Keep staring at the desert, Ash. The answers are always out there, somewhere."

And then, ab-so-loot-ly nothing happened.

Time rolled around, day in and day out, and before anything else came along, I was helping Mona with deliveries a little. In Dolly's house one day there was her calendar on the wall and it was open to September and there was nothing on it and I had that feeling they call déjà vu and right then I knew I had been in Snowflake for a year.

And what had I learned?

A lot, too much. Not enough. But I had learned about getting sick and I had started to learn about dealing with that. I had learned that those folks who think that you can just "pull yourself together" and those folks who think "it's all in your head" and those folks who think that getting sick is for weak-minded people who don't wanna be well, heck, they all have no darned clue what they're talking about.

In the fight between the body and the mind, I had learned this: the body wins, always. Just think about Bly. And those fine folks who teach that the body should obey the mind have got a surprise coming for 'em, sooner or later, even if that's on the day they meet their Maker.

But I had also learned this: that the body and the mind are interconnected, for sure. And I know this sounds weird, but it's only when one of 'em breaks down that you realize they are two *separate* things.

Up until then, I mean the day I arrived in Snowflake, in my eager little scouting through the world's adventures, it had never occurred to me to feel there was any difference between my mind and my body. They was both just ME. And then my body broke down, and yet my mind kept on running, so for the first time I could see they was separate things. And yet interconnected. You cannot have the one without the other. That's the funny part. And it was sickness that made me see both how separated and how connected they are. At one and the same time. And I was thinking, god-darn it, life is truly weird and confusing too, at times. And I started to think that the old-time folks in Stephanie's PhD was right. Only when things go wrong do you learn anything. Like who you are. Like what the world is.

Now, if I'm sounding a mite over-philosophical for your taste, there's a reason. There's a couple reasons. First being that I had been living with a professor of linguistics and philosophy (retired) for a year. That's enough to mess with anyone's head. Someone even as dumb-looking as a Tennessee fainting goat might start to philosophize if they went and lived with Mona.

And the second reason is I am thinking about what happened that autumn.

It started with good news. Well, what sounded like good news. Mona came back from doing the rounds one morning. I had stayed home because I wasn't feeling great. By then, I didn't use the chair anymore to get around. I could do a few more jobs about Mona's place to help out. And on good days I would help with the deliveries, which was nice because I felt like I was actually earning my keep a little, and it took some of the load off of Mona, and though she was mighty strong for a sick fifty-something-year-old, she was still a sick fifty-something-year-old.

But today was not a good day, so I was set in a red plastic chair looking at the desert, waiting for answers to stroll out of it and drop in my lap.

Then Mona got home and she said, "News! Jenny's getting married!" so I said what? and she said, "Sure! Jenny and Steve are getting married!"

So I said huh! that's cool! and the very next thing I thought was, well, I wonder what changed, and Mona was thinking the same thing because she said, "I don't know the details. Fact is, I shouldn't know at all, but Sam, down at the grocery store? You know how Sam can't keep a secret, right? So anyway, Jenny came in a week ago and ordered up a wedding cake and when Sam says 'who's that fer?' Jenny says 'it's for me, dimwit.'"

"Huh," I said. "Wow. Well, cool."

And then Mona and me, we set about wondering what made

Jenny change her mind, and how big the wedding was gonna be, and if she'd ordered a cake in Snowflake then that must mean it was gonna happen here and not in San Fran, and so on.

And then, a few days later, we found out why Jenny was getting married and no, it wasn't gonna be a big wedding. In fact, Jenny and Steve was getting married by themselves with just two witnesses and they was leaving San Fran for good and coming to live out in Jenny's place in the Forties. And the reason for all of that was that Jenny was dying. Of cancer, and it was one she'd had before, even while she was in her forties, and now she was still only fifty but they said it had spread. It was all over her body and they couldn't operate or nothing. Nothing at all.

They said she just had a few months left, but they was wrong. Actually it was weeks, and Jenny and Steve got married and ate their cake by themselves and lived out her last few days in their place just down the hill from Mona and me. Until the end, when the pain was too bad and they took Jenny into the hospital then and that's where she died.

Steve, well, he was a saint.

With all her money and family, Jenny could have been buried in the city, but instead she'd chosen to go into the ground in Snowflake. And so we all went to her funeral, the second of the year, and that was in the cemetery, a block from the library and two from Snowflake High.

The cemetery was as flat as the rest of the land, but there was this one thing about it. It was green. It was all green grass, and they kept that little bit of Snowflake watered, that one place, and it must have took a lot of water but those few acres was the one place in town you could walk on grass. And that was for the dead.

Steve, he did nothing but love Jenny, all that time, before she died and after she died too. When the funeral was over and after we put her in the ground, we went back to their place which was now just his place and I said to him how sorry I was and he said nothing but "thanks, Ash" and smiled and I asked myself could he see what I was thinking? And wasn't he thinking the very same thing? Being this: Jenny, why did you wait so long? What on earth were you waiting for? To be with me? To get married? Why did you wanna wait? Because time does not wait.

Steve said nothing, but I could not stop myself from hearing his voice say it anyway, over and over again. Jenny, what was you waiting for?

UNDIAGNOSIS

Yes, time kept rolling, even with Bly in the ground and Jenny in the ground. Steve stayed on in her place in the desert for a while. She'd left him everything. She had some family, but she left him everything, and the house in the Forties along with it all. And it was plain she had loved him every bit as much as he loved her, but you tell me, what was the use in that to him now? And the desert got to him. It was a rare human that wanted to live in the raw red desert with sand in your soul, day in and out. So Steve, he stayed a month or two and then he moved back to San Francisco. And he sold the house, and since it was a house that was good for folks with MCS, he sold it to one. Me. For one dollar.

Now, a cabin is one thing, but a house is another. And Steve was trying to give me a house, but he said it wasn't a gift, legal-wise, if I paid for it, so he insisted on having one US dollar in return. He said it was what Jenny would have wanted, he said she'd left him more than enough money anyhow, he said he'd already been a rich man, given how he was a lawyer. He said he oughta share some of his good fortune. So I said why can't I just rent it from you? A dollar a week? But he said he was sorry but it was too hard for him to keep. On account of how he missed Jenny. And I argued and I argued with him but he wouldn't take no as an answer, and everyone else was on his team, and in the end I accepted, and I bought his house for a dollar, and I moved in.

By this time, I had lived either on a porch, or in a shed, and then in a cabin, for over a year. And though I hung out with Mona much of the while, it was another thing to walk into a house and shut the door at night and know it was yours, forever, and legal.

Now you might suppose this was the best thing that anyone ever did for me. And I guess it was. But the human mind is a treacherous critter sometimes, and I felt other things besides being grateful.

I felt guilty, for one. Here was me, this dumb little kid, and everyone else in the Forties had fought and struggled for a place to call home when their own homes and families spat 'em out. And now that very thing had been given to me. I had a job, a simple job, where Mona paid me a few dollars for driving a truck with people's groceries in it. And that truck? Well, Jack had let me keep Bly's pickup after he left us, so I'd been given that too.

And with all that fortune, you'd think a body would be happy. And grateful. And I was. I was. But I also wanted something more than anything else in the world: I wanted to walk down a city block again and not have to worry if my legs would give out before I got to the end. That's all I really wanted, and I would have given you that house in the desert for nothing if you could have made it happen.

Now Dostoyevsky, him that was 1821 to 1881, he said, "Man is a being who can get used to anything." But I was not convinced of that fact.

Yet, there was one good thing. I finally won the game with Mona and Finch. I had still been reading stuff about kindness and selfishness, and I read this story in the paper in the library one day. It was about a painkiller called acetaminophen, so I knew that the people who named it had been speed-reading Greek mythology while off of their heads on crystal meth. Anyway, you might not've heard of acetaminophen, but that's because that's not the name they put on the boxes. The names on the boxes would have been things like Actifed or Benadryl or Panadol or Sinutab or Tylenol, or some other god from the ancient mythological land of Pharma. It was in over 600 different medicines, I recall that the article said, and the thing was that these researchers had found that taking it made you less kind. What they said was that people who took it "showed a reduction in empathy" and that using it lowered "a person's capacity to empathize with another person's pain, physical or emotional."

And when I told Mona and Finch about it, well, neither of 'em had heard of it before, and I shouted "hell, yeah!" and punched the air and because I never had told them about my game they both stared at me and I guess they were wondering why I was so damn pleased that over-the-counter drugs were making people mean.

And time went along and still I remained part of the great clan of the Undiagnosed, and I learned that to be sick was one thing, but to be sick with something that no one knows what, well, that's quite another.

Every six months or so, I'd go and see Dr. B, just to mess with her a little. It was my idea of fun, for a time. And it cost me some, but I still did it. By this point, I had given up hope of her having any more answers than I had, but I just wanted her to know that even if it was all in my head, it was *still* all in my head. And body.

One day I made up another new word. I was sitting trying to tell Dr. B that she couldn't go on saying things were in my head forever. Now she started to tell me I had a thing they called chronic fatigue syndrome and I said, "And what does that mean? It's just a fancy way of telling me what I told you, that I'm tired all the time! I could have told you that." And then I went on to say you may as well just say I have an undiagnosed illness but, because I was a little upset, I said, "I have undiagnosis!"

Soon as I told Mona that, we made that the new way we talked about when you're sick but you don't know what with. "I got undiagnosis." I tried it a couple times later, like when a new librarian showed up at the library. "I got undiagnosis," I said when she asked why I was wearing a mask in her library. And that sure was the end of that conversation, real quick, which was more or less what I wanted.

Back in the Forties, when folks got together, they'd still share everything and all they had to know about this thing called MCS, and what caused it, and what might be the way out of it. And I listened to it all, and sometimes, when I was feeling a little better, I'd start saying to myself, see? Dr. B's right. It was all in your head. You was never sick, Snowflake. And then there was other times when it would all come crashing back into me and I laid up in bed for a day or three, waiting for some energy to return to my body. And my head.

One day, a bunch of folks was over at Mona's and Harry was one of 'em. She was all excited because she'd read something and she figured it was why the electrical-sensitive folks were the way they were. Now I was glad I'd never had a problem with that, but Mona did, and Detlef and Harry, and a few of the others. And Harry had read this thing that said that they'd found that bacteria responded to electricity. That they're stimulated by it. And so Harry was thinking that suppose you was infected by some bad bacteria. Then you come into an electrical field and they get stimulated somehow, and that's why you feel sick. On account of all those bacteria having a party in your muscles and in your blood.

While on the other hand, Mary was saying that she thought that lots of people had problems with mold spores, and the Dead Elf agreed, but he said that he felt that toxicant-induced lack of tolerance was the real big issue. He said you had to get your body to detoxify better. And then other people said other things.

And people was listening to Harry, and to Mary, and to Detlef, and I was too but I was also thinking are these the answers? Are they my answers? Are the answers even out there? I know Stephanie said they're always out there, but maybe they ain't. Maybe they're not out there, maybe they're in, someplace.

And the time was coming when I would have to do something about that, I just didn't want it to be in the way that Bly had done something about it.

0 Bly.

What did you do?

See, the thing was this. I had been given a house and by the time Steve had moved all Jenny's stuff out, it was emptier than a shoebox. He'd been generous, of course. He'd left me the bed and the furniture and what-you-got, but all else I had was nothing. The little more than nothing I'd had when I rolled into the Forties, plus one or two books Mona had given me or that the library was throwing out.

And it was one day as I was over at Mona's and collecting the last things from my cabin, trying to fill my house up, and it was almost a year since Bly had gone and left us, and I realized something. I realized that I had not even looked in the direction of those two dang sheds since the night he went.

It was like I had tried to make it not have happened, by not looking at where it did. But it had. And this one day, I looked at the sheds. There was the one he died in, and Mona and Finch had cleaned that one out. But I realized that all Bly's things were still in the other.

"What you thinking, kid?" Mona said and she was suddenly right at my elbow, looking up at me and worrying.

"Nah," I said, "don't fret none. I just thought maybe I oughta go through his stuff."

And Mona sighed and nodded and said, "Yeah, we oughta."

So we did.

I could not look in the sleeping shed. But Mona said there was nothing to see there. But the other shed, well, it had Bly's stuff in it, and mostly that was all his pills. They sat there on a little shelf, and I wondered why they was still alive when Bly wasn't. All the vitamins and all the minerals and herbs and all the stuff that was supposed to make him better, it had all done exactly nothing.

There were some clothes. He was neat, our Bly. The few things he had were all folded up neat and tidy, and when Mona went back to hers to get a sack for stuff we was going to throw out and another for stuff for the thrift store, I stole a T-shirt that had been my brother's and hid it in the box I was taking to mine. It was what he was wearing the day I arrived and I knew it would be big for me, but I wanted it. I don't know why I thought I had to steal it. Mona wouldn't have cared, but somehow I wanted it to be a secret, so I snuck it away when she wasn't looking.

There weren't no books. Bly never did read much. He learned by watching and listening, and that was fair and good enough for him. The only other thing was a plastic solar-powered dancing police officer, still in its box.

Mona lifted it up and we looked at it for a good time, wondering, and then I said I guess he was gonna give it to Jenny and Mona nodded and then we both looked away from each other because it was too much to think of one dead person not getting the chance to give to another dead person something they'd intended to.

And when that passed, I took it from Mona and I said, "I'll put it with the others," because though Steve had moved out of Mona's he'd left me with a collection of ten thousand wiggling solar-powered bits of plastic in my yard.

And see? There was me calling the bit of desert inside my fence a yard, now that it was my bit of desert. All legal, and all for a dollar.

If I mentioned before that nothing happened for a long, long while, well, you ain't seen nothing yet. You are about to see how spectacularly non-happening a long time of nothing can be. Just a world of nothing. And, yeah, we all know now what was happening some places and elsewhere, all the stuff that was brewing and getting ready to burst, but out there in the Forties, it was like time had come to a stop. Period.

Such as.

"The sunflower," Mona said one day, "is seen differently by everyone who sees it."

So I said what? and Mona said, "The sunflower. Snowflake, are you even listening? The sunflower. To a painter, it's the color yellow. To a farmer, it's a crop, a source of oil. The spiral pattern of the seeds reminds the mathematician of the Fibonacci sequence. To someone in love, the sunflower is what? Loyalty, that's what."

"Loyalty?"

"The face of a sunflower follows the course of the sun. Like a lover."

"Oh," I said. "Huh."

Then because I thought it sounded rude not to reply to that any better, I took a guess and said, "Nietzsche, 1844 to 1900?" because it seemed to me he said more things than all the other philosophers put together, but Mona said no, it was one of her own, which I am ashamed kinda took the edge off it a tad. But then I thought why do we think things are smart because they was said by old dead guys, and not by the breathing kind of people all around and about? And I told Mona that and she said Voltaire, 1694 to 1778, had something to say about that, which was "fools have a habit of believing that everything written by a famous author is admirable."

"So who *do* you believe?" I asked Mona and she just grinned at me until I said I guessed that the trick is knowing what to think for yourself, and she pointed her gun fingers at me and said "bam!"

About three weeks later, I said to Mona, "That thing about sunflowers?" and she said whut? and I said, "What did you mean by that?"

So she said how it was all a matter of perception. Life, she meant. That what you saw depended on who you was, and since we're all different, no one sees the same world as anyone else. Not exactly.

And I mention all this just to show the level we had sunk to.

Nothing happened. Nothing, but birthdays came and went and Halloweens and Thanksgivings and Christmases too. Cooper got older and had a couple of falls and we had to take him to the vet. But he was fine. The vet chuckled (mostly to himself) as he told us that there was life in the old dog yet and I got the feeling he said that to everyone with a sick mutt of advancing years, every damn time. And Socrates seemed to be getting dumber, which possibly meant that actually secretly he was getting smarter, but in God's honest truth, we all doubted it.

Mona said, even if he did have borderline personality disorder, that it was only a label and he was still a goat with feelings and we shouldn't stigmatize him for that. And I figured that was right, and I also figured that at least he had a diagnosis.

Still, he may have been a goat with feelings *and* a diagnosis, but that didn't stop him being Socrates. He'd found new ways to annoy, irk, and irritate, from butting the side of Mona's house so loud at two in the morning that I could hear it over at my place, and so could Harry over at hers. For three weeks he banged the siding at two in the a.m., as regular as a clock, and no one could figure out why he started, or why he stopped. But when three weeks was up, he did. Then he started trying to have intercourse with Mona's little clown car every afternoon and Mona said that sort of thing weren't supposed to happen because of how they'd had him "seen to," but maybe they forgot to tell Socrates that.

Mona stood in front of the scene one day, while Socrates tried to mount her car, with her hands on her hips.

"Ash, did I ever tell you how Socrates died?"

So I said uh-uh and she said, "He was forced to commit suicide by drinking hemlock. I wonder if hemlock grows anyplace around here. . . ."

Then, though that was a good joke, we were both quiet and I guess it don't need saying why. Mona coughed and hummed and then I thought I better say something, because I knew she didn't mean anything bad.

"Why did they make him do that? Socrates? The real one, I mean."

"On account of how he didn't believe what everyone else believed. The right kind of gods. That kind of thing."

"Jeez," I said. "They killed him for that? I thought those Greeks were supposed to be smart."

"Real smart about some things. Real dumb on others. But Snowflake, this was a long time ago."

So then I said, "You thinking things have gotten any better?" and Mona nodded and grinned and said, "My work here is done" and pretended to call her spaceship down to Earth to collect her.

Finch finished fixing his house and moved in. Mary told her lawyer to get lost and started looking for another. And time rolled on. I can tell you that in a moment, but that don't make no difference. Years began to stack up on one another and I didn't get better and all that happened was I got a little older.

All things put together, I guess a massive boredom had arrived in the Forties in general, and inside me in particular.

I was no longer the noob. I was getting older and, I feared, like Socrates, not getting any smarter. I'd mostly given up reading stuff, and though from time to time something would grab me, either a book or an article, soon enough I'd be done with it and I'd sink back to being me. Which was what? I was no longer ever in the wheelchair. I had good times during which I drove a lot of groceries around the desert, and I had bad times when I did precisely nothing, unless you count laying in bed staring at the ceiling something, which I don't.

From time to time I thought about the things I'd learned. Like Finch's little gene, no wait, his little polymorphism, the one that meant you was born to be more kind if you had two copies of it, and less if you had none. And then I thought about my mother and why she had never seemed to want me. And I thought about Mona's bacteria, the ones who were actually controlling us and generally ruling the world, the ones who'd be around long after we're gone. I even tried imagining I was bacteria one day and, compared to the four billion years of my species' existence, the life and works of mankind seemed less important and lasting than a snowflake, melting. But when you start imagining you're a bacterium, well, that is when you truly know that you are bored. And all this time, none of us was paying attention. Not to what we shoulda been paying attention to.

I wasn't the only one that felt the boredom. I guess that was why Detlef decided to throw his party.

As you will recall, Detlef being a national of the sovereign state of the Federal Republic of Germany, he did some things a tad different. So his Christmas party was on Christmas Eve, because that's what they did back home. And at Christmas he ate roast goose if he could find it, not turkey. Maybe being German was why most of his diet was Twinkies and hot dogs, though I doubt it. And in midsummer, there was something else he did that we didn't do. Early one June, when the days were so hot you thought that time might melt and stick to the ground, he started going on about midsummer bonfires. He went on about how it was a big time for a big party back in the village he'd grown up in and how he was gonna throw a party this year. And because he'd never done this before I figured it was to relieve the boredom on all of us.

Everyone helped get ready.

The main thing the Dead Elf was excited about was the bonfire. He told us how it was the custom to have a huge fire, and how often you'd make a straw doll and burn it on the bonfire. He said the dolls were supposed to be witches you wanted to get rid of.

So then Mary said, "Where are we gonna get a witch from?" and a moment later everyone looked over at Mona who said "very funny" and sulked for the rest of the day.

But not longer. Mona herself said she'd make a witch and she set to with some old clothes and some of Socrates' hay and three days later she'd made this real funny-looking lady, all ready to be burned. I said to Mona it was a bit weird burning someone, wasn't it? Even in pretend, and she said it was no weirder than lots of things that folk did to have fun and I did not have a smart reply to that.

I drove around in my truck that had been Bly's truck and collected scrap wood from people. Old shipping crates and offcuts from construction. A broken bookcase here, a raggedy chair there. I drove up and down the Forties and the Twenties for two weeks on end and every time I got there, Detlef would unload all the wood and add it to the pile.

Detlef was some kind of human being. He was smart, and though he had his funny ways, everything he did he did real well. So when he built a bonfire, it was not only the biggest bonfire you ever saw, it was also the neatest; somehow he stacked all that ramshackle wood into a shape like a big round drum, ten feet tall. Maybe more.

And other people asked Detlef what food you had for German midsummer parties and Detlef looked kinda confused and said anything was fine with him, just bring anything you want to eat. And I drove into and outta town a dozen times, picking up stuff for the party, and I guess if I had been paying attention I would have seen some things that might have set me thinking. Like, now, I can recall a coupla times I saw a convoy of army trucks motoring through town real fast. But I just didn't think anything of it. There was the party to attend to.

The day came, and we was all so excited and I could not wait for the evening to come because that was when it was all gonna happen, at sundown on the longest day, which meant it was late by the time things even got going.

Mona picked me up in her car and when she pulled up there was the witch sitting in the passenger seat.

"I've given her a name," Mona told me and I said "yeah?" and she said she decided to call her Nancy and I said "why Nancy?" and she thought for a second and then said "why not?"

So Mona and me, we drove Nancy down the dirt turnpike and I had a job stopping Cooper from chewing on her, because he was getting real old by then, and had developed some funny habits. Which Mona blamed on how he had to share his life with a god-danged crazy goat called Socrates, and by that she meant she blamed herself.

Everyone was there. Everyone. The whole gang.

It was getting on for eight in the evening. The sun was tipping down behind the hills to the west, and Detlef had set up all these tables and chairs outside. The tables were covered in food and the chairs were already full of people and the Dead Elf said he had to say a few words. So he told us about midsummer bonfires and how they were a real old thing, going way back before Christian times and they were to celebrate the life of the sun on its longest day. How people thought the fires would keep evil things away and make sure the sun came back again the next year.

He told us he had a surprise for later in the night when it really got dark, and everyone went "oooh" like they have to when you tell 'em there's gonna be a surprise. But first, Detlef lit the bonfire and then yelled because we'd forgotten to put Nancy on top of it, but when he came over to get it I suddenly said to Mona, "We can't burn Nancy!" and Mona looked at me for three seconds, said, "God-durn it. Why did you have to say that?" and I told her it was her fault for giving her a name because now she was in my in-group and she shrugged and then she called over to Detlef.

"Hey, Dead Elf, burning witches is off the agenda!"

Detlef just shrugged and the night came on as the fire took hold and we all started real close to it but soon we was backing off and all saying how hot it was and can you believe it's so hot this far away? and all those kinda things.

Someone had put some music on, real loud, and people started eating and drinking too, and though I was never one to drink much in the way of alcoholic drinks, it seemed the right thing to make an exception, so I had a beer or two. Or three. Then Detlef came over and pushed a glass into my hand, a real little glass, and even though I wasn't a drinker I knew that the smaller the glass, the more you gotta be afraid of what's in it.

"Schnapps!" Detlef said. "Obstwasser! I had to order it specially!"

So then because he said that thing about having to order it, I had to drink it. And it turned out that having just one wasn't gonna satisfy nobody, least of all me.

Now, by this time, I guess it's fair to say I was roaring drunk. Not that I actually roared. I felt kinda far away and swimmy but they don't call it swimmy-drunk. They call it roaring.

And it turned out I wasn't the only one getting a little wasted, because right after that second glass, Detlef grinned at me and shouted over the din of the people and the music.

He said, "Using all the light was how my head got spent!"

And before I could say "what?" he was off to wheel out his big surprise.

He had everyone hush up and then took us around the other side of the house. It was getting on for midnight and there was almost no moon, just a sliver left before it would be gone for good in a couple days. But there was the stars. Did I never tell you about the stars in the Arizona desert?

Those days I slept on the porch, those first days? After the monsoon clouds left, when the nights got clear, then how the stars shone! You could read by 'em, if the print weren't too small. And I never saw stars like that. The Milky Way, you think it's something people have made up, till you finally see it for real, and I guess now most people see much more of it than before, right?

So we all stood there and made some good noises about the sky, and someone said, "Detlef, what's going on?" and he didn't say nothing. He was away off in the distance somewhere so maybe he didn't hear, but a second later we saw the flame of a lighter and something fizzed and two seconds later a rocket whooshed up into the sky. A firework.

It was a big one. Gi-gantic, and when it reached the top of the sky, the explosion, you could feel it on your chest. And he didn't have just one. There were dozens of 'em. He was scurrying around in the dark lighting 'em up, all of 'em, and in groups of two or three they shot up into the sky and it was wonderful. With all their colors and sparkles. All the sounds, the fizzes and the bangs. It was wonderful, and not just because I was as drunk as a horse.

There was one of us, however, who wasn't so pleased. That was Cooper. Now, he was getting old, like I said, and a mite deaf along with it, but those fireworks of Detlef's, they were loud. As soon as the first one went off, Cooper went nuts. He started barking and running about and then he started howling and as I watched the fireworks I tried to make my way over to find Mona to help her calm him down.

Detlef didn't know nothing about it. The noise of the fireworks covered most of it, and everyone going "oooh" covered the rest. And when they was over, everyone clapped and cheered and someone put some music on again but then Detlef found out that he'd upset Cooper.

"I'm so sorry!" he kept saying, over and over. "Mona! I'm so sorry" and Mona said it was okay, but Cooper was still upset. He was shaking and he looked terrified and I said, "Maybe he oughta go home?"

And Mona agreed but I could see something. She didn't wanna go home. She was having a nice time, a ball, and the last thing she wanted to do was haul ass down the dirt turnpike when things were just getting going.

So then I did something dumb.

I said I'd take Cooper home, back to hers and keep him company till he was a happy dog again. Mona looked at me.

"You been drinking?"

And I said "one beer" and Mona said, "Well, I guess the worst can happen is you squash a jackrabbit" and she gave me the keys.

Now I had had more than one beer. And I should not have been driving, but the truth was, I had started to feel bad. It was something I noticed about myself. If we all started having too much fun, I started thinking about someone, a certain someone whose T-shirt I had stolen, and I wanted him to be there, even if it was only the bacteria making me want that. And I think the drink was all making the bacteria make me feel that even worse, so yeah, I was helping Cooper, but he was helping me too, for an excuse to leave.

I bundled him into the car, and sometimes you had to help him get in, these days. This was one of those times, so I lifted his back end while he worked on the front, and then we set off down the turnpike.

Now, as Mona had said, the worst that could happen was that I might squash a turtle or something, it was just one dirt track and it ran straight through the desert towards Mona's. But it was bumpy and had been getting worse after each monsoon. So soon enough, the inevitable happened. I pulled up as quick as I could and opened the door and threw up on the side of the road and as I did I remembered what Mona told me all those years back about checking where you're walking in the middle of the night and what's in your boots in the first place. If I had just vomited on a rattlesnake, however, there was nothing I could do but apologize.

So I was saying sorry, just in case, and pulling myself up into the car again when I saw something coming towards me in the night. Blue flashing lights.

Straightaway I put two and two together, got four, and I was right. It was the Navajo County sheriff's office, come all the way up from Show Low, just to see what all the explosions in the sky was about.

In case you are unaware of the rules and regulations concerning the personal use of fireworks in the state of Arizona in the early years of the twenty-first century, I'll help you out a little.

Simply put, it weren't legal. Sure, you could have little fireworks, but only ones that wouldn't tickle anyone's pickle. And you could only have them from June 24th on. And this was June 23rd, more or less, until a few minutes later. And big ones? Rockets and things that make explosions in the sky, well, they was downright illegal all the darn time. You might wonder, because I did, about how I lived somewhere where it was just fine to buy an assault rifle but setting off a firework was completely evil. Maybe you got a better answer than I do, but them was the rules.

So when the prowler pulled up next to me, and they wound their window down, they said, "Evening. We got reports of some unusual activity out in these parts. You seen anything?"

It is remarkable how quickly you can act sober when you gotta. At least, I think I did, but I wasn't so drunk that I wasn't worried stupid they was gonna arrest me for drunk driving. Even though the land I was driving on was Detlef's and so private and I was desperately wondering if that made any difference or not. I mean, it makes no difference to the person you run over and kill, but maybe it would save my neck in court.

So I said, "Yes, officer, I think we may have seen something."

"We?"

"Me and Cooper."

The officer peered into the cab and couldn't see no one so then he looked at me kinda funny.

"He's my dog."

I thought I was doing a real good job of sounding sober. I'm not sure I was right about that. But on he went, the cop, I mean.

"You know where?"

So then I gave a good old Snowflake shrug.

"I do not," I added, in case it wasn't clear.

"You mind telling me what you're doing out here in the middle of the night?"

I did mind, but you don't get the choice.

"We have been visiting with friends and now we're taking ourselves home."

I said all that convinced it was the soberest anyone ever sounded.

And of course I was thinking my God how can you not smell that German firewater all over me? But they didn't. Somehow.

They drove off looking for terrorists or whatever.

I found out later that when they showed up, everyone acted innocent and said, "Yeah, we saw it too!" and pointed way out into the desert and thank God it was dark enough that they didn't see the remains of the fireworks spread all over Detlef's yard.

I got home, back to Mona's I mean, and I shushed Cooper and he was asleep almost as soon as I put him on Mona's bed. He was one old mutt.

Then I stumbled back out of the door, and there I saw something in the dark, just two shapes, and those two shapes was Bly's sheds.

I could not have told you why I did what I did next. Maybe now, all these years later, I could try to explain. I might try to say that something in me was stuck. Something in me got stuck, or something in me died along with Bly in that shed that night. And somehow, I had not been living since. Somehow, I think my body knew something I could never have worked out with my head. I needed to go in there.

My body needed me to do it. So I did.

I was drunk and I staggered over and I pulled the door open and there weren't much of anything in there. Nothing but the crates he used as a bed, everything else had gone, but drunk as I was, I lay down on the hard crates, and lay there, thinking about what Detlef had said. "Using all the light was how my head got spent." That's what he said and the funny thing was that, at one and the same time, I had no idea what he was talking about and yet I knew exactly what he meant, because I felt the same.

And then it was Bly. I was thinking about Bly, and then thinking I *was* Bly, and yet, before I knew it, I had passed out.

I slept till the early morning.

Mona must've come home, with a lift from someone else, sometime, but I knew nothing. I slept on my dead stepbrother's bed and right through till the early hours when I woke with an ache in my head and my whole body screaming from sleeping on a wooden crate for a few hours.

Then came the thing that happened. The thing that set me rolling off into a whole new part of life.

As my eyes opened and got used to the light coming down from that little skylight Detlef had once put in for me, and as my head thumped and I decided not to move for a moment or two, I saw something above my head.

It was a piece of paper, folded in half, and it was tucked into the ridge, at the highest point of the roof.

Even from where I lay, I could see something else. It had my name on it.

"Ash," it said. And it was in Bly's handwriting.

VOLTAIRE

Voltaire, real name François-Marie Arouet, was born in 1694 and he passed from this world in 1778. He was another philosopher who got in trouble for saying what he thought. His views got him locked up more'n once. Sometimes he got in trouble for criticizing the government. One time he got locked up in that place in Paris called the Bastille. He was put in a cell with no windows for eleven months for accusing Philippe II of committing incest with his daughter. Like Mona always said, you thinking things have got any better?

Anyway, it was just after he was locked up in the Bastille with its ten-foot-thick walls that he changed his name to Voltaire. No one's sure why. My theory is it sounds cool.

Now, why am I telling you all about Voltaire? Well, two things. First, he was all for people thinking for themselves and for governments letting people believe what they wanted to. Just like old Socrates, only two thousand years later. So just like Mona said, who's thinking things have got any better? I ain't sure I am.

And second is on account of what was in Bly's note.

Now, as suicide notes come, I guess it was kinda funny. Don't get me wrong, I was no expert on the subject, but you know, when people take their own life away, you hear stories about letters they leave behind. "Forgive me everyone, I didn't wanna but . . ." or "I'm real sorry, but it's too much for me to bear" or "y'all stink and I'm glad I'm outta here." Whatever it might happen to be.

So when I saw that piece of paper with my name on it, I figured maybe Bly had left something like that for me. I guess maybe a second and one half passed between me seeing that piece of paper and grabbing it and unfolding it and reading it, and in that second and one half there was enough time to think a remarkable amount of things. Things he might have written in that note. Things like "if only we . . ." and "maybe we could have but . . ." or "did you ever wish that . . . ?" but there weren't nothing like that, and I was to be disappointed.

On the one side, it had my name.

On the other side it had three things, and they was as follows:

One: *"All is for the best in the best of all possible worlds."*

Two: *"Eelfoh cooltivay notra jar dun."*

And:

Three, there was a thing I thought might be a name: *Polloo.*

And as Mona might have said, that was god-dang that.

Now, unlike the night before when I only *thought* I was doing a great job of acting sober, in that moment I saw my name, I was as cold as stone and my head clear like water from a well. It didn't make any sense and I needed time for it to make sense. So before Mona could come out and start on interviewing me, I snuck out and shuffled back home to my place, just down the hill.

I spent the morning with the piece of paper unfolded on my kitchen table. I set a chair by it and stared at it and then I stared at the tea I had made and then at the desert, waiting for the answers to roll in.

A couple of times I tried going through some of the books I had borrowed or bought or otherwise gotten from my time in Snowflake, but I didn't have nothing that would help.

And the thing is, you might have spotted that name, Polleux, right off, but I didn't. I had only ever heard Mona say it, and the way she said it was not how it looked on a piece of paper. And I knew it looked kinda French, this word in front of me, and I didn't speak an unholy word of French, not to mention there was that other bit, that looked like gobbledygook, and I didn't speak gobbledygook neither. But in the end, I realized what the name was. It wasn't Polloo. It was Polleux! Polleux, the name of that guy Mona had told me about, the first one to come, the first one with MCS. The guy who lived way out in the deep.

So I stared out in the desert and I knew the answers were out there, after all, just like Stephanie Krokowski had said they would be. Though, to be more precise, I knew I would have to start at Mona's place, because the way to get to those answers, well, that would be in her head.

I waited till the afternoon. She mighta had one ginger ale too many, like me. I told myself it might be best to leave her be, so

I hung around doing nothing but staring at the desert for hour after hour. I kept putting it off, going up to Mona's, because the truth was I didn't wanna share this thing from Bly with anyone. I knew she'd know what it meant, though, and only her, so in the end, around four o'clock it was, and as hot as hell, I drove back up in my truck to her place.

It was funny. It felt wrong. I didn't like finding something that Bly had kept from me, and then I thought about those days when he'd go missing and be acting funny and then I thought about his note and how he'd kept the biggest thing of all from me, that he was gonna kill himself. And then it was too much to think of, because if only he'd, I mean, if only he'd said something, just anything, then I coulda, I coulda maybe stopped him. Maybe. And all that hurt more than I can say.

It didn't take Mona more than a second.

I don't know why for sure, but I didn't wanna give her the paper. In the end I had to, on account of how I didn't know how to say that bit in gobbledygook.

I gave her the paper and said, "What's this mean?" and she stared at it for a while, frowning, but only for like thirty seconds, and then she laughed and said, "Hey! Voltaire!"

"Oh, right," I said.

"1694 to 1778," she said, and I said, "Yuh, obviously" so she stuck her tongue out at me and then I said, "What's that funny writing?"

"It's French. Well, it's not. It's someone writing something down how it sounds. Just like Polleux's name, see? Ash, where'd you get this?"

So then I had to tell her. I didn't tell her how I found it. I just said it was in some of Bly's stuff. And she sighed and took it okay.

She said, "This line. *Eelfoh cooltivay notra jar dun.* That's Voltaire. Only it should be like this." And she grabbed a pen and wrote it out for me.

Il faut cultiver notre jardin.

And I asked, "What's it mean?"

"Well, it don't go straight into English. It would mean something like "we gotta tend our garden."

"Oh," I said. "Uh-huh. Yeah, I got it. Uh-huh." And other stupid stuff like that.

Then I added, "Uh-huh, so. And that other bit?"

"All is for the best in the best of all possible worlds." Well, the bit about the garden, and that bit? They both come from Voltaire's best-known story."

"He wrote books too? Storybooks?"

"Lots of philosophers did. I think it's on account of thinking too much."

"How's that now?"

"Well, the difference between a writer and a philosopher? I reckon they both ask questions, but only the philosopher tries to give the answers too."

"Oh. Right."

"So when a philosopher is thinking, and thinking, and they

wanna say something but they don't exactly got an answer, well, then they write a story instead."

"Oh," I said. "Uh-huh. So what's this book of his?"

"It's called *Candide*. It's about a young man who goes out into the world and has all sorts of crazy adventures. And mostly it's full of all these terrible things happening. I mean real terrible. There's the Lisbon earthquake. That was a real thing. Some hundreds of years ago. Destroyed the whole city, there was a tsunami, tens of thousands dead. It was like the end of the world. Well, it was for the people in Lisbon, right? But it had a big effect around the world too, when people heard about it. Like it was Judgment Day or something. Voltaire put it in his book, because don't ask me why but people always like stories about the end of the world, right? And then he made up a whole bunch of other awful things too. People being flayed alive, people being executed, people getting raped and getting incurable diseases and all."

"Sounds a real giggle."

"Yeah, well, in point of fact it is. It's a real funny book. See, the whole thing is a joke aimed at this other philosopher. Gott-fried Wilhelm Leibniz. 1646 to 1716. See, what Leibniz said was that we oughta be optimistic. No matter what. He argued that since this is the world that God has created, well heck, that must mean it's the best possible one. Because God's top dog, right? So anything He does must be the best. And if it's the best possible world, then anything that happens in it must be the best possible thing that can happen. Right?"

"Right," I said. "I mean, wrong. I mean, it sounds logical and all but who the heck would actually think that for real?"

"You'd be surprised. Anyway, so all these bad things keep happening to Candide but mostly to his friends, and to a woman called Cunégonde who he falls in love with, but there's this real wiseass in the book, name of Professor Pangloss. And what Pangloss keeps telling Candide is—"

"—that all is for the best in the best of all possible worlds?"

"Bingo."

I thought about that for a while.

"Kinda funny, isn't it?" Mona said after a bit, "kinda?" and I nodded but it didn't sound that funny to me.

"This book, well, no one reads it anymore, but it's still important. Like, for one thing, the humor in it? The whole joke aimed at Leibniz? It's called philosophical irony, but you can just think of it as being way sarcastic. Well, years later, it led to a whole raft of books, like science-fiction books, the ones that show a future that everyone thinks is real fine, but in fact is terrible."

I'd read some of those kinds of books. Books about the end of the goddamn world. Like Mona said, people sure must like stories about the end of the world; there were hundreds of 'em. I kinda liked them, but they sure got depressing when you read a stack of 'em back to back.

"Speaking of," said Mona, "you hear about that city they wanna build west of Phoenix? You know that guy, that computer guy, the zillionaire? What's his dang name? Anyway, he wants to build a brand-new hi-tech 25,000-acre city out there in the desert, just west of Phoenix. And this is a place where fifteen days last year it was so hot planes could not take off because of the lack of lift. That's real smart, huh! Trying to ignore the laws of physics. Real smart."

And she burst out laughing, like she always did. Specially when something was dumb.

But I was thinking about something else.

"Mona?" I said, and she said, "What is it, Snowflake?" and I said, "That French thing? What does it mean?"

"I said, it means—"

"No, I mean, what's it really mean? We have to tend our gardens . . . ?"

"People debate that," Mona said. "For instance, some folks think it means we oughta just look after our own business and not meddle with others. And some folks say it means we oughta change the way the world is working."

So I said "huh" and then I said, "Well why's it on this piece of paper?"

Then Mona gave me the Snowflake shrug and said she did not rightly know and I knew I was at the end of Mona's answers.

All is for the best in the best of all possible worlds. That was what had been in Bly's head. And by putting my name on the world's most irritating suicide note, that meant he meant for me to see what had been in his head.

That, and the thing about gardens, and the name of John Polleux. So that's when I knew if I really wanted any answers, then that's where I'd have to go. Out into the desert, out into the deep.

THE WIZARD OF AZ

And what a fine and eager kid I was, I was then. You know how I can still see all the way back to my brightness, my burning brightness, and I can feel it all, as yesterday, my chomping child, me, the eager little scout of the world's adventures! And now there's more than a little tiredness in my bones, but yet I wonder, oh, how did I manage to do what I did?

Even tired as I was then, with years of sickness in my bones, something inside me was stronger, and I guess it was that strong thing that dragged me out into the desert.

'Course, I didn't go right at once. No, not me. Me, I had to set around in my house that Jenny had given Steve that he'd sold me for a dollar. I can't believe that when I think about it now, all these years later. A house for a dollar. And that was when money didn't go very far at all. Now it don't get you nowhere. But you all know that, right? We all know that after What Happened.

No, being me, little old Snowflake, I set around for a day or two, or it might have been three months. Time had kinda lost its meaning for me then anyway, and looking back from here, it's hard to tell whether something took a minute or a year. And trust me when I tell you, truth is, it don't matter.

What I did was this. I would turn my conversations with people around to John Polleux. I didn't want anyone to know I was going, and again, I couldn't have told you for why, not then. I can tell you now, easily enough. I didn't tell anyone because this was something between me and Bly and no one else. It was our private business, and though I didn't know that right out, I just didn't want anyone to know. Now I see it was because if he'd kept his dying from me, I needed to make his secret my secret. To bring us closer again. To stop me feeling betrayed by him. But I couldn't have told you that then.

So, say I might be talking to Finch, or Mary. Or whoever, 'cept I didn't do it with Mona because I knew she'd guess. She was the smartest of the canaries, and she knew me best and she would have guessed. But with everyone else I would steer the talk around to Polleux and pretty soon I found out where he was at, and which road to take, and so on, and then, one day, I put myself in Bly's truck and drove.

I left early morning.

Like I say, I do not know which morning it was, but it was sometime after Detlef's party and sometime before the monsoon came around again. Each year, the monsoon had been getting wilder and wilder. The old-timers said that once you could set your watch by it. But these days, it would arrive late, either that or early, and go early, either that or leave late. And it would hammer the rain into the ground and we thought the world was ending.

So it was the hottest part of the year and that was real smart of me. Still, I thought I was doing the right things. From out of a box someplace, I found my old cell phone, and the charger, and

I charged it up. There was two things about that. First thing, it still worked, and that was weird, somehow. It had been years since I had picked it up. Four? Five maybe. It was still alive, even though I had paid it no attention in all that time, and like plastic bottles of pills, I guess things are more immortal than people. So I turned it on and of course it didn't get a signal. Never had, but what I realized was I had no way of knowing whether the phone company had disconnected me or whatever. If my credit was still good, or whether they let it expire after two hundred years of not using it.

Second thing was, I looked at the photos again. All my old photos. There was about a hundred of 'em on there, and of course they were just the same. The photos of Mary-Beth and Ximeno and Malik. They were all there and they were all the same. They hadn't aged a day. And neither had the guys in the shoe store. The photos of Jack. One or two with Suzanne.

That one single photo of Bly.

And then there was my mom. Who once upon a time I had wanted back in my life. And at that precise time, I knew that was over. In the photos, everyone was just the same. Like before, everyone was from before I was sick. But there was one thing that was different, and that of course was me, because I looked at the photos, but it didn't hurt no more. Not even looking at a photo of my mother, and then I knew I had become someone else. I looked at her and I thought, you are a poor woman and I hope you find what you're after in the end. Because it sure ain't me. But it didn't hurt to think that anymore. It had just stopped hurting.

So what was I doing with the phone? I don't know. I figured maybe there'd be somewhere with a signal someplace up ahead. Well, I was wrong about that. And I figured maybe I'd want to take photos of something, and heck was I right about that.

I took some food and wrapped it up, and I took a couple bottles of water, big ones. And I had filled the gas tank up the day before when I'd done a run to town for Dolly and Sally, so I was all set.

Word was, you took the dirt turnpike past Detlef's, and you kept on to the far end, till you met White Deer Trail. I drove slow past the Dead Elf's place. Not too slow. But just right, thinking I didn't want to stop for talk. Not today. But he weren't home; the 1984 Mercedes was gone so Detlef was out being Detlef someplace.

At White Deer, I knew I had to take a dogleg and then there'd be a trail without a name on it, but with a juniper bush at the corner. Now this was the part that had me worried. It was Detlef who'd told me that and I might have told you that juniper bushes was like rabbits out here: plentiful and multiplying. But when I saw the bush, I knew it was the right one. It was by itself and bigger than most, and right on the corner of an unnamed trail, heading east and a little south.

So off I went. I felt a little bit like Voltaire. A veronaut. A seeker after the truth. Then I told myself I was being stupid, and exactly what truth it was I was looking for, well, I might've been confused about that. Mostly I wanted to know why Bly had

Polleux's name on that piece of paper, along with those lines from Voltaire's book. But I guess also, there was a tiny bit of me, that even after being sick for six years still thought it might be able to get well again. And that maybe Polleux would have the answers to that too.

Now, six years into my sickness, I was doing just fine. I could drive about town. I could spend a few hours reading each day. As long as I wore my mask in town, and ate good, and stayed away from normies smothered in chemicals. I could even walk a half a mile on a good day, without feeling terrible. But any more than that and I was done for. It didn't take much to push things over the edge, and then it would sneak up on me real quick, and everything would come back: the headaches, the rashes, the exhaustion. That was it, the simplicity of it, the damned tiredness. There's still no way to say just how that feels.

So you might think it was dumb to go out into that heat, and you'd be right.

It started out fine enough.

Pretty soon, along the unnamed trail, I came to a fading painted sign that said *private property: keep out* so I ignored that and not long after I got to the site of Polleux's house. His *old* house. They told me about this. This was the first place he'd built when he'd come to Snowflake. But he'd gotten worse when they'd built some power lines nearby, so that was that. He upped-sticks and headed out farther away from town, away from everyone. His old place was just setting there, empty, and unlike my phone and Bly's bottles and the ten thousand wiggling bits of plastic in my backyard, it looked truly dead.

I didn't stop, but I slowed the truck to a crawl and wound the window down for a look that wasn't covered in red dust. Two seconds of that and I put the window back up and cranked the AC a notch higher.

I think it was Finch who told me it was another twenty miles in from here, but I don't know if he'd ever been out here. I don't know if anyone had. Detlef had said how Polleux would come to town every month, maybe two, to stock up. How he spent the rest of his days in the deep.

I rolled on, and the track was okay to start with but soon got a mite rougher. I slowed down and notched up the AC and the desert emptied out around me. There was nothing. I swear, if I thought there was nothing at Mona's, I was lying. That place was a metropolis by comparison. The land was a mite more rolling, and way in the distance there was some low hills. I crossed a dried-out riverbed, and though I guessed in a month or three it would be full of monsoon water, it sure looked like it hadn't seen water since the dinosaurs crawled across what would one day and for a very brief time be called Arizona. It was only the first of many. I crossed dried streams in that old unnamed track, and even the junipers had given up trying. There was just that low scrubby grass here and there. A creosote bush. And nothing. And if any creature save me was stirring abroad that morning, they sure didn't make it plain. At some point I guess I left Navajo County and headed into

Apache County, but they don't paint lines on the sand, so I had no idea when that happened. It just did.

Now, what I hadn't seen was something I oughta have seen. I was getting tired, real quick, and I kept cranking up the AC until I realized it was getting hotter and hotter in the truck anyway. Pretty soon it was obvious the darned thing had gone and broke, and I was just pumping hot air into the cab. I shut it off and thought maybe it was better to open the windows. So I did, and that was the wrong thing to do. I lost the last of any air in the cab that wasn't over 90 and let in a whole bunch that was over 110, most likely.

So I tried to speed things up. I measured I'd made ten miles, getting on for fifteen, when steam started to come out of the hood of the truck. So I sped things up a bit more, and I don't know how much farther I got when there was a bang like someone had hit the engine with a hammer. A hammer that weighed a ton. The truck stopped and from under the hood there was a roar of steam and smoke and the smoke looked angry.

Then I saw a lick of flame and I grabbed one of the bottles of water and jumped out and about three seconds later the flames shot up through the vents on the hood like a dragon breathing fire.

I looked at it, hands on hips.

Then I said "yeah" and then I thought a bit more and said "screwit" which made me think of Finch and made me smile.

But I was starting to realize what a fix I was in.

I looked up the trail. Nothing. And I looked behind me

though I knew there was just nothing there too, because I'd just driven past it.

I started to walk. Towards where I hoped in hell Polleux's place was, because I guessed I was more than halfway, and it made no sense to turn back in that heat.

Please be good was what I was saying to my legs. Please be a good day. Please be okay. You can keep going.

That's how I was thinking to myself. Then I tried not thinking anything, just putting step after step, and trying to look at the desert and see what Jenny saw in it, which I don't know I'd ever managed to do. And yeah, there was plenty of times when she'd say to me ain't the desert beautiful and I would agree, but I was white lying. The desert was not beautiful, it was terrifying in ways I could not number.

Still, I walked and I tried to think like Jenny and I wondered what Polleux would be like and I tried not to think what might happen if this was the one day in a million he went to town.

And I walked and I started to feel the sun burning my face. So I pulled up that faded red T-shirt and put it over my head until I could feel my back burning and then I pulled it down again. I drank some of the water, and some more, and I kept on going and I just thought if only there was one place of shade I could set for a bit, but there was nothing and the sun kept on and very soon my legs announced that they had had enough. Little pains started popping up here and there, and that was always a sure sign they was done. They was getting stiffer and harder to move, just like when you walk through the molasses at the beach, and I started to stagger forwards.

I gotta stop, I said, so I did. I set on the burning sand and took a drink till the sand started burning through my jeans and then I got up and tried to go on and I had gone about I don't know how far when I realized I'd left the water behind and then I knew I was starting not to think right.

Then there was a bang behind me, and I turned and there was a fireball rising over the ridge, probably just about where my truck had once been.

I kept trying to move and had to stop sometimes, and my legs were screaming but my head would not let them stop. And on I went, little by little, and then, though it was getting hard to see with all the sweat stinging my eyes, I saw a building ahead of me.

At least, I thought so. It was a ways off, in the heat haze, shimmering and maybe it wasn't real, but it didn't take many more steps to see it was real. A house, low, and not far beyond it, a rise in the landscape, the escarpment starting to rise. Seeing the house, it brought some more energy out of somewhere, and I knew I was gonna make it. I kept on and inched towards that place, and then I saw something that I thought was gonna make me throw up.

The house was derelict. Not derelict, but I mean, it had never been finished. It was half-built, with the skeleton of wood for the walls, and a wall or two here, but no roof. Not one bit of a roof.

"Well, now you're gonna die," I said out loud. Then I thought about that a bit and said "screwit" but this time I did not smile, and then I said I wonder what will happen next.

I must've crawled the last few feet to the house and I thought, there's gotta be some shade around here, even with no roof, but the sun was way high and I could only find a tiny sliver of a shadow by one wall. So I set myself there and laid down and waited to die and even then I knew that dying of thirst and heat is a real bad way to go.

I shut my eyes and waited and thought about Bly.

Then I heard a voice and it said, "Who the hell are you?"

I looked up and squinted and all I could see was the outline of a man with the sun behind him and I said, "I'm the Snowflake. Who are you?" and the voice said, "I'm Polleux. The Great and Terrible."

I had heatstroke. That was what Polleux told me later. I thought I was dying, but he said the headaches and the vomiting and all that stuff was from heatstroke. But first thing was, I woke up, and I had no idea where I was.

I had more or less passed out and I didn't remember anything after seeing Polleux standing over me in the half-built house. I woke up and I was lying on a couch in a small, dark room. It was cool, it smelt like it might be damp, and that was not something I was expecting.

There was a glass of water by the couch and Polleux nodded at me and said to drink some, if I could. He was set on a chair a little ways off. My head banged if I moved it and it throbbed even if I didn't. But I had to see where I was.

"Just rest, kid," Polleux said. "Sleep it off. I've put aloe on your burns. You'll be just fine."

There was a big plant in a pot on the floor, with fat and spiky leaves and some of 'em was broken and I saw the thick juice inside and I put my hand to my face and it was slimy, but it felt okay. So I slept again.

Next time I woke, he wasn't there. I got a mite panicky. I set up on the couch and my head didn't bang so much, and then I saw what I thought I was dreaming before. I thought I was dreaming that I was in a cave. But I was, I really was. Only it was a regular kind of cave, with flat walls, straight, and even the floor was flat. It was hard to see at first because it was dark. There were no windows, just a little light coming from an open door.

I put my feet on the floor and it was cool, cool rock. I couldn't see my shoes, but I know they weren't on my feet, because I remember how good it felt to walk on that cool rock, in bare feet. And I suddenly thought I oughta be sunburned all to heck but I felt my skin and it was fine and so I guess that was the aloe, worked better than anything you could buy in a plastic bottle. And probably didn't make you a meaner human being.

I pushed the door open and saw a bigger room. Another cave, still with regular walls. But this one had light. There was a shaft, square and regular, in the roof, heading up and it was pouring light down, and under the shaft it was bright, but it grew dark off in the corners, so I didn't see Polleux setting there in a corner, in a chair, and a book in his hands, and it reminded me of the day Mona caught me out the same way.

"Feeling okay?" he said and he put his book down and came over. I knew he had to be old, but he didn't look so old. He'd been out in the desert for over thirty years, that's what they said. And all the canaries who'd come after him, well that was down to him, and Mona, I guess. He wasn't what I was expecting, but then, I don't know what I was expecting. I guess I had been expecting something kinda extreme. In my head, that stuff Mona had said, "the great and terrible" had kinda grown. And hadn't he said that too, when he found me? I wasn't sure what that was all for then, but later I found it was some kinda joke between them, Mona and Polleux. When they was friends. Not that they weren't friends no more. They just never saw each other much.

So, Polleux, he didn't look like a big deal, but then, who does? And those people that do look like something, well, ain't it the case that nineteen times out of twenty there ain't anything so great on the inside? That's my experience. And it's my experience that what's most interesting about people is what's on the inside, not the outside. And Polleux? Boy, was there some stuff on the inside.

"You're Ash," he said and when I gave him a look he said, "There aren't so many people out here. Besides. That was Bly's truck you came in."

"You found the truck?"

"That's how I found you. Column of black smoke a mile high. Came to see what's what. I found you."

"Oh," I said.

"I'm afraid the truck is probably a goner," he said. "But it saved you. Without that smoke, I wouldn't have come out. Too hot out there. Right?"

"Uh-huh," I said, and he was right, I knew I'd been dumb to go out when the mercury was rising in the one-teens. And then I realized just how cool it was in this place.

"You live here?" I asked, which was one of the dumber questions of the twenty-first century, but Polleux shrugged and I wondered if he was the goat that started that whole thing. Passed it on to everyone else, like some kinda virus maybe.

"I was halfway through building my new place. The house you found. And I was jumping through all the hoops of building an EI safe place to live, and figuring out how to keep it cool without using AC. And one day I took a break and I walked a hundred yards away to where the escarpment starts. I knew there were old caves here, small caves. I sat in one and thought about how to keep my house cool and then I realized it was already cooler just a few feet into the cave. So I quit work on the house and I bought the whole hillside and I dug my house out of the ground."

"Oh," I said. "Yeah. Good idea."

So you can see I was making great conversation, but I guess I had nearly died. And yeah, I thought, he did just say he bought the whole damn hill, like I might say I bought a whole quart of milk.

"Where's that go?" I said and pointed a finger at the light shaft.

"Up," he said and I felt even dumber. But he weren't finished. "There was a small network of caves. I dug further into the hill, and where the surface wasn't too far up, I sunk some light wells into certain rooms in the house. Otherwise, the only windows are in the front, which is where I was yesterday when I saw your smoke signal."

"Oh, right," I said, then I said, "Wait, what? Yesterday?"

"You slept it off."

"Yesterday? I oughta let Mona know I'm okay. Heck, she'll be worried about me."

"Already taken care of."

"You have a phone out here?"

"No. But I have a satellite phone I can get up and running in emergencies. Never used it. It's good to know it works. I told her I'd see you're okay."

"Uh, thank you," I said and though he was saying the right things, somehow I got the feeling he wasn't too used to having houseguests, and wasn't too pleased about it neither.

"Well, I better be getting away," I said and he didn't say anything to that 'cept "maybe you need something to eat? Hungry? I promised Mona I'd see you're okay. When you're ready she can come out and get you. I'm not due to go to town for another week or so. I guess I could make an exception."

"Mr. Polleux," I said, "I'm real sorry to barge in on you, but——"

He waved a hand, and it was plain he really wasn't pleased, but he wasn't gonna come out and say it.

"What do you eat? Eggs?"

And I said eggs was just fine and thank you, but what I really wanted to do was ask why Bly had his name on a piece of paper along with those things from the book by Voltaire, and I wanted to ask this before he got tired of me and drove me home.

So he took me out into the kitchen and that was one of the

rooms that was at the front of the hillside and it had a window that was about ten feet wide and three feet high. And five feet deep, through the rock. Through it, it was like looking at a painting of the Arizona desert. It was so still out there, and nothing moved, save the heat haze flickering in the air just above the ground.

There was his half-built house, a hundred yards away, just like he'd said, and beyond it, nothing. I thought maybe I'd see the smoke from the truck still rising, but that was foolish. It was all over now.

While Polleux made the eggs, I nosed about the room, which was even bigger than the one before. There were doors going off here and there and I could see it was a maze. A warren, but for a man and not for jackrabbits. There was wooden entryways, leading out, and you could see how he'd joined the wood into the rock to make a place to set a doorway, which was heavy and thick, and then I felt both scared and protected at the same time.

"This place is some kind of fortress, huh?" I said, and Polleux nodded. He said, "It's very practical. If I want another room, I dig it out of the hillside," but he didn't smile or nothing and I really, really could see he didn't like me being there.

And then that all changed. It all changed in a moment. And that happened like this.

First, I was eating my eggs.

And I thought, if he's gonna put me in his truck and drive me back right after, I better take my chance. He'd recognized Bly's truck.

"You met my brother?" I said, and he nodded.

"Good kid."

"You knew him well?"

"Not really. I ran into him a few times. In town, with Mona, mostly."

"He ever come out here?"

"Uh-huh. He came out here to ask if I knew how to make him well again."

And I said "oh" because I guess we both knew how that turned out.

"He thought I could help him," Polleux said. "And I wondered if he could help me too, with something. He came out a few times. But then he left. . . ."

So I finally knew where Bly had gotten to those times he went missing, and it felt like another secret between us. Then, and I was feeling kinda extra dumb, but I said it anyway.

"Uh. Did you tell him about Voltaire? About that book, *Candide?*"

Now I could not tell what Polleux was thinking. There was nothing on his face. Nothing you could read, at all. But finally he said, "Yeah. I think I might have. It was a long time ago."

He stopped his fussing with the empty egg pan and came and sat at the table with me.

"That would have been Mona's fault, anyway. She got me into the classics. Like I got her into science."

"That was you? Like her thing with bacteria? You did that?"

Polleux nodded.

"Yeah, that would have been me. Did she get carried away? That's so Mona. I bumped into her in town one day and we were talking about the government and I think for fun I told her that people don't rule the world—"

"—bacteria do! Right?" I said, and Polleux looked at me different. But he still was being cagey, even then. It was what happened after. He was still talking, which was better than the silences before.

"So I guess I was obsessed with Voltaire for a while. Obsession is a trait I share with Mona. And yes, I remember talking to your brother about it."

So then I took another chance of really pissing him off.

"That thing about gardens? Why do you think he wrote that down?"

"Il faut cultiver notre jardin," he said and he said it in a real French voice, not like when Mona said it, or me, and I said, "Are you French? Your name's French, ain't it?"

"No. A long way back on my father's side, they say."

"Oh. Uh-huh," I said. And then I have no idea why I said it, but something popped into my mouth and this was the thing that changed everything. What I said was, "You know, ain't it funny? The way you told Mona something and she told you something and she told me something too and you both told Bly things, things that he told me. It's like everyone's infecting everyone else. But with ideas, right?"

Then Polleux was looking at me different, for sure. But he said nothing, 'cept "go on."

So then I had to.

"This is probably just me being dumb and talking without knowing anything. But like Mona was obsessed with her bacteria. For ever. But around then, something got me reading about kindness. You know, how some people do good things for others? Altruism?"

"I know what altruism is, Ash," he said and I said, "Of course you do. Of course you do. What I mean is, Mona told me about how antibiotics are probably the real cause behind a whole lot of sickness and stuff. Like depression and obesity and ADHD and autism and all."

"And?"

"And I wondered whether they might be behind people being meaner to each other too."

Then Polleux looked at me, real hard, and I thought he was angry and that he was so mad he might start shouting but that weren't it at all.

He said, "But people have always been mean to each other. So how does your theory fit with that fact?"

"Oh," I said. "Yeah, you see, I told you I had no idea what I was talking about. Sorry."

Then he put his hand up, and closed his eyes for a second, and then waved his hand from side to side, like he was rubbing out what I'd just said, in the air.

"Did you know that several long-term meta-studies have proven that people are less altruistic than they were forty or fifty years ago?"

And I said, no, I did not know that. And nor did I know what a long-term meta-study was. But that didn't matter. I got the general idea.

"And did you know," he went on, "that in one study, college students were shown to be more selfish and less altruistic by as much as thirty-five percent, compared with just thirty years ago?"

And I said, no, I did not know that either.

Then there was a silence for a real long time, and now I could see he wasn't mad. He was thinking about something, and at the end of the thinking he said, "Ash. I guess you're really tired. Would you like to stay here for a few days, until you're stronger again? We could talk about things. Things like that. If you're interested."

And I thought about it, and thought, well, what do I gotta lose? And what do I have to go back to, 'cept an empty house and the sound of a goat humping a Suzuki every night? So I said yes, that would be swell. For a few days.

And Polleux smiled and a million wrinkles spread out across his face when he did, and then I think he might have said, "Good. Because it's time to tend the garden."

And those few days, out there in the deep? They was the end of times, and though time don't really mean so much anymore, I will always remember those days, like they're precious. I guess we all feel that now. You do too, I guess. About those days, your last days, before the volcano we'd been standing on erupted, before the ground gave way under our feet, before What Happened happened. They was our last days, but you know, whatever yours was like, can't no one ever take 'em away from you.

XEROTIC FICTION

Polleux was a scientist. I mean, before he got sick, he'd been a scientist. And he still was, he'd just changed the nature of the science he was practicing. And I guess he was the richest man I ever met, maybe anyone ever met. You remember back then, how everyone had a computer, or three? How everyone even had a computer in their hands all the time? Smartphones. Or as Mona used to call 'em, dumbphones, because that's how people looked using 'em. So Polleux just let slip one time how, back when downloading music started, he'd written a few lines of code that made sure it all worked as it was supposed to. And he'd been smart because he had a tiny little patent on those tiny little lines of code, and every darn time someone streamed some music, or a film, well, about a tenth of a tenth of a cent would end up in his bank account.

"The money still seems to be coming in," he said. "Last time I looked." And when I asked when that was, he said, "Recently. A few years ago. I suppose."

Then he got sick, like the rest of us.

But he was smart and he was rich, and what those two things meant was a) he figured out what was wrong quick, and b) he could do something about it. So he bought a patch of land in the desert in Arizona and built a house that was well away from the power lines. And when they put more power lines up, he moved out here and built half a house and then gave that one up and dug into the rock.

"I should take that down," he said one day, looking at his old place out of the big window in the kitchen. And I had wondered that, because it couldn't have been for the cost of doing it. No, he said, he hadn't taken it down because it was *a reminder of our foolish optimism*. That's what he said. And I said nothing, because what do you say to that?

Our foolish optimism.

Anyway, he'd built his new house into the side of the hill, and I had no idea how he did that. I guess he paid a lot of people, because even living out in the deep, he was still sick. Not a strong man.

Like he said, if he needed more room, well, he just dug deeper into his hill. He showed me how there was a system of fans to move the air about in the furthest rooms.

"Gets a bit stale otherwise," he said, and when I started wondering about power he told me how the whole place was on DC, just like Detlef's getup, and how all the power came from a hundred million miles away, by which he meant the sun. And on the hill above the house there was a stack of solar panels *made to my own design, I might add*, because they were better than the ones you could buy.

And if you think living in a cave was unpleasant, well, you'd be wrong. You might think different, but what I meant was, a cave was not unpleasant, not if John Polleux had made it. It was cool in the summer and it was easy to warm in the winter. It was quiet, and he had everything you could want in there. And he had rooms for this and rooms for that and some were for being practical like a room full of the batteries for the solar panels and others were for being beautiful like the library, his one room full of books. The shelves were made of beautiful dark wood, and there were little lamps here and there so it felt real cozy, and the floor was covered in fancy rugs, dark red and black, and it had a big leather armchair with a little table next to it where you set your bourbon while you read and thought about the finer things in life.

Then there were the labs. Three of 'em. Big dark places lit by little bright spotlights where he did his science. Full of stuff that was who knew what? To do whatever new kind of science he was doing. To start with, I didn't go in there. He just showed 'em to me and that was that, and when I said what are you working on, he smiled and said this and that, this and that.

Now, I had no idea what this old guy wanted with me in his house, and if you're thinking, oh Ash, you were such a naïve little snowflake, then let me tell you, it weren't anything like that. He was a gentleman, John Polleux. And we spoke about all sorts of odd things. Things like Voltaire and his book. He even gave me a copy to read and I started it though I didn't get much further than the first few pages. Or things like this: one day, as I filled a jug with water for us to have at lunch, I said, "Huh, you have your own well I guess."

Now, Mona had a well too, that was where her water came

from, but Polleux said how it was a mite harder to get a well dug out here, because he was higher up and the water table was lower down underground.

"But it's amazing," I said. "You have the sun for power and you have your own water. You don't need nothing from no one."

Now we had been getting ready to eat and Polleux was fussing in the kitchen like he always fussed when he had to do something hard, such as cook. But when I said that last part he stopped right then and there and he said to me this:

"Well, first of all, I might need some food once in a while. And I do not grow my own food. I considered it, but it would take too much of my time and too much of my energy and I need those two things for other matters. Other matters which are more pressing. You understand?"

And I nodded, quick, because boy was he being serious all of a sudden.

"And second of all, the sunshine is not mine. Even though I harness it. And the water is, for sure, also not mine."

"But it's on your land."

"My land?" he said. "*My* land. What a curious expression that is! Shall we talk about bacteria again?" and I could kinda see what he meant and I was kinda confused as heck too.

"The water table under our feet in this place known as Arizona spreads from New Mexico in the east to California in the west. It is estimated that in the last century it has lost maybe 150 cubic kilometers in volume."

"Oh," I said. "Uh-huh. Where'd the water go?"

"You know the answer to that."

"People?" I said. "Farming? Towns, cities? Watering the cemetery?"

"That's the general idea. People. And . . . ?

"Money?"

"Money," he said and snapped his fingers. "That's it. I see Mona Mochsky has taught you well. People don't stop to think whether something is a good idea, as long as there's money to be made."

"I guess," I said. "You hear about that guy wants to build a new smart city in the desert, west of Phoenix?"

"I did indeed. In a place where the water is running out."

Then we sat down and we started to eat and it was the usual thing he made which was eggs, and while we ate he told me about water. He told me about how it was running out, and fast. Because of the demand for it. And how the world warming up was only gonna make that worse. And even in places where there was water, he told me about places like Glendive, Montana, where a company called Bridger Pipeline spilled 30,000 gallons of crude oil into the Yellowstone River and how the benzene had gotten into the drinking water and was making people sick, and about how two companies called Saint-Gobain and Honeywell had polluted the Hoosic River in upstate New York and how the local people were getting cancer and other stuff and dying, and about how the United Nuclear Corporation let 1,000 tons of radioactive waste and 93 million gallons of acidic radioactive effluent into the Puerco River at Church Rock, New Mexico. Just about a hundred and fifty miles from where we set that lunchtime. Eating eggs. And how that radioactive waste, on top of all the other uranium mines thereabouts, caused sickness and disease and death in the Navajo, but how the scientists and the government told 'em it was because of a *genetic tendency* and nothing to do with the radioactive shit they was drinking and washing in.

"So, you tell me, Ash. Whose water is it?"

And I had no answer to that one. Save it was everyone's. Or no one's. Probably no one's.

"Do you know what a zanjero is?" he asked, and so for about the hundredth time since I'd met Polleux I had to say "no, I do not" and feel dumb.

"A dying art. Perhaps a lost one. This part of the world has been dry for a long time. They used irrigation canals in days gone by, to make the land fertile and bring water to where it needed to be. And it was a fine art, and it took clever men to control the flow of water across the land, to care for those canals. They were called zanjeros. And it wasn't just the men. Being a zanjero was a family business. The husbands rode horses, caring for the water, and the wives stayed home to take orders for deliveries, to do the bookkeeping, fix problems, and so on."

"Zanjero, huh?"

"Spanish for ditch rider. First they rode their horses. Then they rode their trucks. And they cared for the water. They even cared for people. They were sworn in as peacekeepers and would settle disputes between neighbors. It was a real important job. But those days are gone."

He went and fished around and came back with a magazine. A real old magazine. It had the date 1902 on the front and it was called *Century*. He flicked through it and showed me an article he'd found about the zanjero. I remember it still. Word for word. Polleux read it out to me, like it was poetry.

" 'The zanjero. He is the yea and nay of the arid land, the arbiter of fate, the dispenser of good and evil, to be blessed by turns and cursed by turns, and to receive both with the utter unconcern of a small god.' "

Then he laughed and I didn't see anything so funny to be laughing at and he said that he'd read a few books over the years, storybooks about the end of the world and a few that was about the world flooding. I'd read one or two like that myself.

"Foolish books," he said.

But then he said maybe that was unfair. Because they was kinda right and kinda wrong, because yep, the seas will rise, but long before that, finding anything fit to drink on the dry land is gonna be a real big problem.

"Once upon a time I thought I ought to be one of those rare scientists who write a novel. Mona would approve, I think. It would have been about the abnormally drying world, and it would have been written to amuse a small number of men of wit. It would have been the start of a whole new genre. Xerotic fiction!" he said and laughed at himself, and I laughed too but I didn't get the joke until I looked it up in a dictionary in the library later on that night. Then I had a real good old chuckle to myself. (I'm funning you about that last part. It just turns out *xeros* is Greek for "dry.")

Polleux had gone to bed. He always went to bed early and woke early, while I was the other way around. He'd made up a storeroom for me to sleep in and it was just fine. It was better than a porch, or a shed, or even a cabin. I lay there thinking things. I admitted something to myself that I had been thinking for a while: that I would have to sell my house. Jenny's place. It might have cost me a dollar to buy it but there was more to a house than just that. You had to pay for the electricity and there was taxes to be considered and all I had been earning was the few dollars Mona gave me for driving people's groceries around the desert. In a truck I no longer had. And then I thought that if I sold the house the money shouldn't be mine and I oughta give it to Steve and if he didn't want it I oughta give it to charity. And I thought maybe there was a charity that gives help to folks with MCS because the government sure weren't doing nothing to help those folks, folks like that, who'd gotten sick through no fault of their own and didn't have the insurance to pay for it. Because they couldn't afford insurance in the first place. Because of the way the damn government had it all set up with the gods of the land of Pharma.

And I thought about what Polleux had said about writing his xerotic novel and all. I asked him why he didn't do it and he said because he had more important things to do. And then I wondered what those things were, but it wasn't long before I found out, and that's when things got truly weird.

YES, THERE IS A THING CALLED SCIENCE AND IT CAN GIVE YOU ANSWERS

So at first of course I figured that Polleux was trying to figure out how to cure people of MCS and electrical sensitivity. That that was what he was up to in those three dark labs of his. But I soon found out that he'd given up on that one long ago.

"I get by," he said. "Just like you. And the canaries. Now I live out here, in this safe place, I'm ok. Of course, it means I'm not fit to go back to flatland, but I suppose that flatland is overrated anyway."

I think he was funning about that one. Maybe.

"And anyway, if I found a cure of some kind for MCS, well that would just mean I'd found a way to make people cope with living with things that are bad for them, that are toxic, and so on and so on. And what is the point of that? None. In my opinion. Instead, we have to find a way to stop these things happening in the first place."

And when I said, "What things?" he said, "Why, Ash, the bad of the world." And when I asked what he meant by that, he said, and this time I heard him for sure when he said, "Ash, it's time to tend the garden" and then he kinda clammed right up.

We were sitting in one of his labs one day and it was the one with the mice. Now the mice were cute and there were a lot of 'em and they were in cages and some were running around in little maze-like things and some were in pairs and some were alone and he said it was all part of his plan and you won't be surprised if I tell you I started to wonder if all was right with what was inside Polleux's head right then. But he was an easy man to underestimate, that John Polleux. Sure he looked old and frail and a bit sick when he'd been to town, but he was not a man to underestimate.

The mice were running around the mazes on the big table-tops of the lab, or they set nibbling or standing up sniffing the air, and I felt a bit sorry for them, because they sure were cute. Then I thought, why do I only feel sorry for 'em because they're cute? What if they was ugly critters? Shouldn't I feel the same if they was ugly?

And Polleux had just told me how he didn't want to cure MCS.

"Not anymore," he said.

"But you did once?"

"Sure I did. Who wouldn't? To be sick with a long-term illness is not something most people understand. Not until it happens to them. And when it does, it changes the way you see life. Do you not agree?"

And I said, yes, I did agree, and I told him how Mona had told me I would learn to be someone else.

I thought about something Detlef had said to me one day, way back, about how, before you get sick, you just don't have your eyes open. And once you do, once you realize how fragile we are, then everything looks different. You start thinking crazy things, like how, if you stopped breathing for just thirty seconds or a minute you'd be dead, but you never think about it. Not until you get sensitive, which is to say, not until you get sick. And then everything becomes super precious. Even something as simple as a sunrise and a hummingbird. Even a dumb goat. Even a faded red T-shirt.

"Indeed," he said. "But that's not to say that you don't want to get better. Desperately. So for a while, I tried to figure it out, but I admit it was beyond me. You know what they say about MCS? How does it go? At first you're afraid you'll die. Then you're afraid you won't. Right?"

"Uh-huh," I said.

"Well, finally, something else happens. Finally, you're not afraid at all." He smiled at me. "If you get that far . . ."

And then I knew he was thinking about Bly and I said that thing that Mona said that Dostoyevsky, 1821 to 1881, said about a man being a creature who can get used to anything.

"Sadly, this is not always true," Polleux said. "You know, one night, when I was first ill, I mean a year or two into it, and still with no idea why, I went to bed every night and hoped not to wake up in the morning. Every night it was the same, but then, one night, I wondered about God."

"Him?" I said.

Polleux laughed.

"Or Her. Anyway, you should know I am a scientist. I have

been a confirmed atheist as soon as I got to the age of nine and could see that belief in supernatural beings is no less stupid than belief in the tooth fairy. And yet, that one night, I was so desperate, so desperate, so I tried looking out into the dark to see if God was there and if He would help. And I prayed and you know, I felt something come into me. I cannot explain what, but I felt relief, comfort, and that night I knew that God was going to make me better."

"And did He? Or She?"

"He or She did not. By the time I woke up the following morning that momentary feeling of relief had gone. And I was still as sick as a dog and I knew that the only answers would come from the reason of mankind. From science. But I saw for one hour of my life how powerful it is to have faith in some great being looking after you."

"So you still don't believe in God?"

Polleux waved at the mice.

"Do these fellows believe in God? Am I their god? I can decide if they live or die, what happens to them. But do they know I exist?"

"Uh," I said. "I don't get it."

"My point is that I could just about believe in an Old Testament kind of god. The one who punishes wickedness and sends you to hell if you're bad. But who'll protect you if you do what he wants. That all makes sense. Horrible sense, but it makes sense. But a New Testament kind of god? Jesus and Mary and so on? No. An all-loving, all-powerful God is a contradiction in terms."

"How's that?"

"Well, for example. You recall we spoke about Voltaire's Candide?"

I did. We had talked about it a lot in my first days with Polleux, since it was what had brought me there.

"You recall the episode with the Lisbon earthquake? Voltaire put that real-life event in the book for a very good reason. It shook people's faith greatly. That if there was a God, and of course almost no one doubted it in those days, that He could let such a thing happen. Or even cause it. And what made it worse was that it happened on November the first. All Soul's Day. A holy day, when more people than usual were in the city and were attending masses. Many people were crushed inside the collapsing churches. Now, Ash, I can understand an Old-Testament-you-sinned-and-so-I'll-send-a-flood kind of god doing that. But not an all-loving, all-powerful one."

"Huh," I said. Which was more or less the smartest thing I said that day.

So Polleux, he said he would pay me to be his assistant. And I said, yeah, but I ain't staying long, and he said, well, that's ok. Maybe I could come out and see him sometimes. He said that mostly he would need help meant playing with mice. Even if I didn't know what they were doing, it was fine by me. And those mice, they sure were cute, and they sure were ignorant of their god.

A few days later, Polleux went to town to get his supplies, and so I went for the ride and he dropped me off at Mona's.

We rode out, like zanjeros across the xerotic landscape, and we passed Bly's burned-out truck.

"Jeez," I said. "Would you look at that?"

It was a black and burned-out lump of metal and looked like hell.

"We'll have to get it towed," Polleux said, as he drove off the track and around it. But we never did. It sat there, and I'm guessing it still sits there.

Mona was getting along okay.

It was great to see her and I gave her a big hug and she said don't squash me, I'm only little. And she said are you okay and I told her about the mice and the truck and all.

"How's things?" I said and she didn't say anything much. She kinda smiled but I could see her heart wasn't in it.

"You okay?" I said again and she nodded and said maybe she could make some tea and then I said, "Where's Cooper at?" and then Mona said, "Oh, Ash" and she started crying so then I knew Cooper was gone.

She wiped herself up and said, "He did good. He did real good. He was one old mutt. But now it's just me and the goat."

I felt bad and said I oughta come back to be with Mona, but when I told her about staying with Polleux a while she said I oughta do that. She said I had to do my own thing and follow my own path and that path had taken me to Polleux. And that was okay.

"As long as you drop in and see me," she said. "You gotta promise!"

And though she was smiling I could tell there was something else, something underneath.

So I said, "Mona, you really okay?" and she waved a hand and said sure.

"It's just all this stuff in the news," she said and I said "what?" and then she looked all surprised and said "you don't know?" and just the way she said that scared me somehow.

"Ash," she said. "Wake up! You gotta read the papers. You gotta pay attention! Wake up!"

I did not wake up. Not then. But it was not to be long.

ZANJERO

We are all a product of what came before us. A mongrel product, that is. We are this person and that person; we are the brothers we chased across the great nation for, the mothers who never really wanted us, and the fathers we never knew. We are Jack's mean Aunt Zelda and we are our good and honest brother Bly and we are also 4 percent of a Neanderthal cave-kid. But most of who I came to be was down to those years with Mona. She was who I came to be, after I'd finished being Bly. Heck, even the way I speak now. The way I think. Well, that's Mona, not much more nor less. And Mona was what kept me going through the days that were to come.

A little of Polleux rubbed off on me too, in that short time we had together. Stephanie had been right. Well, sorta. Some of the answers were out there in the desert, with Polleux. Just not the ones I wanted. But I played with the mice and slowly, bit by bit, I started to learn what it was he intended to do. And when I understood, well, then I knew for sure he had lost his crazy mind, living out there, all alone in the deep desert for thirty-odd years till I rolled into town.

There was still a war going on. Inside me. For whether I wanted to live or not. The war that Bly had lost. But like Mona had warned me, there were other things going on, things in the real world that I was paying no attention to. And I ain't gonna dwell on that now, because, heck, we all know what came around the corner, and in the end, how fast it came, as we stood on the side of that volcano, me with my mice and Polleux with his bacteria.

For that was what he was really up to.

Bacteria. And it went like this:

It seemed that the reason he'd decided to take me in, well, it was that thing I'd said, about how I'd gotten obsessed with the question of altruism. Of being kind, of doing good for others. Not just the ones in your in-group, but strangers too.

And Polleux explained to me how he felt that this was where the world had gone wrong. That too many people were selfish, and too few were generous with their kindness. And I agreed with that, but then Polleux said something else.

"Now, what is the most pressing matter in the world? What kind of altruism do we need more of, if we are to survive?"

"Well, I am sure I have no idea," I said, and Polleux wasn't in a mood for guessing. So he told me.

"We need to be altruistic towards the future," he said and then I was lost. But he said, "Think about it. All the problems we have discussed, such as things with water, or the climate, or pollution. They are all a result of people wanting money and ease in the short term at the expense of any consequences that might arise down the line. Right? So what we need to do is make people altruistic towards the future, to their great-great-great grandchildren. And to the great-great-great grandchildren of others."

And I said, "Yeah, that seems right," but when he told me how he planned to do it, I knew he was crazy as a coot.

"I am breeding a variety of bacteria that will have two essential properties. First, it will be ridiculously infectious. It will spread with the simplest human contact. I estimate it should take no more than a few years to infect the entire world's population, save for a few remote and outlying areas. Second, it will cause a polymorphic response in a particular length of a certain gene, and anyone thus infected will become fabulously altruistic. It will depend in part on the particular genes of each individual, but the result even in the most modest cases should be enough to turn a sinner into a saint. So to speak."

So then I knew Polleux was crazy. And I also knew I was crazy to be living in a cave twenty miles from anywhere with a total loon. He seemed harmless, but all of a sudden I felt a very long way from home. Not only that, I realized I had no idea where home actually was. I figured I'd only felt at home for one damn night in my whole life, in a small shed in the desert, and that was all lost now, it could not be reclaimed.

"All I need," Polleux said, "is some final tests. And a vector."

And I was about to ask what a vector was, but I never got the chance, because there was a knock at the door and it was Detlef and his Icon Gold Mercedes.

And he was the one who told us.

Mona had told me to wake up. And maybe I had been dreaming, for all those years, and what I woke up to was that the volcano we'd all been living on, well, it had gone off. Erupted, and it felt like out of the blue, but looking back, we can't say we wasn't warned. There was enough folks talking about it, but we was too busy to notice. That or scared. And enough people were talking but too many people weren't listening and the real dumb part? The real dumb part was that, back then, there was still time to do something about it. We could've stopped it all, if only we'd all made just a little effort. It wouldn't have been so very hard for things to have turned out different. But that's what they call wishful thinking, right? When it's too late to do anything.

O eager little scout of the world's adventures! What was I to do then? More than ever I knew I needed to be home, but like I just said, where was home? Snowflake? Maybe. It had felt that way once. But the world had changed. Mona had told me to follow my own path and it was Mona who told me I oughta go back and find my family. Such as it was. The moment she said that, I knew she was right. I had to be back with my tribe. My in-group. But I knew that wasn't my real mother, even if I could have found her, for no one knew where she was at. My story had ended with her long before, that day I'd pulled out my phone and felt nothing but a little sorry for her. Instead, I thought of Jack, and his new Suzanne, and I knew that was where I needed to be, even if it meant I would be sicker. So with the help of Polleux and his satellite phone that was only for emergencies, I made my plans to return to flatland, undiagnosis and all. I had my mask and that would have to do.

O eager little scout of the world's adventures! Yes, I can still see what a fine and shiny kid I was, I was, even then. From here, all these years later, you know I can still see all the way back to that bright and chomping child, that glittering and earnest kid, eyes wide open at the world and happily waiting for what the world would throw at me.

And you know what it threw. Now, yes, you know as well as I do, there's a little tiredness in all our bones, in all our bones, but never mind that, because that don't matter and I wonder, oh, where have I yet to go?

I find I cannot imagine.

Still, one thing comes back to me.

The day Jack made it out into the deep desert, to collect me from John Polleux's house. It had taken him longer than we thought, on account of the police everywhere and the army trucks mobilized and that thing they called the *civil unrest*, as not just the great nation but all the rest of 'em collapsed. Just ceased to be, overnight. As far as bacteria would judge the time elapsed, that is.

This was way early on. It was before the real shit took place. And the days were long and empty and the land was still beautiful. The calm days, days of blue sky and sun only served as eerie threats of the howling to come. No day from then on was without fear.

This was about the time them stories went around, like

that one about the president. How she'd tried to offer her four bodyguards a million dollars each to get her out on a Secret Service helicopter, but they'd already realized that a) you can't eat money and b) there was nowhere to run to. Not that really made any great difference. That was the end of the president.

And all was not for the best in the best of all possible worlds. In the end, we all learned that. And we all learned why, in the end. I guess we all learned it someplace different. The place I learned it was Snowflake.

So Jack arrived that day and he and Polleux nodded grimly at each other and we left, but just before we went, Polleux came out of the house and gave me some stuff for the journey. Some food, wrapped up. And a bottle of water. And even then something tickled at the back of my mind that one little bottle of water wasn't gonna get me and Jack very far. And over the years, I have come to think that wasn't the point of that bottle. That the point of that bottle was something else. That it had something to do with being the zanjero. Every time I think of that day, I hear Polleux's old soft voice saying, "Ash, it's time to tend the garden."

Then Polleux sent me out into the best of all possible worlds, and Jack and I made one stop at Mona's for me to say goodbye and I couldn't say the words, I could only hold her and cry while she told me it was all gonna be okay, and then we, I mean Jack and me, we vectored back home. And? Well, we made the best of it. Just like you did.

But still, I wonder back to the deep desert, and I wonder what happened to Mona and Finch and Detlef and the others. I wonder what happened to Socrates. I wonder if there are still ten thousand plastic figures dancing their asses off in the sunshine. I bet there are, Jenny Krazy-Glued 'em down real good. And I wonder what happened to the mice. Because I wonder whether Polleux is still alive and I tell myself, no, he can't be, that was years ago and he was an old man even then. He couldn't still be alive, out there in the desert, making his mad plans to save the world. But I like to think he is. And now I am old too. Old and, well, did I get better? Like I said to you an age ago, that depends on what exactly you mean by better. Don't it? And anyway, it really don't mean much anymore anyhow, not the way things became, and the real important thing is that we're still here.

And still learning.

You know, just the other day as I sat on my plastic barrel on line at the water pump, I thought, huh, Ash, maybe you was a snowflake, but so was we all. Every last one of us. We were all as fragile as a tiny crystal of ice. And then I thought, but yeah, you put a lot of snowflakes together and what have you got? You got an avalanche. And they tell me that avalanches were real powerful, not fragile at all. And then I thought, hell, there was probably a moment, one last moment in our history, when we coulda all come together, and we coulda been that avalanche, and roared. We coulda changed the world.

And I realized that had already happened once in our history. Remember how we're all descended from that one woman, Eve? How there was just one small family of us left, and in great peril? We musta come together then, and made an avalanche, and we changed the world.

But second time around, we missed that chance. We simply didn't see it coming. We were too many of us, or we were too busy, or we weren't paying attention, or we were just too darn optimistic to believe that our world would end. But it did.

And yet, still, still, maybe there's time for one final chance, those of us who're left: all of us still eager little scouts, staring out into the world, wondering what will happen next. And we was dumb, we was certainly dumb, and I guess I can't say that I am any smarter than I was back then, but I can't help but feel sorry for who we were, no matter how dumb or scared or greedy or kind or ignorant or whatever it was we were.

We were all those things. More besides.

And we were all sick, we were all sick.

We just didn't know it yet.

ACKNOWLEDGMENTS

This story contains references to: the thought of Noam Chomsky (it's an anagram); a song written by Mike Skinner; a number of philosophers, most notably Voltaire (him that was 1694 to 1778); but above all to Thomas Mann and *The Magic Mountain*. I'd like to thank Susie Molloy for her generosity, and Susan Cooper for telling me about Rose Macaulay's book *The Towers of Trebizond* at just the right moment, when I was wondering if it was possible to let Ash be Ash.